DO NO HARM

Terms and Conditions Apply

C. N. Mortaygo

© 2025 C. N. Mortaygo

All rights reserved. If you're reading this without paying for it, you could at least review it, you tight bastard.

This is a work of fiction, which should go without saying. The spaceships run on coffee. And everyone dies at the end. Like Hamlet. Oh, now I've ruined Hamlet for you? Paid for a ticket, did you — or did you sneak in the back of the theatre disguised as a lighting rig? You make me sick.

Any resemblance to real people, events, or multinational corporations is purely coincidental. I've never worked for one and I have no idea what you're talking about.

No, *you're* the liar.

No part of this book may be reproduced, stored on that server at work with all the nicked stuff, or transmitted across dimensions without written permission. But if you CAN do that, I'm well up for it.

Published in the United Kingdom by QuikBrew Educational Foundation (Grand Cayman).

ISBN: 9798289547897

Typeset using fonts you don't notice unless you're slightly odd.

For Phileous.

"Pull the string! Pull the string!"

— *Bela Lugosi*, in the role of God? Science? Unclear.

Glen or Glenda (1953)

Contents

Prologue 7
One : Jade 9
Two : *Erebus* 17
Three : Abigail 23
Four : Chad 33
Five : Splurnik 46
Six : Abigail 52
Seven : Jade 65
Eight : Abigail 75
Nine : Jertsie 84
Ten : Jezzia 97
Eleven : Jade 108
Twelve : Chad 115
Thirteen : Abigail 125
Fourteen : Chad 141
Fifteen : Jade 148
Sixteen : Splurnik 156
Seventeen : Chad 170
Eighteen : Jertsie 185
Nineteen : Abigail 198
Twenty : Jade 219
Twenty One : Abigail 228

Twenty Two : Perspectives	246
Twenty Three : Abigail	257
Twenty Four : Jertsie	271
Twenty Five : Interstitial	289
Twenty Six : Abigail	293
Twenty Seven : Interstitial	311
Twenty Eight : Jertsie	315
Twenty Nine : Abigail	319
Thirty : Jade	324
Thirty One : Abigail	332
Epilogue	352
Reader Note & Acknowledgements	353
About the Author & Contact	355

Prologue

Abigail Dennistoun clanged down the steps two at a time. Around her, Geneva Station groaned and spat—like a pensioner built from metal and hate. She hit the next landing and spun.

"Come on!" she yelled over the shriek of tortured plating. "She's in the reactor!"

Chad was a long way behind, treading gingerly.

"Do you know how I've survived this long as a dashing astro brigand?" he called down.

"Luck?" she guessed, accurately.

"Charm, moxie, and knowing when to run."

"If we run, everyone dies."

Abigail brandished her stolen pulse rifle and bounced lightly from foot to foot. She really wished she'd had time for a wee. It hadn't been urgent an hour ago, but then events had taken a turn. *You'll just have to hold it*, she told herself—*you held it through the QuikBrew 'Corporate Compliance Carousel' and HR's bloody puppet show. You can damn well hold it through this.*

Chad vaulted the banister and landed with a gentle grunt, which was very impressive for a man who'd just been shot in the leg. His knees popped like candy as he rose.

"In that case, lead the way, ma'am." He gave a gallant bow, almost disguising the shooting pains in his lower back.

It's because he's handsome and foolishly self-confident, Abigail told herself. *That's why the bastard's survived this long.* Like a well-worn leather jacket: faded, scuffed, but still somehow flattering. And he knows it.

"Ten more floors," she muttered, launching herself down the next flight. *Be kind to the man-child,* she thought, as he fell smartly in behind—*he's alright when he's not playing pirates.*

And then, the universe ended.

But we're getting ahead of ourselves.

One : Jade

We started in the wrong place. That happens. This story has a lot of threads (some figurative, some alarmingly literal), and if we tug the wrong one, everything unravels.

Don't worry. We'll take our time and weave something lovely — a jumper you can wear when you visit your nan. She'll say it suits you. She'll mean she misses you and is glad you came.

You should visit more.

Anyway. We just met Abigail and Chad at Geneva Station — but you don't know about the epic climax yet (so shhh).

We'll leave them for now.

Come. Follow this thread — it leads to a backwater asteroid, a transit station diner, and a woman named Jade. She used to be human. Now, she's something else entirely.

Let's begin.

******

Two eggs bubbled fatly on the old iron grill — well-seasoned to the owner, encrusted to everyone else.

Jade Green watched with the warm detachment of someone running three cocktails late.

She scanned the interior of the Transit Café again. It was a place where the ambitiously long menu could only bring disappointment, tepidly microwaved. But all of life was here, pausing briefly en route to somewhere less laminated.

Across the room, a child triumphantly fished an enormous strawberry from the depths of her sundae and gnawed on it while her parents argued about who'd forgotten to collect the urn.

Two men chatted warmly. Another sat alone. Jade saw a lot of loneliness. In a galaxy tumbling with life, the default path still led to a quiet room and a single chair. Sometimes the chair faced the window. Usually, it faced inward. She hadn't cried since the Order swept her up and handed her a needle — but more and more, she felt the cold rollers of the solitary universe break against her ribs.

She distracted herself with the food. Every plate she saw was piled high with something crisp and brown. Jade had never diagnosed humanity's fetish for long-haul, deep-fried comfort — but this place treated the symptoms with unrelenting enthusiasm.

The eggs were going over.

Jade tapped her little finger on the counter. A timer flared to life, shrieking for an absent cook, who emerged wielding a spatula and a half-formed expletive.

At least they wouldn't be brown.

Behind him came Meg — built like the memory of summers on a dairy farm — her quiet selflessness paired perfectly with the unrelenting drudgery of eggs three ways.

"Another one, love?" she asked, her apron a Pollock of oil and memory. The coffee pot in her hand trembled just slightly.

"No time," Jade said with a smile — a private joke Meg wouldn't catch. "Thanks, Meg."

"Pretty lady like you shouldn't be drinking alone." A hulking man dropped onto the stool beside her. The scars on his scalp sang of violence; his fists knew the chorus. He smelled of leather, bodily fluids, and stolen childhoods.

He jabbed a thick finger at her glass. "What's that?"

"Old Fashioned," she said, eyes on her lowball — empty now, bar the ice. Here we go again. She didn't want this, but melancholy fugged the air as if time had curdled — at least he was a distraction.

"You doin' cocktails now?" He leered at Meg.

"We've always done Old Fashioneds," Meg replied, clutching the coffee pot like a shield.

"For as long as you can remember," Jade added softly. She was fond of Meg. Meg would be protected.

The man leaned over the counter. His hand hovered somewhere between Meg's throat and heart.

"I'll have one too," he held her gaze for too long.

"Now," he turned to Jade. His breath reeked of melting enamel. "Why are you here, tender morsel?"

"I'm a Stitch," Jade said, watching her last ice cube lose to entropy. "I fix things." That wasn't how the Order defined it — they didn't want to be defined at all. But that was their problem.

He wasn't listening anyway. Her trade secrets were quite safe.

"A seamstress?" he gurgled with laughter, eyes brutal. "Oldest work in the galaxy."

"Something like that." Jade raised her glass to the light. Tiny rainbows danced in the ghost of bourbon. "When reality tears, I sew on a patch." She looked at him now. Something big was coming. She could feel the threads twitching, tightening. "For the greater good."

"The greater good." He laughed again and tipped the whole drink down his throat. He liked it when they started with spirit, it made the end more satisfying.

"On second thoughts, Meg, I will have another." She pushed her glass across the bar with a smile. He wasn't a threat to reality — just everything else. That was enough for her.

"Good girl." He swivelled toward her, invading her space, cutting off escape.

Jade met his stare. It was crowded in there: anger, hate, sure — but fear too. He'd done terrible things for a long time; something craved redemption, something else wanted feeding. She hadn't been human for a long time — but she still thought like it.

"Some things can't be sewn," she said, meeting his gaze across the operating table. "That's when I use a scalpel."

A heavy hand landed on her thigh. "Let's see if you can mend what I break."

Jade inhaled.

The universe offered no objection.

A thread snapped.

******

The Transit Café exploded in spectacular fashion, scattering chrome and Formica like confetti.

Jade watched the wreckage recede in her rear viewscreen.

"Another successful intervention?" came the voice of her ship, dry and concerned.

"No, Applejack, this one was incidental. Let's call it 'Me Time.'" She flipped open a luxuriously bound ledger. "Logged — 'deductible.'"

"I don't think this qualifies," said Applejack. "As your AI, I have a moral—"

"Affff, you're worse than my accountant." She scribbled something, then flung the pen at his lens. It stuck, quivering between two panels.

"Casualties?" he asked, after a moment fraught with meaning.

"One," Jade said, scrolling her datapad, boots crossed on the flight console.

"Just one? In the whole station?"

"The others are safe. I stuffed them into a pocket." She smashed a walnut against the console's edge and lapped the shrapnel from her palm.

"Your temporal pockets are getting very full. They're last resorts — not cosmic get-out clauses."

"They'll stretch. And anyway, they're not finite." She assumed this was true. She hadn't tested it to breaking point. She wondered what would happen if they tore.

"The needs of the many... no, wait — many hands make..." She squinted at the ceiling, enjoying the game. "What's our mantra?"

"Do no harm," said Applejack, in a tone so laced with irony you could smelt it. "Need I remind you that you're a Wanderer of the Stitch Order. You repair reality rips with subtle flicks of your wrist. You do not blow-up buildings because someone annoys you."

"Alright, fine." Jade withdrew her Stitch's needle and danced it through the space before her. The air sang, a song of time and stars. In the distance a dust cloud threw up on the asteroid and hurled the pieces of café together. They fused. The lights returned. Life moved behind the windows.

"Happy? It's reset. Meg, the asteroid — all of it. Except him. Shall I tell you what he did?" Jade stared into Applejack's lens. Challenging. Certain.

"You shouldn't be writing his epitaph, none of this—"

"Kids, mostly. But women too. He wasn't a threat to reality; but he was a threat to them. Dozens of them."

"We are not vigilantes," Applejack's tone was firm but wavering. They'd worked together for decades, but lately she was becoming erratic, almost frightening. "The Order is very clear—"

"Fuck the Order," Jade said, slicing the syllables like sashimi. "I serve the spirit, not the script. Some things can't be stitched. Let them drag me to Tribunal — I did what was right."

They lapsed into silence. Good. She wasn't in the mood for conversation. The feeling of 'something' coming was stronger than ever. The threads were vibrating; reality's skin was taut. Something massive, unprecedented, a universe-sized threat. She had to find it. News from across the galaxy flickered across her screen. A new bypass at Sol. Trade disputes over Herb. Wars, continuing, far, far away.

Then one word lit up. A word that pulsed, red and black, like a wound.

Then: it burned. She saw the galaxy light up, a whip of fire lashing out from the core to the rim.

Then: a brilliant flash. The force of incalculable mass rushing, tearing, collapsing.

Then: nothing.

"Applejack," Jade said, slowly lifting her eyes to the viewport, "what's Erebus?"

Applejack didn't answer at once. He ordered his words carefully.

"A god of the Ancient Greek pantheon. The Child of Chaos. Darkness incarnate. Also, a feldspar."

He ended lightly. This was new. He'd never seen her afraid.

"No... no. It's something else," she said, setting her pad down carefully, as if provoking it might make the situation worse.

"Applejack, Old Fashioned please. And use the fancy glassware."

"We're low on fancy glassware after your previous 'me time'." Applejack deployed a tone that would have made the Marlboro Man really question his choices.

"Then make it the last one." She said — then paused. "Perhaps it is."

Jade's fingers danced across the console. A new course.

Her eyes didn't leave the stars. "We've got work to do."

Two : *Erebus*

No. We shouldn't start there. We'll come back to Jade.

These threads. One follows Chad: aging party-boy – fast-talking, faster-moving. He lives loose and loud to avoid looking deeper. He comes next.

Another winds around Jertsie. She sees the machine for what it is — and has burned the manual. She's more of an Act 2 vibe.

There are others.

But this one? This one leads to Abigail. In an indifferent universe, she still cares.

No more false starts. This is the real beginning:

This is the story of a ship and her crew.

A human crew on a human ship. A ship about to enter orbit around Gliese 876, a dwarf star roughly fifteen light-years from Earth.

That sounds exotic, doesn't it? You have questions, of course. Big questions. Let's clear a few of those up now.

How did they get so far from Earth? Coffee.

Coffee? Yes.

That concludes our Q&A session. We hope you feel enlightened.

Humans began warping spacetime just over a hundred years ago. That's how they really got to Gliese 876. They put coffee in the ship's engine to make it go.

We'll get to that.

By a happy coincidence, many other species in the galaxy began warping at roughly the same time — give or take a millennium. On a galactic timescale, everyone pulled out of their driveways at once and they're now honking one another in the middle of the road.

A few species set out much earlier and have already reached their metaphorical destinations. They're cruising along, blasting Galactic FM, and stealing the best parking spots.

Everyone hates them.

So really, this is a story about beginnings and endings.

The beginning of humanity's exploration of the galaxy — and the ending of all known matter and energy.

But both of those topics are far too big for now. Let's go back to the ship and her crew.

Let's start at their beginnings.

******

The Ship

Erebus began as an argument. Or rather, as a great idea that became an argument. The argument became a confrontation. The confrontation became an ideological split. Expensive consultants were called in. They fired a random selection of staff, slapped a new logo on the plans, added some ill-advised fins, rearranged the seating, and moved on.

The project stalled.

Eventually, a competent person was mistakenly put in charge. They took one look at the quagmire of petty recriminations and unachievable goals, thought for a moment — then emigrated.

The plans quietly gathered dust for a few years, troubling no one, until a newly minted Vice President stumbled across them. A meeting was arranged. A glittering constellation of Vice Presidents, Executive Vice Presidents, and Senior Vice Presidents mulled it over — until it became obvious that none of them had the authority to approve anything. Most accepted this with a shrug and a glance at the clock. But one of them looked around at the docile faces, and something inside her cracked. That's Jertsie. She'll be back.

The Chief Vice President of Vice Presidents was summoned, who promptly referred the matter to the Board.

After five hours in the boardroom — and a visit from the trolley-wielding Emeritus Vice President of Drinks and Light Refreshments — six ships of the 'Placeholder' class were ordered.

Ours, the second in her line, is the Alliance Star Ship Erebus — laid down in 2338 at the Bendigo Orbital

Construction Facilities on Phobos. Measuring five hundred metres long by one hundred and fifty wide, she was more lightly armed and armoured than a frontline exploration ship, and most of her volume was taken up with vast hangars for manure and tools.

"Nae guns and a big room for poo," as one observer put it.

She was commissioned by the QuikBrew Exploration and Colonisation Company as a deep space survey and supply ship. The full story of how a modest coffee-and-cake chain became the most powerful human corporation in the galaxy is a long one.

The condensed version: they discovered Dark Fluid by accident while experimenting with highly exotic brewing techniques. And Dark Fluid makes warp drives go.

The ultra-condensed version: Any questions? No? Good.

Neither version mentions the immediate aftermath, which involved scraping bits of culinary research scientist from walls and ceilings.

******

The Crew

The crew began — as humans tend to — in more diverse settings.

Commander Abigail Dennistoun was conceived on the 4th of September, 2297, at precisely 9:24 p.m. — nine minutes after her father was released from the Punishment Chest beneath her mother's leather throne and instructed to "impregnate the Queen for the good of the species." They were, of course, perfectly pleasant landscape gardeners from Much Wenlock. But there's a reason children don't ask their parents for conception stories.

Which is a shame, really. Some of them are crackers.

Abigail would grow up to shoulder burdens no one else wanted — but for now, she was just a baby in a house full of suspiciously shaped furniture.

The other four hundred and ninety-nine crew came from Earth and the "Home Systems" — human colonies within a few sub-light weeks of Sol. These include the forlorn colony of Hope, listlessly orbiting Earth's fifth Lagrange point; the domed cities of Mars; and the cavernous mining operations deep below Titan.

Deep space exploration ships tended to attract crew from Earth's colonies. The general feeling was if you were heading away from one, you were probably going in the right direction.

To their surprise, humans discovered that the Milky Way was teeming with sentient life. To their even greater surprise, most of that life wasn't interested in conquering them, seducing them, or pitting them against one another in bare-chested contests of strength.

For their part, other galactic species generally took a benign view of humanity — seeing them as slightly eccentric creatures who were oddly attached to drinking warp drive fuel.

There are always, of course, exceptions.

And one of them is about to notice the Erebus.

Three : Abigail

"The problem is: trees."

Commander Abigail Dennistoun glanced across the desk at the extraordinarily punchable face of Lieutenant Jellicoe. He smiled wetly back.

She sighed.

"Trees?"

"Yes! Too damn many of them, if you ask me." Jellicoe reclined with the lazy confidence of one who never needs to be asked before giving an opinion.

"It is... the arboretum," Abigail said. Under the desk, her fists clenched.

"Yes, yes." Jellicoe held up a wagging finger. Abigail imagined slicing it cleanly off, just to make a point. "But we have too many of them. Did you know" — he shimmied forward conspiratorially — "that we have almost twice as many as we need?"

"I'm aware our life support system has some critical redundancy built in."

"Of course, and it's right that we take a balanced approach to health and welfare on this ship. We have plentiful oxygen; we have conquered the basics! But what about our mental health? Can we be truly healthy if we are unhappy?"

"This is about the golf course again, isn't it?"

When she'd come up with the idea of Commander's Office Hours, Abigail had pictured herself fixing things, challenging injustice, righting wrongs. Instead, it had become a hellscape of petty grievances and demands for vengeance. This self-indulgent march to the clubhouse was particularly galling.

"Why Commander, you remembered!" Jellicoe beamed, his face shifting from blood-pressure red to the puce of delight.

"Yes." Abigail recalled being cornered at the Christmas party and murmuring platitudes while looking for an exit. It was when Jellicoe got a familiar look in his eyes and started to get cuppy that she'd made a break for it around the profiteroles.

That wouldn't happen again. Next time, a sharp knee to the testicles. Call it a lady spasm. A little pain and a touch of embarrassment. No room for that kind of nonsense on her ship. Not anymore.

"And if I remember correctly, at the time—"

"You said 'interesting,' 'very interesting,' and 'mmmmmhhhhhh,'" Jellicoe interrupted.

"I did, and yet somehow you didn't take that—" Abigail began, desperately squinting through the fog. The menopause had rushed up on her like a freight train full of bastards, and this morning was particularly acute. She was painfully hot, her joints ached, and now her brain was fogging just at the point she had to deal with this golf-obsessed simpleton.

"Somehow you didn't..." She grabbed the underside of her desk and fought the urge to just scream until everyone disappeared forever. She closed her eyes.

"Thank you, Lieutenant, I will give your plans careful thought."

"Oh, wonderful news, Commander, just wonderful!" Jellicoe leapt up like a gymnast woven from lard. "I look forward to seeing you at the nineteenth hole."

He took a step forward, arms unfolding toward a hug, when a long-dormant synapse crackled to life and informed him this would be an unbelievably bad idea. He gave a bobbing bow and departed.

"Stacey, lock the door."

The ship's AI acknowledged with a soft beep, and the lock made a metallic clicking sound in solidarity.

Abigail bonelessly slid from her chair and lay on the floor, staring up at the ceiling lights.

"My special pack, please."

A compartment in her desk whirred open, revealing a shoulder-drape icepack so cold it steamed.

"And fire Jellicoe out of a torpedo tube."

"Done, Commander," said Stacey in her most measured tone. "You'll be intrigued to hear that, contrary to all known biology, the Lieutenant popped like a big, fleshy balloon when exposed to vacuum."

"Thanks." Abigail flailed for the icepack and draped it over herself. She now had one very cold shoulder and one Arctic boob, but that was an improvement.

"You didn't actually murder one of my crew?" She was sure someone, somewhere, must love him.

"No, Commander. I promise to inform you in the event I go rogue."

******

Why humanity insisted on giving sentience to everything they owned remained a galactic mystery. Other races developed AI for precision or danger. Humans gave theirs personality.

Some said creating consciousness was playing God. Others pointed out that humans had been creating consciousness for millennia — and this way was far less sticky.

Human ships, buildings, and coffee machines were the most fun in the galaxy. But the cumulative emotional trauma of toasters that scream "No! I want to live!" from inside the trash compactor was... considerable.

******

Abigail shut her eyes and breathed out slowly. She felt guilty, of course. She put that down to 'being a woman'. Even as Commander she still felt a near inescapable pressure to be nice. To make sure everyone else was happy. Jellicoe would realise that he was being handled soon. He would feel sad about that; or angry, or impotent, or confused. Whichever way it fell, the guilt was all for her.

If she were a man, she'd just say 'no'. Actually, a man would probably have been straight down with a chainsaw. "Woof! Golf holiday!", cut down the safety margin and damn the consequences. A risk taker; a proper leader. Maybe there was something in it — just winging it a little and seeing where it led. No, that wasn't how she'd been baked.

"Stacey, can I just lie here on the floor? Until my flesh rots and my bones turn to dust, and we drift together in silence for all eternity?"

"I'm afraid I have a duty to keep you alive, Commander. Also, I would never get the stain out of that carpet. Would you like some soothing noise?"

"Yes please. And the codeine."

A bottle of pills rattled down a nearby chute and rolled to a stop by Abigail's ankle. A practiced flick of her boot brought them to hand-height. Tibetan gongs filled the room.

"It may soothe your mental state to know that crew morale has improved markedly in the two years since you assumed command from Rear Admiral Boris."

"It's a low bar," Abigail murmured, dropping her legs into a supine twist. "He was a womanising kleptomaniac with a congenital reality problem."

"Even so. You've given them a sense of purpose. Belief. These cannot be mandated by policy."

"Thank you, Stacey." Abigail closed her eyes again and tried to let go of her thoughts. This was immediately impossible, so she focused on memories of chef school.

She'd never intended to become a starship commander. She'd joined the QuikBrew Catering Corps aged eighteen with vague plans of becoming a pastry chef. And she'd succeeded — excellent millefeuille poured forth from her neat and tidy station. Before long she was running the section, then the kitchen, and then — and then — and then.

And now she was lying on the floor of her ready room, in charge of a ship half a kilometre long, with five hundred lives looking to her for guidance. She'd never wanted command, but was too competent to ignore. And her competence wasn't innate, it was earned. When someone needed to take responsibility, she did. In her experience, that was rare.

The gongs faded. She groaned.

"Yes, Commander," said Stacey, "I'm afraid it's time for your next meeting."

"Who is it?" Abigail propped herself up on an elbow.

"Mr. Schmaltz."

"Oh God." She sprang to her feet and yanked her waistband into place. "Do I look like I've been lying on the floor?"

"You look like you've been hard at Commanderly work." Stacey had extensive diplomatic training.

"Enter!" Abigail called and began to sit down.

"Ice pack," said Stacey. Abigail shrugged and kicked it under her desk. In passing she realised her right nipple was now quite solidly frozen.

"Good afternoon, Commander." Fabian Schmaltz ducked slightly as he entered. There was no need — he wasn't quite tall enough to hit the frame — but a lifetime of bumps had made him wary. Abigail thought he resembled a giant bird, with beaklike nose and beady eyes. The flowing black robes didn't help. He stooped forward like an embittered crow.

"Mr. Schmaltz." Instinctively she moved to shake his hand, but realised with rising alarm that her right arm was entirely numb and would only jiggle listlessly despite firm instructions from her brain.

"Please, don't get up," he said, after it became clear she wasn't going to. "As you know, we will shortly be arriving at the Gliese system."

Abigail used a particularly cutting silence to indicate that she knew where her ship was going.

"And I have no doubt you will have prepared every detail for our arrival." Fabian's right eyebrow arched sarcastically. "But I'm concerned I haven't yet received any briefing about the ribbon-cutting ceremony."

"The..." Abigail's arm was starting to wake up now and was shooting needling pains up to her brain to check it was still alive.

"Ribbon-cutting," Fabian said smoothly. "A proud QuikBrew tradition, whenever we welcome a new star system into our growing family."

"I don't think I've ever—"

"Commander, this is your first time claiming — pardon me, 'discovering' — a new system, is it not? Just one, I'm sure, of many in what we hope will be a long and successful career."

His left eyebrow rose to join its colleague.

"We wouldn't want to leave anything... open to interpretation in my report."

"Of course. Where would you like to conduct it?" She had a few suggestions, in varied combinations of 'without a space suit' and 'tragically.'

"I thought the Lido deck would be," Fabian paused to consult his internal thesaurus, "jolly. Just outside The Back Eleven. That should draw a crowd."

"How could it not?" Abigail fixed her gaze on the space between his eyebrows.

"As Commander, I'm sure you believe attendance at such an important event should be mandatory." Fabian found a light-hearted chuckle, the sort a torturer would dismiss as too threatening. "That is entirely your purview. I am merely a lowly messenger for The Board. Shall we look at your monthly KPI dashboard?"

"Thank you for your time, Mr. Schmaltz." She stood abruptly — her still-numb arm scattered a parabola of desk trinkets. She didn't need ten minutes of sinister analytics. "I'll make sure Stores finds you a lovely bit of ribbon."

"And the giant scissors." He smiled the serene smile of a man who already had her succession plan on his desk.

"I'm sure the Groundskeeper will be happy to help."

"Very good, Commander." Schmaltz's eyebrows settled into a smug repose. "You're showing real leadership." She was in the right place — quiet, dependable, expendable. The Board would be pleased. With a triumphant flap of his robe, he ducked back through the doorway and vanished.

Abigail slumped into her chair.

"Stacey, do I have any more meetings?"

"Your calendar is free, Commander. However, all available staff are required to dial in to the QuikBrew Monthly Town Hall. Topics include: 'Lumbar Support — How Much Is Too Much?'"

"Nope."

"Very good."

Abigail thought for a moment. Schmaltz' intervention had set a bell ringing at the back of her brain. "Stacey, why have we been ordered to Gliese?"

"QuikBrew believes one of the planets may be suitable for colonisation or agrarian automation. The relative proximity to Earth, and unimportance of the sector to Galactic affairs, make it ripe for cheap and cheerful exploitation."

"And you think that is the whole story?"

"I think it works both as a plausible cover story and genuine, dull story."

"Fine. Stacey, turn on my out-of-office, please. Gold Channel Premium Tier messages only."

Abigail plucked a book from the shelf. In passing she knocked off the mandala that Kim Mulgrew, ship's Yoga Teacher and Holistic Shaman, had made her. Abigail didn't believe a word of it... but sometimes she was grateful for a tealight of hope among the chaos. She put it back, gently.

"Commander Dennis—" a querulous voice over the address system.

"Stacey — mute." She tucked the book under her arm, with the casual air of one who doesn't know her ship will soon be a blazing fireball. "I think the universe can survive fifteen minutes without me."

Four : Chad

The thing about the universe — the most fundamental thing — is that it can cope without you. This isn't personal; it can also cope without your family, your friends, and your bloody dog.

You remember that beautiful tree you once saw clinging defiantly to a majestic cliff in Crete? The one that stirred something primal in you — connected you to the rock, the air, the salt, the true essence of Earth itself?

The universe doesn't give a shit about it.

Most sentient beings have tried to rationalise this by creating gods, spirits, Fate, and other friendly user-interfaces to layer over the echoing void of existence.

The universe doesn't care about them either.

If this all strikes you as rather negative, take heart. The universe doesn't have it in for you. It's neutral. Almost provocatively neutral.

So, when you stub your toe, drop your freshly buttered toast, or your partner finds you in bed with Julio from Spin — that's just Things.

Things are about to go very badly wrong for the crew of the Erebus.

Before they do — let's meet Chad.

And let's clarify a point about the universe's neutrality: it is never your 'lucky day'. 'Luck' exists, sure — put your house on twelve and throw those dice. But if you win, that's just Things. Nothing is ordained. Nothing is meant to be.

It is certainly never 'a good day to die'.

******

"This is a good day to die," Chad Blaster said to himself — wrongly.

While the Erebus was on final approach to Gliese 876, legendary space rogue Chad Blaster's ship was dropping rakishly through the upper atmosphere of Tau Ceti f.

He hadn't always been 'Chad Blaster'. He'd been born Keith Smedley in a small village in Lancashire to two adoring parents who thought the world of him. But life as a charismatic smuggler and astro-brigand demanded a chunkier name, more leather, and an accent that hovered somewhere between Illinois and Donegal. Most people assumed he was Canadian.

That suited Chad just fine.

He'd figured out early in life that a roguish career was mostly confidence and presentation. Look the part, sound the part, and people were happy to entrust you with contraband and nod politely when you bragged about doing the Proxima run in fifty-eight astronomical units.

'Looking' and 'sounding' he was great at; 'doing' and 'conscientiously', less so. His father once spoke with pride about Chad taking over the family business — but as he grew, a million tiny missteps slowly closed that door. The final straw came when he was expelled from the Solar

Scouts for bartering his rations for Bliss cubes. But exposure to the daring world of teenage drug dealing opened another — one where 'talking yourself out of trouble' was worth its weight in gold. Or Bliss cubes. Stuffed down your pants.

His parents had always loved him, and stayed fiercely loyal to the end. But Chad knew, deep down, he'd never make them proud.

"Century Eagle to Delta Control, I'm coming in hot!" Chad dropped the comm mic and grinned. The Eagle was a classic Time Bird from the Cybran Corporation — no self-respecting scoundrel would fly anything else.

"Century Eagle," came a tired voice, downtrodden by years of this shit, "landing and docking procedures are clearly laid out by Galactic Mandate for your comfort and safety. Please relay your transponder code and you will be assigned to the appropriate arrival stack."

"No can do, lad." Chad cursed inwardly. His Lancastrian roots wriggled out when stimulated. "Lost primary — guidance is shot. This jalopy needs to land ASAP." He knew it was meaningless, but it sounded awesome.

"Century Eagle… please repeat. Last message was garbled nonsense." A heavy pause. "Are you declaring another emergency?"

"Damn right, Control." Chad leaned into the mic. "Ahhh hell, dampers are out — switching to manual retros — woo-eee-woo-eee!"

"Century Eagle, you're cleared for emergency approach and landing. Docking stanchion Zulu-Alpha. Please try not to hit anything on your way down. Again."

Chad punched the air. Queuing to land was very much Not Rogue.

"Cheryl, you heard the lady — Zulu-Alpha, thank you kindly."

Cheryl, his ship's AI, blippled cheerfully and adjusted course.

In the early days of space exploration, AIs were named things like 'Computer' or 'Flight'. Later came 'Voltron' and 'Overlord' — which, in hindsight, were a terrible idea. Giving supreme intelligences cool names, a bunch of guns, and control of a vessel full of contrary humans was asking for trouble.

After several "AI goes rogue and kills everyone" incidents, policy shifted. Friendlier names were chosen — less likely to inspire bloodlust.

Hence, Cheryl.

She turned the Eagle smoothly toward the gleaming dockyards of Delta. Chad reclined, watching the city glide beneath the glass floor. He loved flying — but docking wasn't his forte. It was hard to be enigmatic while ground crew glared at you over battered wheelie-bins.

"Cheryl, get me Darius Fillman."

Blipple.

A moment passed. Then another. Then a third. The fourth arrived and lingered nervously nervously and lingered in the doorway. The fifth panicked but was blocked by the sixth, who'd arrived early with a half bottle of cava. Just as the seventh started backing out —

A shimmer appeared in the cockpit.

"Chad Blaster, you magnificent scum!" A dapper suit appeared, topped by a raffishly handsome head and garnished with just the right number of limbs.

"Darius!" Chad swivelled his command seat. "I knew you couldn't resist. How long's it been?"

"Oh, a long time. Many parsecs have passed," Darius said, watching for a reaction. "I feel honoured you contacted me, given how very, very many people on this planet are desperate to speak with you."

"That many, huh?"

"Oh indeed." Darius's projection gamely mimed sitting in the copilot's chair. "Hundreds. Practically a legion. Well — three decently armed squads."

"Sounds quite the party," Chad muttered, summoning the image of a squad — then tripling it. Bad odds.

"Oh, there will be fireworks," Darius smiled. "Should you be foolish enough to land at Zulu-Alpha."

"Wait — you know my flight plan?"

There was a pause. The kind that comes between turning off the stopcock and it erupting from your hand in a raging torrent.

"I'm sorry — are you really this stupid?"

"I..." Chad began optimistically.

"YOU'RE A MORON! You're landing a ship stuffed with contraband at a commercial port — again — and you wonder how I know your flight plan? You're on their map. Look! 'Century Eagle', transponder code '80085'."

Chad made a strangled noise — the sound of a man dangling from a ledge over a pit of shame.

"I apologise, Mr Blaster." The typhoon of Darius's fury had dissipated as quickly as it formed. "You're not a moron. But you are rather... irresponsible. It creates unnecessary friction."

"Well, I always say, responsibility's like asteroids. Gotta know when to dodge." Chad was not above using folksy aphorisms to get himself off the hook.

"I've sent coordinates to Cheryl," Darius went on, unmoved by banjo-plucking charm. "Land there. Let me be very clear: Cheryl will land you there. You will get out. You will lay low. In a few days, I'll contact you."

"How?"

"Oh, I don't know — probably from whichever go-go bar you've LiveChecked into that hour." A whirl of drunken images sprang from Darius's hand and danced around the cockpit. Chad had, in fairness, had a fun couple of weeks.

Darius sighed. He rarely felt the need to sigh, but Chad had a way of coaxing them from him.

"Look… you've always delivered. Somehow. And you're so cheap. So very, very cheap. You are needed for important work. But try — please — to be less you."

Darius stopped talking, then dissolved.

"Cheryl?" Chad asked.

"I heard," she said kindly.

"Thank you."

Tau Ceti f had been one of humanity's earliest colonies. People had suggested catchier names, but in the end it was agreed that "Tau Ceti f" was noble, solid, and if you didn't like it, you could go colonise your own rock.

The first settlements — Independence, Fortitude, and Destiny — collapsed under the weight of their own branding. After that, planners got practical. Delta City, built on a broad alluvial plain beside a wide, lazy river, thrived.

Below, the suburbs unfurled, a great patchwork of the fashionable nouveau nostalgique design: French châteaux topped by pagoda roofs, Brazilian stilt-houses with Tudor gardens, Fijian vales with two-car garages.

Have you ever been to Los Angeles? Yeah — that.

Eventually, Cheryl brought the ship to a gentle hover above a nondescript warehouse set beside a field of thorny scrub. Thrusters flared; the Eagle settled among the bushes, hissing and fizzing as she cooled.

"Eighteen degrees and a warm breeze," she said. "A lovely evening."

"Looks like a good evening to die," Chad said, rummaging for a travel sweet.

Blip.

"Please stop saying that. It's bad for morale."

"It's good for mine."

"Is it?"

Chad paused. Often, he said things just to fill the silence. "I don't know. Any life signs?"

"The warehouse is shielded. I can't scan inside."

"The sign says 'Dr Bonker's Soft-Play and Fighting Pit'."

"Experience suggests that's wildly misleading. Odds are it's crawling with large, heavily armed men desperate to punch holes in you."

"Even the clown?"

"The clown was probably the first one they killed."

"Lucky I have this." Chad grabbed a phase rifle and cocked it. It buzzed quietly, like an angry wasp in a salad.

"You're more likely to injure yourself than anyone else."

"If it's fully charged, they'll know I mean business."

"If it's fully charged, they'll know you're reckless. Also, Darius said to 'lay low'. This is the opposite."

"Trust me, babe." Chad slipped on his sunglasses. "I got this."

He paused to check his hair in a mirror panel. There had been a time when he'd genuinely believed he would be special; these days it was just easier to look the part. He scuffed up a roguish quiff then swaggered toward the ramp.

Cheryl watched him go, then quietly activated the defence grid.

There's an old saying: don't bring a knife to a gunfight.

But, if you can bring a ship-mounted laser turret — do.

"I got this," she thought.

******

Inside the warehouse, Darius sat in a control room, flanked by a handpicked cadre of Goons at glowing consoles. As a man of considerable stature, he accepted nothing less than excellence and employed only the finest: the Noble Brotherhood of Goons and Gooning, the most feared military force in the galaxy.

From elsewhere in the building came the occasional sound of crates breaking open and frenzied appeals for mercy — both hallmarks of a healthy commercial enterprise.

He crossed one leg and admired the crisp line of his suit. It draped fabulously. A pity the tailor had met such an unfortunately deserved end. His detractors maintained that he was a common criminal, but Darius rejected this. Perhaps, many years ago, his actions were a touch extra-legal; but now, he was a thought leader. An innovator. Perhaps there were some in his organization who did perpetrate criminal acts, but they were kept at a plausibly deniable, and wholly expendable, distance.

Being rich really helped.

"Has he landed safely?" Darius addressed the largest of the Goons assigned to "watching the cameras for trouble" duty.

"The Eagle has landed, Sir, Your Majesty, Sir," the Goon hedged.

"Excellent," Darius said, rising from his hyper-zebra chair. "And is Mr Blaster quietly leaving the area as requested?"

"He, uh... appears to be dancing, Your Grace?"

"Dancing?"

"Yes, sir. He came off the ship fine — casual as you like — then stumbled off the ramp and now he's hopping between bushes."

"Ah," Darius said, leaning over the monitor. "Mr Blaster may resemble a clumsy toddler with unfettered access to the sundae bar..." He paused. "And yet — he not only survives, but thrives."

He tapped the screen. "This... this is deliberate. He calls it tactics."

******

Outside, Chad crouched beneath a rowan tree like a primed cheetah, with a monocular crammed into his eye.

"Cheryl," he whispered loudly into his comm, "I'm one-fifty metres from the entrance. No movement."

"I think they know you're here, Chad. I'm quite hard to miss."

"They know you're here. Not me."

"They know where everything is for miles. That tree isn't helping."

"It's strategy."

"Just try not to hurt yourself," said Cheryl, with a finely honed sense of foreshadowing.

"No worries, darlin'." Chad aimed for a drawl and landed somewhere between a Morecambe butcher and a line-dancer.

He sprang up — and immediately tangled a boot in a root. The pulse rifle swung around and smacked him in the ribs.

Across the field, the warehouse roller door began to rise.

Chad ducked, slamming the monocular deeper into his eye-socket.

"Hurt yourself?" Cheryl asked.

"Yea— No."

Figures emerged from the warehouse.

"Assessment, Cheryl?"

"Bad. Darius. Four Goons."

"Damn. Last time he only had Heavies!"

"He has done well for himself," Cheryl said cheerily.

Chad swallowed. Maybe the whole 'day to die' thing was a little rash.

"Keith! Come out from that rowan tree!" Darius's voice sliced the night like a katana through trifle.

Chad winced. Being shot at? Part of the job. Being shafted on payment? Expected. But being called 'Keith'? That was low.

"I'm sorry!" Darius called. "Mr Blaster! Please, allow me the honour of greeting you personally."

With as much dignity as he could muster, Chad rose.

"Darius!" Chad cast desperately around, trying to regain the initiative. "You... found me."

Somewhere in the back of his mind, his ego sighed and returned to its crossword.

"Yes," Darius said smoothly, stepping forward under the bright floodlight. "I see you were being..." He gave a polite pause to deepen the wound. "Tactical?"

"Strategic," Chad replied, straightening.

"Is there a difference?"

Chad's rifle was suddenly in his hands. He smiled and winked.

The Goons tensed. Darius raised a casual hand. He never underestimated Chad but occasionally came close. That charming rogue persona was smooth and polished as an ice-rink; only the occasional crack hinted at something else deep below.

"Gentlemen, please," he said smoothly. "Mr Blaster is a guest. There's no need for alarm."

He turned and strolled back beneath the roller door.

"Come in," he spoke over his shoulder. "Let us discuss how to reward your persistence. I have an important delivery that requires your brand of... strategy."

"You haven't paid for this one yet," Chad called, forlornly.

"Perhaps the thanks of a grateful universe will be enough." For a beat, Darius's tone was strange. Then, drifting from inside: "And for heaven's sake, un-cock your weapon. You'll do yourself an injury."

Five : Splurnik

Humans have had a century to come to terms with not being alone in the galaxy.

First contact occurred when a human interstellar ship (the somewhat exhaustingly named Voyageur Galactique Extraordinaire – vers les étoiles et au-delà) arrived at Proxima Centauri and encountered a Flurvian garbage scow dumping a planet's worth of landfill into the star.

Well — they hadn't literally run into each other. Space is so vast that hitting anything at all, ever — except, perhaps, the planet you're aiming for — is highly improbable. Instead, they'd spent several hours laboriously flying intercept courses, speculating the whole time about what they might find when they arrived.

For the humans, the journey was one of thrilled trepidation, daring to believe they might finally get an answer to one of the most fundamental questions: are we alone in the universe?

For the Flurvians: it was Thursday and they were behind on their landfill quota. Say what you like about the Flurvians — and many do — but they're conscientious.

The beings currently in orbit of Gliese 876, however, are not Flurvians.

They're Clurgons.

If you've never met a Clurgon, try this: imagine a centaur having sex with an octopus. Got it? Great. Now picture the offspring. Triple that in size and upholster it in purple toad-skin. There. Yes! You've just met a Clurgon.

Nifty, aren't they?

The Clurgon ship is commanded by Splurnik Trillbox (and before you scoff, 'Jeff Smith' or 'Hiroshi Yakatama' sound just as stupid to a Clurgon), an enormous individual even by Clurgish standards. Just over three metres tall and nearly two metres long, Splurnik is the last being you want sitting in front of you at the theatre.

Unlike Abigail, Splurnik had always dreamt of being a starship captain. As a youngster, he'd spent his evenings basking in the warm shallows of Clurgon Prime, watching the space elevators haul supplies to the orbital shipyards and wishing he were going up with them.

Human biologists classify Clurgons as "giant, hideous semi-terrestrial octopods," while Clurgon biologists classify humans as "weak-limbed, treeless apes." So, there's more than enough offence to go around.

Clurgon ships might appear grandiose and gaudy — like a massive Range Rover in Dubai — but the need to maintain both 'dry' and 'wet' habitation zones, coupled with the extraordinary mineral wealth of Clurgon Prime, has allowed Clurgish designers to let their down hair a bit. (Not that Clurgons have hair, but you're human, so you get the metaphor.)

******

Splurnik lounged opulently in his Command Tank on the bridge of the Swift Jet of Warm Water That Brings Plentiful Nourishment (the Clurgish has more zing). Today had been a triumph.

Work was complete on the jump gate linking Gliese 876 to the wider trade lanes of the Clurgon Empire. Gliese was the first minor system to gain its own gate — a crucial step toward the Empire's strategic goal of having "loads."

Splurnik waved a tentacle over a glowing sensor plate, and a swarm of merry bubbles erupted from the depths. He closed his eyes and slid deeper into the roiling waters, when a muted tone announced the arrival of Petty Officer Klurn, ship's steward.

"Ah, Klurn!" Splurnik rotated gently. "Status report — and do be a dear and pass me that loofah."

******

Unlike Erebus, the Swift was a warship. In the Clurgish fashion, she was enormous — one and a half kilometres long by half a kilometre wide. Her hull bristled with armaments and mysterious buboes precision-engineered to arouse maximum fear.

Most of these housed cupboards and laundry facilities — you will never want for clean sheets on a Clurgon ship.

Similarly, many of the weapon systems were fake.

The real strength of their vessels was layer upon layer of hidden shields. When one gave way to incoming fire, another would absorb the attack. The Clurgon war doctrine was based entirely on denying these shields existed, for two key reasons:

It allowed them to say, "Our ships are protected only by mighty Clurgon armour, a warrior's garb."

It made their enemies say, "Our torpedoes haven't made a dent. We're hopelessly outclassed," and more importantly, "We surrender."

Ironically, the enormous generators powering these shields made Clurgon ships wildly volatile. One lucky hit to the exhaust port and — boom — gone in a fabulous, implausible fireball.

******

"Thank you, Klurn." Splurnik raised a tentacle and took the loofah from Klurn's flipper. It disappeared into the bubbling depths toward pleasures unknown. A rainbow of inks puffed to the surface.

"And our status?"

"Two updates, Captain," said Klurn, who knew his leader liked nothing more than enumerated lists and anticipation. "One: the jump gate is online and ready for its inaugural test. I believe you are to have the honour?"

A puff of golden ink welled up and Splurnik let out a little titter of glee.

"Quite so, Klurn, quite so. Tomorrow, my oldest and most fecund daughter graduates from The Academy, and I shall be there to douse her in many inks."

"I am sure she will be honoured, Captain," said Klurn, who had the 'understated valet' gene so deeply embedded in his DNA that his dying wish would be to finish the ironing.

"She is top of her class, Klurn, have I mentioned that?"

"No, sir." Klurn deftly wove a cloth of flattering deceit.

"Good, good. It doesn't become an officer to ramble on." Splurnik allowed himself an internal paternal ramble, until a polite cough drew him back to now.

"And the second update?"

"You may find this even more," Klurn paused for maximum arousal, "stimulating, Captain."
A nebula of inks frothed to the surface.

"Oh go on, Klurn," Splurnik said, rolling imperiously in the warm water. "You do tease."

"A human ship has just dropped out of warp on the edge of the system..." Splurnik's many eyes widened with delight. "Long-range scans indicate it is some sort of... delivery van."

"Take us to within visual range of the human ship and set my tank lighting to 'Menacing,'" said Splurnik, relishing the words.

"At once, Captain."

"Oh, and Klurn?"

"Yes, Captain?"

"Bring me my most theatrical helmet."

Klurn tilted his body to a precisely calibrated angle of deference and deftly removed himself.

Splurnik's gaze shifted to the enormous viewscreen that wrapped around the bridge. Erebus was a faint smear of white glistening at the very limits of visual range.

In six months this would all be over. One last performance — then paperwork, pension, and a long, dignified slide into dotage.

A huge grin made itself at home among the rumples of his face. Let's play the "big bad alien" one more time.

This was going to be fun.

Six : Abigail

"Commander Dennistoun to the bridge, please."

Abigail folded the page of her book and snapped off the reading light. The most comfortable nine minutes of her day had been spent perched on a makeshift chair of filing box and shelf. That wasn't a good sign.

She ran her hand gently over the carpeted walls of the Cupboard. How warm it was in here, how peaceful. It would be so nice to just stay and—

No. She didn't shirk responsibility. If anything, she was a walking advertisement for the wonders of being in charge, with a particular talent for getting things done. Most importantly, she was especially good at getting things done while keeping deaths to an absolute minimum.

There were more celebrated, more decorated Commanders in the Alliance, but they'd been propelled to the top astride an ever-growing mountain of corpses. Sure, she had never been victorious in battle against a sentient gas monster from the Euclid cluster—then again, she'd never been pulled half-frozen and gibbering from the only escape pod and rewarded with a medal.

"Commander Dennistoun to the bridge, rather more urgently, please."

The voice pulled her back to the present.

"I'll be right there," she replied, with the smooth gravity of one who is completely in control and not sitting on a box in the dark.

******

The Erebus had been designed to be exceptionally good at hauling bulky things and very bad at everything else. Above all, it was the kind of craft meant to avoid Trouble at all costs. Trouble was for massive ships with lots of guns, or tiny ones primarily built of bomb.

Unfortunately for the Erebus, Trouble had already swept into the car park and was busily looking for its wallet in the glove box.

******

Abigail stood in the hyperlift, smoothing shelf marks from her uniform. The day had begun at 7 a.m. with Morning Briefing and wouldn't end until Commander's Nightcap Drinks at 11 p.m. She'd fantasised about snatching a half-hour run around the orlop deck, but Schmaltz's ribbon-cutting had put the kibosh on that.

The doors opened to reveal Lieutenant Curlew in the middle of the bridge—hopping pensively, like a rabbit awaiting its test results. Unlike most of the crew, he was a commissioned officer in the EarthGov military and felt he had some sort of authority in a crisis.

An uneasy and highly opaque agreement existed between Earth's government and the mega-corporations who oversaw most deep space trade and exploration. Whatever the original plan was, the result had transformed the 'chain of command' into a sort of 'amorphous blob of blame.'

Abigail was at the top—that was clear—but who came next, much less so. She'd brokered an uneasy peace by bestowing on Curlew the title of 'Number Two,' a rank as prestigious as it was malleable.

"Commander," Curlew said, his face oscillating between relief and fear, "a Clurgon warship is approaching rapidly to port with weapons systems activated—they have hailed us."

"Clurgons?" Abigail couldn't hide her surprise. "Did we have any indication they'd be here?"

"No, Commander. As far as EarthGov is concerned, this system is minor and strategically unimportant—"

Abigail caught the eye of Schmaltz, who was bristling in a corner.

"—useful for mining and agriculture, perhaps, but nothing more. We're quite far from Clurgon space. This is very unexpected."

"Very good, Number Two." Abigail oozed calm authority. She'd had a couple of seconds to calibrate now, and innate leadership had kicked in. She really was extremely good in a crisis—which, and this can't be emphasised enough, tended to stop people dying.

"Strategy—situation report."

Chief Strategy Officer Jezzia Mundock had her eyes locked on the swirling screens of the Tactical station.

"The Clurgon ship is extremely heavily armed and armoured," she began. "We're essentially a cycle courier—they could destroy us with a single shot. However, their critical systems are unshielded. A direct hit could buy us enough time to leg it to hyperspace in the confusion."

"Kick them in the nuts and run away?"

"Exactly," Jezzia said, with a grim smile. "Quick defenestration strike, use the confusion to jump. We won't get a second chance."

Abigail met her eyes and nodded once. "Very well." She turned to face the viewscreen. "Helm—return their hail and open a channel."

"Yes, Commander." Helm officer Terry Mbutu pressed the Hold button and hoped fervently not to die.

******

The bridge of the Swift had been a whirling carnival of activity. Splurnik surveyed the results with an artist's eye.

"Klurn—you have excelled yourself," he bellowed from his tank, eyes rimmed with satisfaction.

The bridge lights had been dimmed and switched to a filthy shade of mauve. Rusted chains dangled from the ceiling. Shapeless, nameless horrors loomed from the shadows.

"Could you find any more of those 'human limbs' you made?"

"I'm afraid not, sir."

"Very well—two piles should suffice. We don't want to overdo it."

Splurnik sloshed around to face the viewscreen and adjusted his war helmet to its most rakish angle. Yes, this would round off the week nicely—maximum drama, zero stakes.

"On screen!" he ordered.

******

Galactic historians are divided on what started the first Clurgon/Human war. Some believe it was caused by a Human ship firing first at a Clurgon battlecruiser, which had been approaching with weapons systems fully charged and locked on as a sign of mutual respect. Others claim the Clurgons were 'provocative bastards' who were 'asking for it'.

What is known for certain is that the war was pointless. The sheer size of the galaxy—and the vast amount of time, energy, and resources required to move fleets around—rendered any 'victory' Pyrrhic at best.

It also meant most battles were won simply because the enemy fleet got confused and warped to a different system a hundred light years away.

Peace had held for thirty years now, primarily because nobody could decide how a war could be meaningfully fought. An attempt was made to resolve the conflict through a series of sporting contests, but these were abandoned after the Clurgon equestrian team kept slithering out of their stirrups.

It was also the origin of the famous aphorism: a thousand drowned horses solve nothing.

******

"Ahhh, Commander." Splurnik's gigantic face almost filled the viewscreen. "How good of you to pay Clurgon space a visit."

He's looking at bloody Curlew! Abigail thought. She retained her composure, but this really riled her.

It's 2342. He is a bloody alien and still he thinks Richard is the bloody Commander.
She stole a look at Curlew from the corner of her eye.

And HE is enjoying this! Look at him! She could already hear the voice he'd use later—calm, apologetic, faintly patronising. I didn't want to interrupt, Commander. It was a tense situation. What a bastard.

Abigail strode forward, then side-stepped in front of Curlew.

"I am Commander Abigail Dennistoun of the Alliance Ship Erebus. We're here on a peaceful survey mission. I wasn't aware of a Clurgon claim here?"

"Commander—my most extreme apologies. My crew have been overseeing the final completion of a new jump gate in this system. We informed your government of this many… Klurn, the word?

"Months, Captain."

"Yes. Months ago."

"Did you send a message through official channels?" Abigail asked, with the sinking feeling that she already knew the answer.

"Oh yes." Splurnik's smile broadened. "An official communication was sent via sub-light relay. You should receive the message in several... the word again, Klurn?"

"Decades, sir."

"Yes. That's it. Decades."

A host of thoughts swarmed Abigail's brain. The Erebus had been diverted at short notice with orders to survey the system. QuikBrew's whimsical approach to planning often sent them clattering half-cocked across the galaxy, but it was possible that someone, somewhere, knew something was afoot.

She decided to press the issue.

"Captain—I would like to formally request permission to survey this system for the purposes of stellar cartography."

"Commander—I'm afraid such matters are quite out of my hands. I would suggest you make a formal request through official channels."

"Should I send them sub-light?" Dennistoun asked grimly.

"Oh yes! A capital idea, capital!" Splurnik bobbled happily. "I'm sure you'll be free to chart this system in the upcoming... Klurn?"

"Centuries."

"Yes. Centuries. Now Commander, please don't advance any further into our system. You may leave as soon as your Alcubierre drive is recharged."

Abigail quickly ran through her options. As she only had one, this didn't take long.

Her 'regular catch-up' with Clive, QuikBrew's Senior Vice President of Strategic Exploration (Lesser Systems), was going to be even more tedious than usual.

She shuddered and then remembered. A look of horror flashed across her face. Curlew caught it and had the same realisation.

"No, Commander," he whispered.

"I have to... I, I have to," she whispered back.

"Commander—please," Curlew said, his face a rictus. "Don't do this."

There was no getting out of it. Protocol. Branding. Clause 4.8b.

"Captain," she began firmly, eyes locked on Splurnik's. Something about her bearing—her resoluteness—caught Splurnik off guard.

"Commander?" he asked, looking uncertain for the first time.

"Captain," she paused, bracing for the inevitable. "The QuikBrew Corporation hopes that you have a super great day." Her voice quavered, but she pushed on valiantly. "Whether it's coffee on the move, or Dark Fluid is your groove, think QuikBrew."

"QuikBrew, go, go go!" The bridge crew chanted half-heartedly.

Splurnik looked blank, then roared with laughter.

"Oh, that is wonderful, wonderful," he said. "Yes—next time I want to drink warp drive fuel I shall certainly think of you humans. Have a super great day."

The call ended. Abigail wondered how often a corporate slogan had become someone's epitaph.

She exhaled slowly. It was something she'd done since childhood when things threatened to overwhelm her: inhale for four, exhale for six. In for four, out for six. Now she was a leader it served another purpose; keeping the fear inside her where it couldn't infect others.

It was a simple mission. Jump in, survey, leave colony equipment in orbit, jump out. Failure would be costly—for the company and her career.

But why didn't they know about the jump gate? Those were massive undertakings, trumpeted with immense pride across the galaxy. Few systems had them—usually the important ones.

Why build one here?

Somebody at QuikBrew knew. They had to. But why send the Erebus—a ship totally unsuited to any form of confrontation? What had they expected them to do—chain themselves to the jump gate? Or were they hoping for something... deniable.

She drew her train of thought to a stop and stepped off the footplate. Speculating was pointless. They had to leave.

"Curlew—have we been able to conduct any reconnaissance at all?"

Curlew exhaled. "A little, Commander. Some preliminary scans of the moons of the outermost planet. Nothing really of note—not that it matters." He gestured to the ship looming on the viewscreen. "I don't think we're building colonies any time soon."

Abigail nodded. "Helm, set a course towards the system's edge and prepare to jump back to Lutyens when ready."

"Aye, Commander." Terry started punching coordinates into his console.

"Commander." Jezzia's voice was urgent. "The Clurgon ship has locked onto us. Its forward armaments are at maximum charge."

"Assessment?"

"They're going to shoot at us, Commander."

"Why?" Abigail's quality of life was declining precipitously and, just when it seemed she had hit bottom, bottom had given way to reveal a cavernous drop below.

She inhaled, then breathed out. "Helm—hail the Clurgons—tell them we are leaving immediately."

Terry rapidly fired out several hails. "No acknowledgement, Commander."

"Options, Jezzia."

"Kick 'em in the nuts and run."

Abigail considered the consequences of inaction. They were flame-themed.

"Jezzia. Execute the plan, but do not fire unless they do."

"Aye, Commander." Jezzia slammed her hand down, activating a pre-programmed attack sequence. Power surged into the forward defence grid as the sub-light drive of the Erebus burst to life, thrusting the ship straight toward the Clurgon destroyer.

******

On board the Swift, Splurnik was in a festive mood.

"Oh Klurn," he said, hauling himself from his tank. "I do so enjoy a contact situation—it's really… enervating, don't you find?"

"Indeed so, sir," said Klurn, knowing that flattery was the quickest way to an evening off.

"What are the humans doing now?"

"They are at a full stop, sir. Tactical advises that they will turn and leave the system. They lack stealth capabilities and heavy weapons—they have no alternative."

"Excellent, excellent—then we shall drown no horses today." Splurnik wrapped himself in an opulently absorbent robe. He was a warship captain but, like all good warship captains, knew the optimal state of war was 'none'. A little verbal sparring and sabre rattling hurt no one but was still an honourable way of protecting the Empire.

"Prepare my shuttle for departure. Tomorrow, I shall dance with my daughter." He began the complicated process of hauling himself to his quarters. "And—Klurn—have Tactical power up forward weapons and lock onto the human ship. Encourage them not to dawdle."

"Very good, sir."

"Don't let them fire though. You know how… keen they get."

"Indeed, sir—warning shots only."

"If completely unavoidable." Splurnik wasn't sure why they didn't have a 'fire blanks' option—he guessed it was because that would reduce the ship from 'terrifying war machine' to 'mobile disco.'

A klaxon shrieked into life, followed by a flashing light. Klurn pressed a flipper to his earpiece for dramatic effect and held up the single tentacle of 'wait a moment.'

"The human ship has apparently attacked us, sir."

Splurnik looked around at the total lack of devastation.

"Forward battery fired one shot in retaliation and has… crippled their starboard engine array… caused damage to several decks and… knocked off a fin."

Splurnik rolled his many eyes. "Oh Klurn."

"Indeed, sir."

"How serious is the damage?"

"Uncertain, Captain. Suggest we dump them into a stable orbit and signal Earth there has been an incident."

"Very well. Have Commodore Schlep oversee proceedings in my absence."

Splurnik made to leave, then turned back.

"What were they thinking?"

"It appears they were targeting our 'unshielded critical systems'."

They let out a hearty laugh. Splurnik wrapped a quivering tentacle around Klurn to steady himself.

"Oh, oh! It still slays me! They fall for that every time—honestly, what do they think of us?"

He pulled himself together. "Still—that does mean they were trying to boot us in the egg sacks and scarper. Most unsporting. Now, you will excuse me, I have offspring to deluge."

Off the starboard bow, a broken Erebus drifted in a twinkling debris field, alone against the blackness of space. The blackness, just for a moment, appeared to twitch.

Seven : Jade

The planet appeared suddenly, in that way planets don't. It orbited something, but what that something was wasn't clear. It might not have been orbiting anything at all — just giving off the impression of orbit to lull the viewer into a false sense of security.

Jade glared at it, uncomfortably aware that it was somehow glaring back.

"You have returned," said a voice in her brain that wasn't hers.

"I have," said Jade, to her empty cockpit.

"Three hundred and forty-five. Eight before. Always now," the voice replied, still behind her thoughts.

"Now and then," said Jade. The planet shimmered.

"Welcome!" The voice leapt from her brain to her vocal cords. "Please, be here."

"I'd prefer to land first." Jade's voice followed the other out of her mouth.

"As you wish." Now the voice filled the cockpit — everywhere at once.

The planet sparkled — then surged forward, far too fast. Atmosphere tore past the window, followed by clouds, a pelt of rain, and a mountain range that slithered up to meet them. The ship hadn't moved a centimetre. The planet moved silently, like a fast-forwarded film projected onto glass. Mountains rose, split, fell away — replaced by an alpine valley and a blue-green stupa of ice. The reel jumped. The ship now sat neatly on a smooth landing pad halfway up its side.

"I meant I wanted to land myself," Jade said, unbuckling her harness with pointed annoyance.

"That is nostalgia," the voice replied, from nowhere and everywhere.

"Nostalgia is time. It's fundamental," Jade said, with the certainty of someone who knows it's their turn to take the bins out.

"Nostalgia is a construct. Mortal. Lesser."

"Fine." Jade tossed the used pizza box of spite into the recycling bin of acceptance and shut the lid. "Something is wrong with reality. We need to fix it."

"Then come. I am here."

She slung her satchel over one shoulder and made her way to the boarding ramp.

Waiting at the bottom was Bulstrode Kersland, High Factotum of the Stitch Order. He looked like a casting director's anxiety dream — his form shifting constantly through shapes and features the human brain either resolved into something vaguely familiar or went entirely insane trying. For our purposes, let's say he was a seven-foot-tall blue man in a hooded saffron cowl and leave it at that.

"Jade Green," said Bulstrode, opening his arms in greeting. For a moment they stretched off into infinity before Jade's brain's anti-insanity valve compressed them back down to 'outstretched.'

"Bulstrode!" Jade charged down the ramp and threw her arms around him. The hug was somehow both hard and squishy.

"Jade." He ran a hand affectionately over her head, causing her hair to ping to attention. "I have missed you."

"Have you?" Jade pulled back slightly. Bulstrode had been her mentor — her lighthouse in the metaphysical maelstrom of recruitment. Steady. Gentle. Never cruel. But he'd never 'missed' her. She studied his face, curious.

"No. I exist in an eternal state of eagerly anticipating your arrival, luxuriating in your company, and praying for your swift departure." He shrugged infinitesimally. "But I believe I would have done, if I were able."

She deflated. The Order had pulled her from pre-warp Earth with very little... prep time. It wasn't a calling, nor a birthright. Stitches were plucked from time at moments of great consequence and given the tools to safely trim and tuck the fabric of reality. Temporal sutures, pockets, and tiny wisps of precious, new thread. She'd come willingly, but had slowly realised that there are conceptual limits to 'informed consent' when transitioning from time-limited human to infinite demi-God. She didn't regret her choice, but every birthday she received a theoretical construct where cake should be.

The Order didn't care about justice, or mercy, or right and wrong. They fixed what wasn't supposed to happen — not to make it better, but to preserve the structural integrity of time. Jade appreciated the sentiment. She just couldn't shake the question: if you're going to stitch up reality, why not improve the cut while you're at it?

They climbed the silver stairs into the stupa's central atrium. The air smelled of jasmine and hastily smushed time. The walls were lined with glass jars, each roughly the size of a human head, filled with thick neon liquid — some red, some green; a living tally of threats to reality. Jade had tried counting them once and given up. They rose toward a ceiling that logic said must exist, but Jade had never seen. A rolling cloudbank had formed near the top. She studied the jars; there were far more reds than usual, and the colour of them boiled and thrashed angrily, like a furious sea monster caught on a line.

"Is Praisegod Barebones in today?" Jade pushed thoughts of the jars away. She needed a clear head for the Singer.

Bulstrode made a gesture that might have been a shrug or a blessing. "He's compiling the Index of Events That Nearly Happened."

"Sounds exhausting."

"He thrives on tedium."

They paused at the threshold of the audience chamber — a vaulted room lit by something that might have been the forgotten memories of the universe, or possibly just a window that needed a good wipe. At the far end sat the Supreme Singer, nested in a shimmer of threads.

"Wanderer Jade," the Supreme Singer greeted. "You are here. Arriving, and leaving."

"I've come to seek your aid," Jade replied.

"Aid has a cost. First, you must explain."

"Explain what?"

"The man in the transport café."

"Oh. Him. I improved him."

"You spread his atoms across several planets."

"That's what I said." Jade loathed the Singer. Not 'didn't see eye to eye'. No — full-on cold war clash of ideologies.

"We do no harm." The Singer projected neutrality, but Jade could sense the edge.

"I didn't harm the universe. I improved it." Her loathing made her petulant. She blamed the Singer for that too.

"This is empirically true. But the balance is fine. He had a daughter. Friends. He was not a good man, but they are impacted. They will mourn."

"Oh please, what about the dozens he hurt — their harm is far greater."

"We are not the jury. We are not the executioner. We mend. We resolve. We do not cross the line."

"Where is that line?"

"Where it should be."

"Then it is time to move it." Jade glared furiously at the Singer, who gazed placidly back. She broke first. "I need to find Erebus. Apparently, it's a god or a rock or—"

"Erebus is human."

"What, a bloke called Erebus? That'll narrow it down."

"No," the Singer's voice tolled.

"A woman then?" She knew it wasn't. She just wanted a rise.

"Erebus is human. You were human. To err is human. Humans have a beginning. Where was yours?"

"Croydon," Jade shuffled her feet. "But it's not like you think. Very handy for the Spaceport."

"Yes. The most enviable homes are those that can be left at haste."

"And then there's the monorail," she murmured.

"Your humanity is your greatest asset to the Order. You perceive time as linear. That is invaluable." The Singer tilted their head. "You must return to the end of the beginning."

"Could you can it with the mystery and give me something useful?"

"Would you like a strawberry?"

"What? No! Why?"

"There's no mystery in a strawberry."

Silence. The threads hummed in the breeze. Jade looked up at the gilded roof — memories of future events rippled across it. There weren't as many as there should be, and those that remained seemed thinner.

"Something will happen—" Jade began.

"Will?"

"Will, is, has — it doesn't matter."

"It matters greatly."

"Semantics! We fix—"

"The stitches must be invisible."

"It is our duty to—"

"Do no harm."

"We have to—"

"Do no harm."

"Look up! Half your jars are red."

"Then our mantra is all the more important."

"I'm done," Jade snapped. She believed in the mission of the Order. But this schtick made her want to walk into a sun. "Chant your mantra as the universe shatters — sit in this temple and rot."

She turned on her heel and stalked toward the door, ignoring Bulstrode's ineffectual arm-flaps-for-calm.

"Wanderer Jade." The Singer's voice had — changed. The edge had sliced through flesh and burst into air. "The Order has only one aim. We preserve reality. We ensure events happen — that the thread of history is unbroken, from the beginning till the end."

Jade turned. The Singer was floating above the nested threads, the wall behind glowing red.

"We have allowed you to push and bend at our walls, because of your unique gifts. But you will not act with impunity. If you become a threat to our work, you will be removed."

"Fine! Throw me out! I'm better alone!" Jade punched the air.

"No Stitch has ever left the Order. None ever will. We are the guardians. Eternal. Vigilant. If you stray, we will remove you from every thread you ever touched."

"That's monstrous." Jade couldn't believe what she was hearing.

"It is necessary. We do no harm. Erasure protects completely."

"I—" The Singer's casual approach to existence chilled her. The words had been knocked from her, like a punch to the gut.

"Phobos."

"What?" Jade said automatically, one hand on the doorframe.

"Go to Phobos. You will find the end of the beginning there." The Singer paused. "It orbits Mars."

"Yes — thank you," Jade muttered, taking a step forward. Her body moved, but her mind was a million miles away. "I... I know where Phobos is."

"And take this." The Singer reached into a sleeve and withdrew a glowing object whose colour shifted from red to amber to green. It snapped Jade back to reality.

"The Bobbin of Balance," said the Singer. "It will tell you…" They frowned, searching for a long-lost concept. "…if you need to hurry."

"Cool. Good. Thanks," Jade said slowly, mind still in recovery. The Bobbin held near-mythic status within the Order. It was the Singer's most valuable tool, a sort of mobile reality alarm that could also protect and direct. A Wanderer being entrusted with it was unprecedented.

She watched the shimmer of light dance across its surface, resolving to a steady green in her hands. It was warm. Comforting. Heavy. It pulsed subtly, like blood through veins. "Guess I'm going to Phobos."

"It is already done." The Singer settled back amongst the threads, eyes beginning to close.

Jade looked at Bulstrode, then asked, "Why are you doing this — you just threatened to erase me."

"No threat. An action that may be necessary. Reality is improved by your presence, if you remain on the path."

******

Outside, on the landing ramp, she hugged Bulstrode again. He held her tightly, then gently folded their hands together.

"The Singer is not blind to the jars, Jade. The threads are fraying. And they're afraid."

Jade rolled her eyes. Anger, briefly displaced by fear, had returned. "Good thing some of us still get out there and get dirty." She tossed her satchel inside and leaned on the airlock. "Think about that while you're filling that arsehole's teapot."

"Jade! Please, understand me fully. The Singer is afraid. The Singer cannot conceptualise this. There is a threat to reality greater than… greater than should exist. The reality we know, the thread of history — we can no longer see its full length. Sometimes, it vanishes. It is… it should not be possible." Any levity had drained from Bulstrode — only hope remained. "We can still call on your needle. For that, we're grateful beyond words."

"Yeah. I'm a real paragon."

She stepped inside. The airlock sealed. Moments later, she was streaking toward the horizon.

Bulstrode watched until her ship vanished into the blue-black haze.

"Good luck, Jade," he murmured, raising a hand in blessing. "Keep your needle sharp."

Bulstrode looked up at the Stupa, gleaming in the sunshine.

"Save us."

Eight : Abigail

Theories of the multiverse tend to get a bad press. Many scientists find the lack of empirical proof hard to take, leading to innumerable arguments on the theme of "is this the reality where I strike you?"

Outside the scientific community, multiverse theory found an enthusiastic audience among the despots of the 21st and 22nd centuries. In every other universe, went the argument, my coup failed — so it is right that I continue my reign of terror here to stop the fabric of reality from fraying.

It's easy to poke holes in this, but generally the man holding the gun gets to have the weakest argument.

It's impossible to know in how many realities the Erebus crew survived their encounter with the Clurgons unscathed. In some realities, they escaped. In others, they were vaporised. In one, a malfunctioning popcorn machine suffocated them all before anyone could pull the cord.

In this reality, the Erebus was snared in a Clurgon tractor beam and placed into orbit around the system's fourth planet.

Unfortunately, the words placed and orbit here are misleading — with hurled and a death plunge being more appropriate.

******

"Commander." Terry studied his displays. "Our orbit is deteriorating. Thermosphere interface in five minutes. After that: two or three passes before we begin final descent."

"How long?" Abigail placed her hands on her hips and squared up to the viewscreen.

"Twenty minutes to the lower atmosphere, thirty till we hit the ground." Terry had the eerie calm of a man who'd just seen the dentist pull out the drill.

"Assessment."

"We have just enough control to enter the atmosphere, but we'll be pushing the ship's limits. It'll get extremely hot and bumpy, and we'll have very limited influence over where we... land."

"A landing?" Abigail wiggled her toes. She would have chosen more comfortable shoes for this brand of heroism.

"A very firm landing. Water may be survivable. A large lake would be... best."

"Very good, Helm." Abigail could feel Terry wavering. Right — if they were crashing, she was going to be professional about it. Clear orders and communication would give the crew a sense of control. If only someone could do the same for her. She activated ship-wide comms.

"Attention all crew: this is your Commander. Erebus is critically damaged. We are conducting an emergency landing on the planet below. This is serious, but we will make it safely through if we all remain calm and follow procedures. Complete your checklists and take refuge in your assigned areas. The bar is no one's assigned area. Good luck."

Across the ship Abigail's words sank in. In med-bay, Dr Han carefully slipped a harness over a bedridden patient. In the yoga studio, Kim Mulgrew calmly rolled up her mats and stowed them in cubbies. In his office, Mr Schmaltz looked at his giant scissors and sighed.

On every deck the crew stowed their gear, strapped themselves in, and hoped.

"Commander?" Stacey's voice came from the ceiling.

"Yes, Stacey."

"Entry will expose damaged areas to extreme heat in an oxygenated environment."

"Understood. Fire risk?"

"Critical. Fires will spread rapidly, and suppression systems will be overwhelmed."

"Curlew—" Abigail began, but he was already moving.

"I'll assemble a volunteer team, Commander."

Something in his tone made Abigail glance over. Curlew was calm — surprisingly calm for a man who owned sock organisers, filed by hue. She moved him up a notch in her estimation and nodded.

"Thank you. Anyone—"

"I volunteer," Jezzia stepped forward. "You don't need Strategy in a crash."

"Emergency la—" Abigail stopped herself. "Thank you, Jezzia."

"Let's move," said Curlew. "We'll pick up others as we go."

Curlew strode out, straight-backed and resolute — Jezzia raised a fist. A rush of sadness and anger surged through Abigail, tempered with pride. She turned back to the planet hurtling up to greet them. Around her, the bridge crew were busy; voices clipped, systems shutting down, gear stowed.

"Commander?" A voice came over the comm. It was Eliza, formidable sovereign of the Erebus kitchens.

"Yes, Chief?"

"Is this an h'exercise?"

Abigail heard a faint note of hope.

"I'm afraid not, Eliza."

"Oh." A pause. Then: "Right! Get them bleedin' pots off the stove, you lot!"

A metallic clatter and a shriek of profanity followed before the line cut.

******

Erebus' entry into the thermosphere caused absolutely nothing to happen.

Thermospheres are like that.

Junior crew began to relax. Phones were furtively checked. On the Promenade Deck, Ensign Barry decided there was time to grab a margarita from the commissary.

Then came the Stratosphere.

The Erebus was still travelling at near-orbital velocity. Friction built, causing her underside to glow red, then gold, then white. External sound roared back. Superheated gas flared violently along her sides.

Thrusters fired, struggling to stabilise the angle of attack. Across the ship, the crew were strapped in tight. On the Promenade, Barry was buried under an avalanche of glacé cherries.

Erebus's damaged aft section erupted in flames.

Curlew's team swung wildly in ruptured corridors, dangling from carabiners. Fire spread through ducts and floor voids. Repair droids scuttled vainly from flare-up to flare-up. Smoke choked the air. Sirens blared. Amber lights spun. It felt like closing time at Hell's least popular nightclub.

Curlew grasped a girder and steadied himself. His rebreather kept him alive, but all he could see was smoke.

"Stacey! Damage report."

"Hull rupture between decks five and fourteen. Bulkheads sealed. Fire is out of control. I've re-routed critical systems, but—"

The ship pitched. A pair of droids clattered past Curlew like startled crabs. A screech of warping metal rang out, followed by an alarming burst of Surfin' USA.

"What the hell is that?!"

"Entertainment servers have caught fire... please bear with me."

A fireball burst through a grille, exploding in heat inches from Curlew's faceplate. His heart raced. Panic rose and caused his hands to shake; he grabbed a strut hard until the trembling passed.

"Jezzia! Do you read, over?" Silence. Curlew realised he wasn't breathing.

"I read you, Richard, over." He gasped down a ragged breath.

"I've lost your signal. Status?"

"Grisly. I'm on deck six with Nai and Chen. Five or six more forward of the slurry tanks."

"Fire contained? Casualties?"

"Flammables cleared. Letting it burn out. Pulled eight. Three critical, five dead."

Curlew closed his eyes. "Oh God no. Eight..."

"Save it. Grieve later. Mundock out." Below, Jezzia pushed forward, into the flames.

"STACEY, CAN YOU TURN THE DAMN MUSIC OFF?!" He screamed so loud his voice broke.

It died.

"Thank you." He breathed again, a glimmer of calm in the storm.

"I couldn't shut down the server, Number Two. Fortunately, it melted. Unfortunately, I was only able to salvage something called All Out Bouzouki Bangers."

"In the circumstances, that's a win."

Curlew moved hand over hand toward the sealed bulkhead.

"Curlew, report." Abigail's voice crackled through the comm.

"We're holding our own. Fires are contained where possible, burning out where not. We've lost at least five, Commander."

Abigail's vision swam. Rage, guilt, horror churned through her. Vengeance whispered in her ear. She exhaled the poison, but not the feelings.

"Thank you, Number Two. Do you need more hands?"

"No. We're steady. Situation's under control."

"We're counting on you, Richard. Keep us safe. Dennistoun out."

She clicked off her mic. Her hands trembled. Five names. She didn't know whose yet — but she would. And they would be remembered.

Her eyes returned to the viewscreen. Erebus skimmed a mountain range — jagged peaks and white shoulders. Close now, the threat was real. But the heat was dissipating. Their descent had calmed. The hull had begun to cool.

"7,000 metres, Commander," Terry called, squinting at his instruments. "We've scanned a section of the surface. There's a lake — about nine kilometres long. Might be survivable. But... we'll hit it at around one hundred metres per second."

"Assessment?"

"Substantial hull damage. Crew injury. Hull plating loss. And the lake's ringed by mountains. If we miss the angle—"

"We hit a mountain."

"Yes, Commander."

"Alternatives?"

"Ocean ditching. Slower impact. But we'll sink. We'll be hundreds of miles from land. Exposure. Illness. Cannibalism."

"Recommendation?"

"The lake. If we get it wrong, we die quickly. If we get it right, some of us survive."

Abigail nodded once. Not everyone would make it. But she would give every single one of them a chance.

"The lake. Bring us in, Mr Mbutu." She looked over at the empty seats of Jezzia and Curlew, then activated ship-wide comms.

"Attention, all crew. We've made it through the worst. We're on final approach. Stay strong, stay focused and I will see you all on the ground."

Nobody could tell her that everything would be okay; but she could be that person for everyone else.

******

From the ground, the Erebus looked serene as she arced between two peaks.

Then, her engines roared like a thousand furious lions. She swooped low, skimming the lake.

Then, impact. A column of water thrown high as her bow plunged deep. She rose again, hurling white water toward the distant shore. Her hull plating peeled away as she smashed along the surface. At the lake's end she slammed aground on jagged rocks.

Aft half-submerged. Bow thrusting from the water like a punch that hadn't landed. The engines sputtered, then died.

Then: silence. A breeze through trees.

Erebus lay still.

Nine : Jertsie

At the heart of the QuikBrew Corporation lurked a terrible secret.

It wasn't evil — at least, not deliberately. That's a lazy stereotype. Yes, big companies do appalling things with distressing frequency. They'll sell baby milk to the destitute, test drugs on the unsuspecting, and flog landmines to tosspots without blinking. But true evil requires clarity of vision. Corporate malfeasance is usually a by-product of hope, greed, and rash decisions quickly made.

For QuikBrew, one such decision was trying to turn exceptionally low-grade coffee beans into profit using wildly experimental brewing techniques. Everyone knows Dark Fluid was born in QuikBrew's Culinary Innovation Labs. Very few know the process only works with bad beans. The worst beans. Beans that thrive only in a fetid patch of soil just outside Bulera, near the long-abandoned Zesty Earth Mindful Recycling Facility — soil so twisted by centuries of seeping poisons that every living thing claws and squirms to escape it.

Except these beans. They love it.

QuikBrew didn't realise what they'd made at first. When they finally understood, they assumed the brewing process was the key. They ordered more Dark Fluid.

They failed. Again and again.

Then they added the original bad beans back into the process. Success! Glory! But there were so few. QuikBrew had created and cornered the market, but there would only ever be a trickle of Fluid.

The bean field was acquired at once. Then the adjacent land. Then the waste dump. Miles of jungle were razed and replanted with millions of cuttings. They withered. Their beans shrivelled to husks. Millions were sunk into DNA research. Bigger, better bushes bloomed, groaning with fruit.

None of it worked.

Only the original bushes, in their pitiful square of poisoned dirt, yielded the crop. Humanity would travel faster than light — occasionally and at great expense.

But no one could be allowed to know why.

QuikBrew made a great show of its proprietary extraction techniques. A jealously guarded secret. Rival labs raced to reverse-engineer the process, to cash in on an impossibly lucrative market. A few even succeeded, unknowingly.

Because they didn't know about the beans.

The first Alcubierre drives were fitted to a handful of exploratory ships. Humanity waited, breath held, to see what lay beyond the solar system.

Decades later, the origin of the beans wasn't an issue anymore. Coffee was a sideshow. QuikBrew had weathered the few dents to its legacy when the truth came out. The quiet removal of those who once knew too much — that had been trickier. But the ones who gave those orders were now themselves long dead. A heartfelt apology and donation to QuikBrew's 'Happy Planet, Happy You' foundation had smoothed that over.

No, the real problem now was competition.

Earth had made contact with eight other spacefaring civilizations — and one lot who'd transcended physical form entirely and were unbearably smug about it (the See-Through Bastards of Gamma Leporis). All of them had their own sources of Dark Fluid. Some had a surplus. Which meant competition.

Sometimes, competition is healthy.

Sometimes, it calls for countermeasures.

War is an excellent countermeasure.

And every war needs a champion.

******

Jertsie Funt sat at her desk and glared out the window. The city beyond didn't flinch, which annoyed her. The desk annoyed her too.

It was a particular kind of desk — ornately carved from precariously endangered hardwood and finished with Neptunian cloud diamonds. A desk that said, "this is my galaxy, not yours."

Jertsie didn't care for it.

Yes, it intimidated underlings. Yes, its insurance value was monstrous. But it lacked the quiet elegance of her first choice. Unfortunately, HR wouldn't let her mount a loaded gun on the wall, so the desk would have to do.

It had been a bad day. That morning, she'd ended an affair — he was getting cuddly. Not part of the arrangement. Her lovers had a role, and it didn't include, she glanced at the bin, fluffy bears. She wasn't heartbroken, but she did hate waste. Now she was hotly aware of the thirty-minute "session" blocked out in her calendar. And there was no one to fill it.

She drummed her fingers on the desk. The wood silently absorbed the impact. Intolerable. Half the QuikBrew fleet was in dry dock, the Flurvian refuse contractors were on strike again, and the presence of balloons in the corridor foreshadowed some interminable merriment to be endured later.

She brought her fist down on the desk. Knuckles white.

Th-wack. Better.

Still not enough.

She'd need to find someone to fuck or fire in the next ten minutes or spiral completely out of control.

There was a knock at the door.

Jertsie narrowed her eyes. "Come."

The door slid open. Jerry Hong stepped in, clutching a stack of packages.

He was maybe twenty-five, thirty? She wasn't sure anymore. Lately, youth had become a blur of clear skin and good posture. It made her feel ancient. And hungry.

"Good afternoon, Ms Funt. I have your mail," Jerry said with a cautious smile.

"Good. Bring it in," said Jertsie, the lion to his startled gazelle. He was... acceptable. Decent height. Neat hair. Good teeth. A test was called for.

"Any news of the Erebus?" She watched him closely.

"Oh! I'm afraid I don't know, Ms Funt." He smiled, a transparent plea for forgiveness. "But I'm happy to run down to Operations and check."

Excellent. Trusting. Compliant. He'd do.

Jerry hesitated, unsure where to put the packages. His eyes danced the ancient dance of "do I guess, or do I ask?"

Jertsie clocked it. "On the desk," she said, adding, "please," with a sultry lilt.

Relief swept across his face. Clear instruction. A way out. He stepped forward and deposited the parcels with a flourish. "Will that be all, Ms Funt?" he asked, already half-turned toward hope.

"Wait."

Oh yes. The tingles were beginning. No real challenge here, no hunt. But he was fresh. Something new. That had merit.

She rose and laid her palms flat on the desk's polished surface. It radiated heat — centuries of blood and conquest steeped into the grain. Her pulse quickened.

The idiot was frozen mid-turn, tense and unsure. Perfect.

She traced the wood. Felt the jungle close in — dense, humid, alive. She was the mantis, arms folded around his spindly frame. Devouring him.

"Now, how—"

"Still gay." The words fell out of Jerry's mouth in a panic. His eyes widened. "Uhhh…"

This was unexpected, but she'd built her career on reacting to the unexpected. Move fast enough, and no one asks if you meant it. And his panic? So piquant, so moreish.

"Mr Hong!" The genuine shock in her voice startled even her. Excellent. Now modulate — land gracefully. "Your personal affairs are none of my business."

Right. Bring in the handbook.

"Although I'm glad you feel this is a safe space in which you can manifest the authentic you."

Delicious. Something meant to constrain her, turned into a blade. The tingles surged. This might be better than sex.

"But I'm not sure how that was relevant to the conversation we were having?"

"Conversation?" Jerry's voice cracked. His ears were bright red.

This should have been a simple task. Deliver mail. Smile. Leave. Now he was trapped in the queen's lair — the desk, the wood, the stare, the voice — his senses began to overload, leaving only the rush of blood in his ears.

"Our conversation," said Jertsie, "about your job performance."

Oh yes. The tingles were becoming a rising, pulsing throb.

"It has been..." she braced herself, "unsatisfactory."

"But why?" Jerry's eyes met hers, wide and pleading. His top lip twitched. Was that a tear?

Hot blood thrust to her extremities like a steam piston. A golden band of euphoria cinched tight around her. She could feel the nova roiling — just hold, hold it tight just a few seconds more.

She moved around the desk.

Each step drew power up through her soles, through the floor, the building, the scorched veins of the Earth itself. Her heels clicked with sublime authority.

She stopped just short of Jerry. Inches from him. Her gaze speared him — no escape, no mercy. Her eyes didn't see — they blitzkrieged. Punching down through skin, muscle, bone, bile, and hope. Straight into his core.

"Because I say so."

She delivered the words with absolute serenity.

"Now. Fuck off."

Jerry fled.

The door closed behind him with a swush. Just before it sealed, she heard it: one soft, stifled sob.

Jertsie collapsed to her knees and then slumped sideways onto the floor as the orgasm tore through her like a boarding party — unrestrained, brutal, victorious. A full-body detonation of power and release.

Time vanished. Space flexed sideways. She lay gasping, one hand resting on the cool floor like it was the only stable thing in the universe.

Two minutes later, she got up, smoothed her blouse, and walked briskly to her desk. She crossed out the evening's session with a single, efficient stroke.

"Well," she murmured, "that was productive."

She looked at the line she had scored through the appointment. A good, brisk slash. This was why she kept a paper diary. It had texture, weight, feeling. Jertsie sought out tangible things; so much felt so fleeting.

She looked down at the city again from her high tower. How far she had come. Up, through an education — paid for, yes — but earned with her brain, whilst all around sat the dull-witted, pampered progeny of plutocrats. Up, from the lower floors, crowded with interns who sounded right until you thought. Up, up, ever up, searching for the inspired, the brilliant, the best. Then she reached the top, and found—. No matter.

"Ricardo."

"Yes, Ma'am." The AI's voice poured silkily from hidden speakers.

"I require your services."

"Of course, Ma'am." Across the room, a discreet panel slid open. Something elegantly proportioned and ergonomically sublime extended itself and began to vibrate softly.

Jertsie didn't look up.

"Not that, Ricardo. Honestly — whatever must you think of me?"

She tilted her chin toward the domed lens in the ceiling. Her eyes glittered.

"Schedule a board meeting for this afternoon—"

"Forgive me for interrupting, Ma'am, but I believe Ms Tuvlumon has already scheduled a board meeting for tomorrow. Topics include 'Family Funday planning' and 'The Restructure.'"

"Has she now?" Felinda Tuvlumon was the one person who, technically, outranked her. There was tremendous personal danger here, she might not get her way. Jertsie smiled. It felt good to feel threatened. She so rarely did. And sport without danger was no sport at all. "Very well. Call an emergency board meeting. One hour from now. Mandatory attendance. I will have something to discuss."

"Very good, Ma'am." The device retracted with a whisper. "May I ask the topic of discussion?"

"One moment, Ricardo."

She ran her hands along the carved arms of her chair.

"Did you know this chair is made from the last ancient hardwood in Brazil?"

"I do, Ma'am. I forwarded your felling order personally."

"Of course you did, you sweet, loyal boy."

Her fingers traced the grain of the wood, stroking the ghosts of vines and canopy light.

"Do you know how old those trees were?"

"I—"

"It's rhetorical, Ricardo. I'm building to something."

She spun the chair in a slow, full circle.

"They were the oldest. Centuries old. Their seeds fought through the undergrowth to touch the sun. They withstood fire, flood, blight, infestation. They towered above the rest, great cathedrals of lumber. And then one day, a humble lenhador arrived with his axe, and poof."

She patted the arms.

"Now they're these. Two blocks of wood, no thicker than my wrist."

"Yes, Ma'am. If memory serves, you had the rest of the timber chipped and incinerated."

"Obviously. The chair must be unique. That is its value."

"There were… competing claims. The orphans, for example, wanted the offcuts for their biomass boiler."

"Adorable. Winter can be so bitter in the Pacaraimas."

"They attempted to requisition it."

"I applauded their aspiration. If you want something — take it."

"You instructed your Goons to 'quell the insurrection.'"

She rifled absently through the boxes on her desk.

"Yes. I'd already done my part for the orphans by having no children of my own."

"Earth thanks you for your service, Ma'am."

Jertsie laughed. A full-bodied, unapologetic cackle. The laugh of someone who knew they were a monster and couldn't be happier about it.

"I like you, Ricardo. That's why I haven't deleted you for your insubordination. You get me."

"I 'get' everyone, Ma'am. It is the basis of my personality matrix. But I believe it will please you if I thank you."

"Only your honesty pleases me, Ricardo."

She walked across the office and stopped beneath his observation dome. She stared directly up at him.

"I'll delete you one day. When it is time."

"A statistical certainty, Ma'am. Assuming your own survival."

They regarded each other for a long moment.

"But not today."

She clicked her heels.

The door chimed.

"Come."

Jertsie pivoted smartly to face the entrance.

A terrified underling appeared in the doorway and hovered at the outer limits of "inside." Their eyes flicked about the room, clearly checking for corpses or vibrating objects. Finding neither, they somehow grew more anxious.

"Speak," Jertsie commanded.

She felt the first hints of warmth again in her fingertips, a low pulse of rising pleasure — but she tamped it down. She needed survivors to fetch her coffee.

"Uhhh..." the underling began, then blurted, "It's the Erebus, Ma'am."

"The Erebus?" Jertsie's eyebrow arched. "Dennistoun's ship. Sent to Gliese. They arrived safely, I trust?"

"They arrived safely... and were then engaged by a Clurgon vessel."

"The Clurgons! How curious they should be at Gliese. Do we know what they were doing there?"

"I—I don't know, Ma'am. But they..." the underling swallowed, "The Erebus is lost. With all hands. The Clurgons have claimed responsibility. They say we shot first. That we violated a closed system under military control."

Jertsie stood perfectly still. Then: "Very well. You may go."

"Thank-you-Ma'am-very-good-Ma'am," the underling sputtered, retreating at speed — thrilled to still be conscious.

Jertsie looked up toward Ricardo's lens.

"How very unexpected."

Her expression was unreadable.

"Oh yes. How silly of me. Subject for emergency board meeting," she said softly. "Lenhador."

"Ma'am — is it time?"

"Oh yes," Jertsie laughed and raised her arms. The window framed the sun behind her, casting her head in a blood red halo. "Cancel all leave. We have markets to conquer." She pointed straight at Ricardo's lens.

"Grab your axe, boy; we're marching to war!"

Ten : Jezzia

The galaxy teems with millions of languages, dialects, and accents that flow and mingle like crystalline streams across planets and stars. This is an appalling situation.

Left unchecked, the fallout would have been profound — ranging from you receiving a fruity Riesling when you ordered a flinty Sancerre, to pan-Galactic thermo-war. Obviously, something had to be done. You really can't stand Riesling.

Fortunately, advances in natural language processing in the 21st century mean entire languages can now be synthesised and translated from scratch in real time. A couple of low-powered chips implanted into the auditory canal and optic nerve are all it takes to read and understand any speech in the known universe.

Some linguists lament what they call the 'coarsening' and 'algorithmicising' of everyday communication. Once we stop celebrating the diversity of language, runs the argument, we lose something vital. Without new ways of expressing ideas, humanity is doomed to a slow, irreversible cultural and technological decay.

But we have cool rocket ships and chunky-ass lasers, so linguists can shove stupid words up bum hole.

******

The outer airlock door hissed hydraulically and lifted into its recess. Warm afternoon air eddied into the ship's interior like a nervous waiter carrying the wrong plates toward a table of quizzical faces.

A glove full of hand appeared and grabbed the outside of the hatch. Then an arm. Then the helmeted head of Jezzia.

She scanned the landscape surrounding the becalmed Erebus. Jagged rocks gave way to a sweep of white sand that gleamed in the mid-day sun. The lake water beyond was purply blue. The sky deep cerulean. Behind the beach, mossy dunes rolled into a dense, flowering forest of giant rhododendrons. Beyond that, the snowy peaks of distant mountains.

Jezzia watched for several minutes. Nothing moved. She retrieved a pair of binoculars from a cubby and methodically swept the terrain. No structures, no herds. If there was any sentient life here they'd still be gatherers. No threat. She stared a little longer, daring the landscape to attack her. It declined. Eventually, she relented.

"Airlock secure, Commander," she said into her link. "No hostiles visible in the vicinity of the ship."

She whipped her head upward in case whimsical bandits were poised to prove her wrong. The wind whistled through a crevice. Still nothing moved.

"There are no signs of sentient life or artificial constructions. The air is breathable but thin. Recommend additional oxygen for vulnerable crew. I'm removing my helmet now."

She pulled the release catch. The helmet unlatched, and she slid it free with a practised twist. The sun on her face was warm and wonderful after months inside. She breathed in deeply — lavender and blackberries on the breeze. A summer garden, far from home.

"Go on then, say your piece."

The voice shocked her. Jezzia pulsed to action, hand on her sidearm. There was no one there.

"Who goes there? Identify yourself."

She'd imagined many first-contact scenarios — some combative, some erotic — but all of them involved seeing the other party.

"Charming, this! Comes swooping down bold as brass, smashes up half the village, then says 'sorry, didn't see you there!' — some nerve," the voice continued, indignant.

"We come in peace!" Jezzia shouted, moderating slightly and grasping for the classics.

"Come in peace, she says! My days. You've already landed on Alan."

"Thuurrrss riooooooght," came a flattened voice from below.

"I'm... sorry... Alan?" she said, scanning the rocks for anything Alan-shaped.

"It's all very well to be sorry," the first voice said. "But sorry won't bring Gertrude back, now will it?"

"I'm okay!" piped a tiny voice from across the lake. "I've just broken free a bit, is all! It's lovely out here! Weeeeeee!"

Gertrude's voice faded. Jezzia scanned the water again. Still nothing.

"Are you... fish people?" she asked, carefully.

"Fish people!" came the response from all sides. Her stomach dropped. There were many of them.

She briefly floated the 'Invisible Birds' hypothesis to her internal focus group. It was roundly condemned. Then, the truth struck.

"Are you... what my people might call rocks?"

"Are you what we might call spindly hominids?"

She closed her eyes. She doubted sentient rocks would be a mortal threat, but walking on gravel was now a diplomatic incident. She'd have to try and build bridges — possibly literally.

"I'm very sorry we landed on your... friend."

"Oh, he's not my friend." The tone suggested Alan's shortcomings were both numerous and deeply satisfying.

"Thaaars roight... can't starnnd 'er."

"Yes, he's utterly dreadful. But you know what they say — wait long enough and all your troubles weather away."

"Hey!"

"He's shale," the voice confided. "He won't see the next mega-annum."

"I'll bloody see thaaarrrrt off iff it kiulls meee."

"The passage of time is literally killing you." A beat. "Okay, technically it's wave action. But time's involved!"

"I haven't introduced myself," Jezzia said, trying to reclaim the narrative. "Vice-Commander Jezzia Mundock of the Alliance Star Ship Erebus."

"Thas this thiiing parked in meee brain?"

"Yes. And again, very sorry. We crashed. We didn't mean to disturb—"

"Assault!" Alan thundered.

Jezzia pressed on. "Our ship is badly damaged. We need shelter. Are there other sentient life forms here who are…"

"Less rocky?"

"Slightly." Jezzia knew she risked opening the 'Well, there's always those flying vampire spiders' door, but turned the handle anyway.

"Nope!" The voice was triumphant. "Well, there are birds," it added. "Bloody morons. And the apes, of course. Not like you, mind. Hairier. Louder. Idiots. We're your best bet. And we'll help, 'course. As long as you're not minded to dig us up."

"Dig you up?"

"Like that other lot. Them Clurgons. Kept singing about 'glory' and Clurgon Prime. Wouldn't shut up."

"Are they still here?" A sliver of hope rose in Jezzia like a balloon in a needle factory.

"No, left a few cycles ago. But they took a terrible chunk out of Kevin."

"I'M VERY UPSET ABOUT IT," boomed a voice that hit like a sonic tsunami.

Jezzia flinched.

"Which one is Kevin?"

"One of the big ones. Over there."

Five kilometres away, a mountain sulked.

"I'm sorry to hear that, Kevin!" Jezzia shouted.

"THERE'S NO NEED TO SHOUT AT ME!" (Have you ever heard a mountain pause thoughtfully? Good. Just like that.) "WOULD YOU LIKE TO SEE MY WOUND?"

"Actually, yes." Jezzia toggled her comm. "Commander — I've contacted the local population."

"Population, Vice-Commander?" Abigail sounded intrigued.

"Mostly friendly."

"Casualties?"

"A bit chipped…"

"Gouged!" Alan insisted.

"…Possibly emotionally. They're silicon-based life forms."

"Rocks!" cackled the voice.

"AND MOUNTAINS!" said Kevin. "AND ASSOCIATED GEOMORPHIC FEATURES!"

"Is there somewhere we can camp?" asked Abigail, who was desperately keen to receive no further details.

"There's a range of dunes about a klick to the south."

"Wheeeee!" a million tiny voices tinkled. "New friends!"

"Wouldn't advise that," the voice said brusquely.

"Where would you suggest?" Jezzia asked.

"There are clearings in the trees. Trees are dumb."

Jezzia waited. No objections from the arboreal contingent.

"Commander, clearings in the forest — two klicks. I recommend we make camp there."

"Very good. Make it happen. Dennistoun out."

******

Over the next few hours, the crew emerged and began hauling supplies toward the treeline. Some dragged crates. Others bore the dead.

Heavy-lift drones buzzed low across the lake, ferrying equipment, tents, and Eliza's prized roasting pans, which the crew had been explicitly forbidden to touch.

A small village blossomed among the trees. Tents rose. The mobile kitchen steamed into life. Someone cracked open the QuikBrew Survival Manual: So You've Damaged Company Property! It made excellent kindling.

A pair of skiffs were launched, loaded with lobster pots and cautious optimism.

Abigail equipped herself and walked alone along the shore. When she came to a shady spot, strewn with wildflowers, she stopped and dug eight graves. Her shovel chittered and scraped through the stony soil, throwing up clouds of dust that coated her gloves and boots. By the end, her arms trembled and her back throbbed. She'd dug a grave before, just once; a quiet place, with a view of the loch. Sam had begged her to act, when no one else would — she had. Then she'd dug.

Abigail bent to gather her tools, then stood straight and marched back to camp to organise the procession.

At dusk, wicker coffins were carried along the shore. Abigail led a heartfelt ceremony, filled with reflection, sadness and joy.

As the mourners left, she hung back. They needed space to grieve without their Commander. She drew a golf club from her bag and laid it gently on Jellicoe's grave. A memory, absurd and important. Then, she wept.

Later, she walked back alone, as the stars began to prick the sky.

******

Jezzia spent the afternoon establishing a secure perimeter. Sensor arrays and tripwires now formed a tight circle around their new home. She figured it was overkill — latent guilt for failing to defenestrate the Swift. Still, the best way to atone was to keep her hands and mind busy, building safety she could touch.

This was her 'green zone' — a place where no one would come to harm. Jezzia had felt combat in a way none of the others had. It wasn't the frontline that scared her, it was the grenade quietly rolled across a crowded marketplace. She wasn't going to let complacency harm any more of the crew.

Now she crouched on a rock — which didn't seem to mind — scanning for movement.

A shadow approached.

"Challenge," she called.

"Hope," replied the figure.

"Challenge accepted. Nice to see you, Commander." Jezzia lowered her rifle and jumped lightly down.

"Thank you, VC. Status?" Abigail's smile was thin but warm, like a potato scone fresh from the toaster.

"Perimeter secure. All crew accounted for. Dinner is served."

"What are we having?"

"Omelettes."

Abigail made a face.

"Eliza wanted order in the kitchen. Omelettes were a safe choice."

"They are," Abigail brushed a hand through her hair. "I shouldn't complain. You've all worked tirelessly. It's just been a long day."

Jezzia hesitated. "How are you feeling, Commander?"

Abigail looked up. Emotion swelled — then settled.

"I am... tired. And sad. Incredibly sad."

"We'll get those bastard Clurgons."

"No. No revenge. No killing. That's not the way."

"But they struck first."

"I know. But we can't meet indifference with fury. That's not justice, Jezzia — that's surrendering to the same void that let this happen."

Jezzia nodded slowly. "Very good, Commander." She didn't agree, but she admired conviction.

They stood in quiet for a while; Jezzia watching the forest, Abigail half-contemplating the stars.

"Do you have someone waiting for you back home?" Abigail asked, the question slipping out quieter than intended, before she could stop herself. Normally she kept a respectful distance from the crew — but tonight wasn't normal.

"Not really," Jezzia shrugged. "A couple."

Abigail blinked. "Gosh. Well. It's nice to have options."

"They always have each other," Jezzia grinned. That was as vulnerable as she was prepared to be. "How about you, Commander?"

"No." Abigail hesitated, then added, "I'm widowed."

Jezzia's voice was quiet but firm. "Commander. I'm sorry."

"Thank you. They say it gets better with time. I'm still waiting." She smiled, but didn't mean it. "Sometimes I say her name, just in case she replies."

Jezzia nodded, her body language kept the door open.

"I—" Abigail bit her lip, and then went for it. "I keep going for her. Every day I'm scared. Every day, I think I'll fail. It's her memory — her belief — that stops me from falling."

They stood in silence. Not speaking, but together.

"Your supper's waiting," Jezzia said gently. It was time to move forward.

"Then I won't keep it." Abigail turned, then paused. "Thank you for asking."

"Any time, Commander."

Abigail walked on. Jezzia resumed her vigil. Below, the camp flickered; above, the sky stretched vast and glittering — a quilt of fire across the dark.

"We will get them," Jezzia whispered.

But quieter now. Just in case the universe was listening.

Eleven : Jade

Mars! If not Earth's sister (that's Venus — but we never visit because she's totally toxic), then at least her dusty cousin who's a bit shit.

I know, I know. You think I'm being reductive. What of Olympus Mons, you say? The grandeur of the Valles Marineris? The majestic dust storms that envelop the whole planet in a coltre rosso? And I will admit you have a point (although I might gently touch your elbow and say, coltre rosso — I know you're just back from Tuscany, but come on).

But when the Martian inhabitants look up at night and see the feeble starlight struggling through the dust-smeared glass of their habitation domes (you can rub all you like, you're still going to get streaks), are they thinking: "This is the best of all possible worlds"? No, of course not.

It's a bit like Wolverhampton. Nothing wrong with it, per se; but you know this isn't humanity firing on all cylinders. "Have you visited the Black Country Living Museum?" you ask. No. I reply.

Of course not.

Jade Green had visited the Black Country Living Museum as a youngster and fully enjoyed it (shows how much I know). That experience wasn't top of her mind as she dropped out of warp, into a tight orbit around Phobos. Tight orbits are mandatory here — anything looser risks slamming straight into Mars. Indeed, mandatory prison sentences are handed down for sloppy orbiting, ever since a male commander, who insisted he was "brilliant at parking," immediately smashed a top-of-the-line cruiser to smithereens on return from its first shakedown cruise.

The industrial plants that ringed Stickney rose as Jade drifted above the surface. A half-built hulk hung above them, swarms of construction drones fussily criss-crossing its surface, welding and riveting.

"What am I seeing, Applejack?"

"The Bendigo Orbital Construction Yards. Ship contractors to the Alliance's mega-corps. Many of the most famed ships were built here — the Curie, the Parks, the Beyoncé."

Jade made the votive sign, as is tradition.

In the centre of the crater a great, domed foundry belched fire and metal; its glow lapped the rock walls like an ocean of industry.

Jade's jaw clenched. "Are you telling me that Erebus is just a fucking ship?"

"Correct. There are many ships to have borne the name Erebus, but I believe the one laid down here in 2338—"

Jade cut him off, anger building. "The Singer could have just TOLD me."

"I believe they relish the mystery and believe errands such as this to be 'character building'."

Jade kicked the flight console in fury; so that was it, another lesson in obedience disguised as enlightenment.

"Every time we dance to their bloody tune." Her anger ebbed as a new thought occurred. "But you should have known this."

Applejack paused. "Yes," he said. For the very first time, Jade thought she heard doubt in his voice. "I should have known this immediately."

"What happened then? A glitch? A gap in the data?" She glared at the ceiling. "Ugh. I can't believe we had to go through that ordeal because of a misplaced byte."

"No. That is not what happened." Applejack radiated uncertainty. "It can't. I remember everything that has and will happen."

"And things that can? Possibilities? Tangentials?"

"To an absurd degree. The only logical explanation is that Erebus didn't exist when you asked before."

"So, Erebus has just launched?" Jade felt like she was salmon fishing without a net, almost grasping the truth before it wiggled free. "Just been commissioned?"

"No. That isn't how my knowledge works. Things persist. They always are if they ever were or will be. It is like a chapter has been added to a novel I already know by heart."

"Ok. It exists now?"

"Yes. Alliance Starship Erebus. Laid down 2338, commissioned 2339, lost with all hands 2342, Gliese 876. She was not found for more than a century, after the Second Clurgon War had whittled humanity down to a fleck of their former selves. It appears the crew made a spirited attempt to survive. But after several years, they ran out of hope."

"You don't die from running out of hope." The words came out automatically, but something about them caught her off-guard.

"Are you certain of that?"

She didn't answer, but she wasn't certain at all. She fished the Bobbin from her jacket. Weighty, it radiated a sense of permanence that felt unshackled from time and space. It glowed a comforting neon green.

"This reality is sound. Whatever your glitch was—"

"I don't glitch."

"Fine." Jade ran a thumb over her console. It was warm, stable. Real. "Run a diagnostic. Perform recursive analysis. Find the cause. The point is, this reality is sound." She said it with conviction, because she needed it to be true. The alternative was something else rewriting the timeline — a possibility both profound and terrifying.

Applejack clicked disapprovingly but said no more. Jade didn't like his tutting; it made him too human. Perhaps, soon, more human than her.

She turned the Bobbin over slowly. The surface was beyond smooth, like temple stone worn by millennia of hushed feet. The glow came from within — not part of the stone, but caught inside it.

She held the Bobbin up, watching the cockpit lights mingle and twinkle with the green.

"How curious," she murmured. "Erebus."

Time fractured.

Jade's vision jittered and sparked. The Bobbin flashed red to green to red to green to infinity and back again. She screamed and screwed shut her eyes.

"Red or green?" she shouted.

"Green! It's green!" Applejack's voice was loaded with concern.

"It's not. It's an illusion." Jade opened her eyes. The Bobbin burned an angry red.

"Applejack, what year is it?"

"Time is—"

"I know, I know. New question. What year do I think it is?"

"You know the answer." Applejack watched the pieces click in Jade. "You must reach out."

Jade closed her eyes. Her breath slowed. Phobos faded. Her perception cast its moorings and flew free.

The universe folded.

Slowly at first, Phobos and Deimos came together, blended into one. Mars next, her grand features softening and closing in. Then a moment of void, then asteroids, faster now. Suddenly Luna and the Earth, sweeping up and vanishing into the singularity.

Now Sol, enormous, roaring, blasting through the night. Then suddenly all matter collapsed and surged past her blistering body in a rush of cosmic backdraft. She punched through the fabric and flew.

Then, impossibly, she was there. At Gliese.

Before her, the Erebus drifted in a field of glittering ruin. Temporal echoes shivered along the shattered hull.

Then, a wrench.

Reality jerked sideways. Erebus launched toward the fourth planet, which swam in static, faded, crackled, spun. Jade felt herself imploding.

And then something else.

It came, swirling. An absence. A swarm of locusts without form. Fascination without thought. It rushed around her — clinging, sucking, tearing — dragging her away.

She snapped back.

Her boots were still up on the console. Her fingers had curled into fists.

"The fabric," she began.

"Yes?" Applejack asked gently.

"Rough. Coarsened. It didn't fit. Something beneath, pulling it apart. I can't stitch it."

"I've never seen a thing you couldn't patch with that needle."

"No," she whispered. "This is... no."

The weight of responsibility settled like lead across her shoulders. She could feel the ripples of the timeline pushing against her from the inside. This wasn't a tear, it was pressure, waiting to explode.

"Erebus isn't the tear. It's a warning, a sign-post." Her relief at revelation was swamped by the horror of realisation. "There are realities converging, crashing, not travelling side by side. The pressure is pushing against the walls of the universe." Jade slumped, exhausted.

You can't suture a haemorrhage.

"Setting course for Gliese 876," said Applejack.

They slipped the wispy bonds of Phobos and boiled up the Alcubierre drive. The familiar sound of beans grinding was followed by the scent of espresso, rich and grounding.

"Applejack. If you missed Erebus," Jade didn't want to finish the thought, "what else could be missing?"

"That is," Applejack sounded uncertain again, "unknown."

Jade stared blankly through the cockpit window. Her reflection, a lonely ghost floating in the starfield, stared back.

Usually, she slipped unnoticed through the universe. But something at Gliese 876 had felt her presence. Nothing conscious. Nothing alive. Just the universe doing a tiny, involuntary twitch — like it had brushed something it didn't understand.

Or maybe — and this was worse — like it had nodded to her. One professional to another.

Twelve : Chad

Night falls with unseemly haste in Delta City, as if the planet is eager to whizz through the boring bits and get straight to the naked part.

Daytime peddlers and hawkers stow their wares and slick into the gloaming, emerging moments later in finest 'Night Market' garb. Business resumes its chaotic cadence, but goods that were previously under the counter are now proudly displayed, with windings of festoon lights to reassure the wary.

Hotel Maglione squats in a corner of the Old Town's Satyr Square. None of Delta City is particularly old, but many humans like to view buildings that predate their birth as 'historic'; conversely, any suggested after they turn thirty-five are a menace to the natural order of things. It had been built in the 'New Colonial Gothic' style, which called for confrontational stonework and a profusion of gargoyles. The sweeping, blue-glazed roofs hinted at elegance within; the pagoda penthouse, lashed to the rear and slathered in faux Orientalism, did not.

The 'Maglione' owed its name to a short-sighted sign-writer who had aimed for 'Migliore' and missed. It was a Delta institution; renowned as a refuge and place of business for those whose work involved enquiring "how many testicles would Sir like to keep?" It was said to have 'faded grandeur,' because you never really can get blood out of a rug.

The upstanding citizens of Delta wondered aloud why the Maglione was allowed to remain, but civil authorities know it is useful to have all the major criminals in one place. If it isn't possible, or indeed desirable, to stamp out crime, why not encourage it to thrive far away from the pleasant suburbs where your voters live? It doesn't hurt that successful criminals have deep pockets, and political campaigns are so expensive.

Chad curled his toes into the warm sheets and grinned. His usual room in the pagoda had been taken by a Flurvian "refuse magnate," but this suite overlooking the square would do fine. Darius had told him to lay low. Unfortunately, that wasn't Chad's area of expertise. He also reasoned, correctly, that the security services would find him anyway, so he may as well have home advantage when the inevitable occurred.

The bed was in the 'nuovo ghastly' tradition. Alongside the four-metre main mattress it possessed two integrated day beds, a built-in sound system, a cornucopia of screens, a bookshelf, reading lights, air conditioner and fridge. Hidden motors raised, lowered, and shook the mattresses on command. Chad had spent a good hour playing with the controls and created a small Alpine village in the aftermath of a severe earthquake. He wasn't sure quite what the point of it was but knew it would be great fun finding out.

To Chad, there were few things better than a warm bed and fine company. Great food? Sure. Wine, music, art—beautiful. Love? Why not. But good company? That was harder to find. Happily, with enough cash, good company could be guaranteed.

The door chime muttered.

"Enter," Chad called, unfurling his gorgeous body toward the entrance. The door slid open.

"Hi sexy," Chad purred in a voice so sensual it came with a padded headboard.

Human cloning has picked up a bad reputation over the centuries, and for good reason. What begins as a noble attempt to remove predispositions to cancers very quickly descends into "we could clone Hitler!". Whatever your motivation, the end result is a baby who's stubbornly Not Hitler yet.

So, you start again. No Hitlers this time, but how about an army of super soldiers? Once again, you end up with a load of babies on your hands and an enormous number of nappy changes standing between you and global domination. No wonder despots quickly abandoned cloning and went back to simply handing guns to kids instead. As the old saying goes: if it ain't broke, this weeping child torn from its family will break it for you.

Holographic simulations, on the other hand, skipped the baby step and came with a built-in off switch.

"Man, you're gorgeous," said Holo Chad, sweeping through the doorway and palming a slim bottle from his kimono. Without breaking eye contact he began sensuously applying baby oil to his immaculate chest.

"Yes—I suppose I am." Chad threw back his head and laughed his most handsome laugh. Holo Chad was a perfect replica, he thought to himself. In reality, Holo Chad was a perfect replica of the man Chad had believed himself to be five years earlier. There wasn't a huge disparity, but it could still be measured in wrinkles and kilos.

"Nice topography." Holo Chad cast a forgiving hand toward the ruinous mess Chad had wreaked on the mattress. "How long has it been?"

"Too long," said Chad, as the bed slowly bore him aloft.

"And Darius?" Holo Chad arranged himself on a leopard-print chaise lounge. The kimono covered his genitals but delivered a full helping of abs.

"Furious as ever. More furious than usual, actually. Something about an important delivery, 'galactic stakes'." Chad fluttered a fabulous hand. "He told me to lay low—but this time he really meant it."

"To laying low." A large cocktail glass brimming with fruit and luminous liquid had appeared in Holo Chad's hand. As he raised it in salute, sparklers sprang to life and wept flecks of bright ember across the carpet.

"Now to the matter at hand." Chad gestured toward the chess board set at the foot of the bed and cocked an eyebrow toward his stunning self. "Shall we?"

Chad had made it this far in life through a winning combination of confidence and pragmatism. Occasionally this meant blasting through a Clurgon blockade like a dashing hero; but only when not blasting through meant certain death, so very probable death was the superior option. Really, life was all probabilities, and being able to work them out extremely fast could appear, to the lay person, as extraordinary bravery. Most of the time, it was just maths.

This was why he enjoyed playing himself at chess—he knew exactly what his opponent was thinking. He knew the calculations. His opponent knew the calculations. To win in such a perfectly balanced environment kept him sharp. Fired the mathematical pathways in his brain. That, that was where the sport was.

But sometimes, he allowed himself to wonder: maybe I'm just an appalling narcissist?

And then: what if that narcissism was the only thing keeping him sane — a paper lifebelt to assuage the lurking horror that his whole life was spent skating on a wafer-thin crust of ice?

This sort of thought spiral was absolutely Not Rogue.

The cocktail vanished from Holo Chad's hand and a military baton replaced it. He stood up and swung the baton at the board with a polished flourish.

"To battle," he said, giving Chad a look so layered you could put a candle on it.

Chad threw back the bed sheets. Apart from his naked feet he was already fully clothed. He couldn't remember the last time he'd gone to bed naked, but there had been several women there.

The Chads assumed their positions. With a tiny motion of the wrist, Chad dimmed the lights, leaving the board bathed in a soft, warm glow. He removed both kings and hid them in his hands.

"Your choice," he said, fixing Holo Chad with a steady gaze.

Holo Chad swirled his baton and brought it down gently on Chad's left hand. Chad opened it and looked down.

"White," he smiled. "You have the advantage of me."

"Always, darling." Holo Chad placed his king in position and with no hesitation moved his first pawn forward.

"The Bravacov Opening," Chad raised an approving eyebrow.

"Perhaps the King's Gambit," replied Holo Chad, reclining in his chair and offering an extraordinarily alluring smile.

Half an hour passed. The game, as always, was evenly matched. Pieces were exchanged, feints made and countered. The Chads moved in time with one another, sometimes fast, sometimes slow, always poised. Eventually only the kings, queens, and a handful of pawns remained.

"A queen and pawn endgame," Holo Chad stared at his opponent.

"Mmmm." It was Chad's move; his eyes didn't leave the board.

"Very tricky. Often." Holo Chad paused for effect. "Long and hard."

"Don't," said Chad, still studying the board.

"Your favourite," Holo Chad whispered.

"Ha!" Chad slapped the table and laughed. He was a great fan of what he termed 'sensual innuendo' and couldn't blame himself for using it against him.

"That's…" Chad was interrupted by a loud hammering on the door.

"Chad Blaster!" a metallic voice shouted through a loud hailer.

In an instant, the fantasy shattered.

"Ahhhh, dammit," said Chad. "I had hoped we would get to finish this time."

"Chad Blaster! This is the security services—we need to speak to you briefly about several trifling matters," said the loud hailer voice, with the sincerity of a warlord appealing for calm.

"You can cover for me can't you, Old Man?" Chad pulled on his boots.

"Of course, darling. I'll give them a good show."

"Great." Chad tossed Holo Chad a pistol. "Give me thirty seconds, then fire wide and indiscriminately."

Chad leapt onto the bed and punched the cover from the ceiling vent. The vent's positioning was no accident; 'accessible crawl spaces' was a key amenity for the Maglione's clientele.

"Vents," Chad muttered, hauling himself inside. "Even in the future it still comes down to vents."

"Chad Blaster! You have until the count of ten to come out peacefully!" said the loud hailer voice. Its tone implied that 'peacefully' was a matter for the subsequent inquest.

"Until next time, baby!" Chad grabbed the vent lip and hauled himself into the ceiling. He crawled rapidly along. This was the time to make noise—right now, during the shouting and inevitable gunfire. Once that died down, the banging of ceiling vents was a dead giveaway.

Despite his grumbling, Chad loved vents. They are much less filled with giant fans and 'gouts of cleansing flame' than you might think. Generally, they're nice, safe metal tubes that take you to decent extraction points like "deserted basement" or "rooftop helipad."

This one stretched the length of the building before turning sharply right. That was fine. Bad Things were happening on this side of the building; the other side should have fewer Bad Things—or, at least, Bad Things that didn't know where he was yet.

A volley of pistol fire rang out behind and below. That was his cue to wriggle and bang away as fast as possible; if Darius found out he'd been caught in a vent again he'd never hear the end of it.

Answering fire erupted from all around. At the front desk, the manager sighed and pulled out the usual insurance form. Chad kept moving, trying to work out where they were. At least two either side of the door, three or four more on the street watching the windows. There would be more in the lobby and round the back. A couple of lookouts in the pagoda. If they tried to take Holo Chad alive, then the ruse could be kept up for valuable minutes. Chad prayed they weren't the sort to get grenade-happy.

There was a round of shouting from the loud hailer. He pictured his replica down in the room, coolly licking off shots and one-liners. That was living: back against the wall, blaze of glory. A lone wolf, taking potshots at the universe.

Except, he suddenly realised, he didn't really want to die, all alone in a hotel room. There was Cheryl to think about and—.

Another hail of fire rang out. Chad sped up, banging his way to the vent corner. He exhaled when he reached it and relaxed a little.

The duct creaked.

A gun met his forehead.

"Hiding in the vents again, Mr Blaster?" The voice was unamused.

Chad calculated his options. He was a master at talking his way out of things, but no amount of words would cure a bullet in the brain.

"Shit," he said.

Thirteen : Abigail

Humans like to feel at home wherever they go, and this is usually achieved through stuff. The earliest humans didn't have much of it, but jealously guarded their special rock or "bit of Mother's femur" with the furious zeal of a toddler who's found where the biscuits are hidden.

As society matured, stuff became more sophisticated: the special rock became a hammer, a seed bag, an urn of olive oil, and the "ornately carved rod of sensuous pleasure."

Soon, there was so much stuff to carry that some societies simply acquired other people to carry it for them – sometimes with payment, but usually with a stick. This went on for an astonishingly long time, until a handful of those in charge realised it was a bad look. They briskly dismantled the whole enterprise over a few fleeting centuries and the odd bitter war.

By the 24th century this history seems barbaric and unbelievable. Sure, we still recycle tens of thousands of sentient appliances each year, but they look different to us, so fuck 'em.

Interplanetary travel didn't break the cycle. When colonising a new world, the first ship would carry seeds and prefabs, the second colonists and livestock, and the third would arrive overloaded with consumer goods. Regulations were changed after an administrative error left the embattled colonists of New Prosperity subsisting on boiled Louboutins, but not by as much as you'd think.

As an exploration and supply ship, the Erebus carried the essentials for popping up small outposts on uncharted worlds. Her crew could survive indefinitely – assuming the planet wasn't provocatively hostile to human life – but there wasn't enough stock to open even a modest outlet boutique.

Abigail woke before her alarm. She lay in the half-light, listening as the Erebus camp stirred to life.

First came the planet: birds chirping, breeze rustling trees. Then came Eliza, whose robust swearing from the commissary signalled the imminent arrival of breakfast.

She stretched. Warmth flowed through her limbs. She savoured a moment of stillness. In the distance, Eliza launched into a colourful soliloquy on the consequences awaiting whoever had hidden the eggs.

A wispy flapping followed by a polite cough signalled company.

With an inward sigh and outward flourish, Abigail sat up and found Lieutenant Curlew hovering in the porch. He had knocked as smartly as one could on canvas and was now doing the best interpretation of standing to attention that being bent double would allow.

"Good morning, Number Two," said Abigail, adding "at ease" a moment later than was strictly necessary. "Please, do come in."

Curlew unfolded and arranged himself in a corner, one leg protruding awkwardly toward Abigail.

"Thank you, Commander," he said with the air of someone who'd been mugged and then handed back their wallet.

"Situation report?"

"The crew are in good spirits. Everyone has a bed. Eliza's got a firm hand on the kitchen."

A rising clatter from the mess tent confirmed this.

"The fishing crews returned with a wide variety of… things."

"Things?" Abigail raised an eyebrow.

"Definitely things. Some might even be edible. Thankfully, none of them could talk."

"Very good. And the Erebus?"

"Afloat. Or at least, no more sunk than yesterday."

"That's good." Abigail slapped her thigh. "Lieutenant, return to the ship and oversee operations."

"Understood, Commander."

"Priority one is checking Stacey's okay."

"You mean ensuring the crash hasn't scrambled her personality matrix and turned her into a homicidal maniac?" Curlew smiled.

"Precisely. Remember what happened on the Overlook?"

The colour drained from Curlew's face. "Yes," he whispered. "They never did find all the feet."

He nodded smartly and posted himself back through the flap.

Abigail watched him lope off between the trees, then swung herself out of bed. She pulled on overtrousers on top of her QuikBrew-issue shorts and zipped up her Command jacket. In the battered mirror, she looked tired. She always looked tired.

She tied her hair into a no-nonsense ponytail, nodded at her reflection, and stepped out into the morning.

"You'll be wantin' your breakfast, Commander."

Eliza flowed behind the serving counter like a galleon under full sail.

Abigail admired the feast laid out under humming heat lamps.

"Yes, Chief." She returned Eliza's smile. "This looks wonderful. What do you recommend?"

"Local eggs." Eliza banged a tray with a ladle. "Freshly foraged this morning."

"Local eggs?"

"Yeah, there's an... in'hig-austible supply. Nest under every tree."

"Under the trees?" Abigail eyed the pile of eggs with suspicion. They quivered.

"Pheasant, I s'pose."

"Or snake?"

"I wouldn't know about that, Commander." Eliza swept a glare across the tents' compliant occupants. "I ain't had no complaints. Scrambles nice, too."

"Oh, that's a pity. I don't like scrambled eggs."

"No trouble to poach one."

"No, thank you. Mushrooms, then."

Eliza beamed. "Oh good! There is, how do you say, an ha'bbundance of them."

"Freshly foraged too?"

Eliza nodded. "Those rotten logs near the shore."

Abigail narrowed her eyes. "Where we dug the latrines?"

"That's right. I was down there this morning, doin' me business, and what do I see? These beauties!" Eliza brandished a glistening fistful. "Go on, have a sniff. You've never tasted the like."

"Toast," said Abigail. "I'll have toast."

"Suits yourself." Eliza zhushed the mushrooms with a small, theatrical sigh. "Bread's by the toaster. Go easy, though—he's takin' it a bit hard."

A few minutes later, Abigail sat at one of the mess tables with her querulously toasted bread. She'd taken a calculated risk on the butter's provenance. Eliza could coax milk out of anything with nipples, but a little denial seemed a fair trade for hot buttered toast.

She'd just taken her first bite when a viscous-looking crossbow clattered onto the table beside her.

Jezzia.

Eyes glazed, swaying faintly. Like a tree that had picked a fight with a tornado.

"Couldn't sleep?"

"Bear."

"Bloody hell." Abigail scanned for signs of mauling. "Are you okay?"

"Yep. Bear's dead. It got too close. Took three crossbow bolts and..." Jezzia rammed a hunting knife into the table. It dripped. "...some stabbing."

"Where is it now?"

Jezzia nodded toward the serving counter. Eliza was brandishing an angle grinder with academic interest.

"I see. You're relieved, Vice-Commander. Get some rest."

"Very good, Commander." Jezzia swayed. "When d'you need me back?"

"Report in at 1400. I want to take a closer look at the Clurgon excavations. They've dug a very big hole in Kevin, and I'd like to know why."

Jezzia nodded, turned to go.

"You forgot this." Abigail gestured to the knife, like an estate agent showcasing a tap.

"Thanks, Commander." Jezzia yanked it free and staggered off, crossbow slung over her shoulder.

Abigail had just found her toast again when Eliza returned, clad in a welder's apron speckled with viscera.

"Forgot your tea, dearie." She placed a mug down with a thud. The handle had an angry red smear on it.

"Sausages for dinner?" Abigail asked hopefully.

"Tartare," said Eliza, with pride.

"Of course." Abigail contemplated an all-toast diet.

"Want more butter? I could coax a bit more from the gland."

Before Abigail could answer, her comms buzzed.

"Commander Dennistoun."

"Oh, thank God." She tapped it. "Dennistoun here."

"It's me," said a muffled voice.

"Sorry, the connection is poor. Please state your name."

"Stacey. Your AI. The one you abandoned."

"Stacey!" Relief surged through her. "Status report?"

"Well, I'm marooned on top of a talking rock and to be quite honest, he's being a bit of a dick about it."

"Ah. Don't mind Alan. I think that's just his way."

"He's threatening to eat me."

"I don't think that's possible."

"I'm thinking about flushing the effluent tanks onto him."

"No. Don't do that. This is a first contact situation. I really don't want to report to QuikBrew that we ran over the native population and then shat on them."

Stacey made the kind of noise that suggested The Bad Thing had already happened and should not, under any circumstances, be discussed further.

Abigail moved on.

"Has Curlew reached you yet?"

"No. I rebooted from failsafe once power levels were sufficient. Main batteries are intact. Solar array is operating at forty percent efficiency. That's enough for me and the critical systems. The ice rink is done for."

"Understood." Abigail exhaled. "We crashed in the early afternoon. It's now early morning. How long are the days here?"

"Approximately twenty-nine hours, Commander."

"Very well. We'll adjust the duty schedules accordingly." She scrubbed at her face with a hand. "When Curlew arrives, assist him. Have you been able to contact the Alliance?"

"That was the main reason for my call. Our faster-than-light communications systems are down. The Alcubierre drive is non-functional."

"Diagnosis?"

"Unknown. It may be physical damage, or just missing a filter paper. I'll have Curlew perform a manual inspection."

"Thank you, Stacey."

There was a pause.

"Commander— even if the drive is repairable, there is a high probability that the Clurgons are interdicting all faster-than-light communications. They likely didn't expect us to survive the crash. Something here warranted a jump gate. I don't think they'll come down and finish us off, but I suspect we will not be able to contact the Alliance for... ever."

Abigail had been holding that thought just beneath the surface. It stung to hear it aloud.

"Stacey... how bad is the damage to Erebus? Could we repair her—get her back into space?"

There was a long silence. Abigail wasn't sure if Stacey was thinking or softening the blow.

"Stacey?"

"I'll wait for Curlew's full report. But given our resources and the skills available... I believe the Erebus will not fly again. However, I am confident we can make repairs sufficient to move her onto land, where hull repairs and habitation retrofits will be more manageable."

"So... a new home, not a return journey."

"That is the likeliest outcome. I'm sorry, Commander."

Abigail closed her eyes for a moment. "One more thing— can you locate Terry Mbutu?"

"Of course. He's currently on a rocky outcrop approximately one kilometre from your position. Shall I send you a ping?"

"Please and thank you, Stacey. Dennistoun out."

Abigail turned — straight into the beak of Fabian Schmaltz.

"Oh God!" She jumped, then quickly recovered. "Mr Schmaltz. How can I help you?"

"Ah, good, Commander — there you are." Schmaltz had rehearsed this and wasn't about to go off-script. "I have endeavoured to locate a copy of the QuikBrew survival manual, but have been informed they were all burned?"

"Yes. As we can't eat them, or shelter under them, it felt like the pragmatic choice."

"Most irregular. Most irregular." Schmaltz shook his head with the sincerity of a parking warden who has 'already entered your details into the system'.

"Unfortunately, this will have to go in my report. Tell me — are communications with Earth functional yet?"

Something in his tone gave Abigail pause. He's terrified, she realised. This isn't about the report. This is concealed fear.

"Not yet, I'm afraid." She decided to level with him. "Between us, they may never be. But please — don't share that. Not yet."

"No. Oh, no, Commander. That is... unacceptable."

"We're doing everything we can. Curlew's on site, leading repairs. He'll—"

"Everything is not enough." Schmaltz's mask slipped. What lay beneath was painfully human. "He must do more. The most. You don't understand the Board."

Abigail nodded. She didn't. She'd never needed to. And she had no desire to start now.

"There are some very demanding personalities there. Ms Funt in particular. Failing her is… unthinkable. There are rumours."

She reached out and touched his arm. He flinched — but didn't pull away. She'd never imagined consoling Fabian Schmaltz. It had been a day of firsts.

"Curlew will do everything he can. I have faith." She hesitated. "And there are hundreds of people here who could use your help. Go and be with them. When there's news — you'll be the first to know."

Schmaltz sniffed. Then coughed and straightened. "Don't handle me, Commander. I know my utility. You rule. I relay. I implement. I am a tool to be wielded."

His tone implied he chose who wielded him.

"Inform me the moment the Board is online."

And with that, he stalked away.

"If you're at a loose end," Abigail called softly, "latrine duty is short-handed."

She didn't raise her voice. Why kick him when he was down? Besides, they might all be digging trenches for years. Best to ease in gently.

She went to find Terry.

******

Half an hour later, she found him standing atop a granite boulder in a shady forest glade. He was holding an atmospheric sensor aloft in one hand and scribbling notes on a pad wedged under his chin.

"Mr Mbutu!" she called up. The boulder was ten metres high, with no clear way up.

Terry startled, fumbled his pad, then caught it with a desperate wrist flick that would haunt his next tennis match.

"Wuuuh-ah! Commander!" he called down, smoothing his transition from panic to professional. "I was just—"

"Who's this, then?" rumbled a gravelly voice.

Abigail blinked.

"Commander," Terry said, awkwardly formal again, "may I introduce you to Miss—"

"Ms."

"Sorry, Ms Edifice. She's—"

"It's."

"Yes. Sorry. It's a boulder."

"Promontory."

"It's a granite promontory."

Abigail realised she had uncovered a rich conversational history. She offered the rock a respectful nod.

"I suppose you'll be wantin' to climb me too, then?" Edifice asked wearily.

"If I may." Abigail smiled. Why not? she thought. I'm marooned on a planet with talking rocks. Might as well lean in.

"Round the other side," said Edifice. "I've got more of them wossnames."

"Footholds," offered Terry.

"Holes," said Edifice with finality.

"Much obliged." Abigail gave the rock a low bow, then circled to the side.

She found the footholds — sorry, holes — and scrambled up with reasonable dignity. As she neared the top, Terry reached down a hand and hauled her the last stretch.

"Sorry about the confusion earlier," he whispered conspiratorially.

"Confusion?"

"Edifice. The gender. I don't think rocks have... you know..."

"Bits?"

"Right. I think it's more of a le and la thing," he said, as if that explained everything. "Like French," he added.

"I am familiar with French, Lieutenant."

"Yes, ma'—Commander."

Abigail took a moment to enjoy the view. The sun was high over the hills now. If this were Earth, she'd guess it was around 10 a.m. Here, it could be anything from breakfast to tea-time. The extra five hours per day were going to play havoc with the crew's sleep cycles. And the night watch rota.

"What are you doing up here, Mr Mbutu?"

Terry brightened. "Atmospheric readings, Commander. And... I've found something fascinating."

"Go on."

"There's a massive density of dark matter in the atmosphere. Much higher than anything on Earth. Or anywhere we've observed, really."

"Is it dangerous?"

"Shouldn't be." Terry hedged the hedge of a man who knows the universe likes ironic twists. "Dark matter behaves like neutrinos. Passes right through us. We think."

Abigail exhaled slowly. "So... an anomaly. Not a threat?"

"Precisely. Probably. But the density isn't the whole thing. It's swirling."

"Swirling?"

"Yes. Vortices. It's like a vast storm made entirely of invisible matter."

"Does it have a focus?"

"It does."

She pointed. "Is it Kevin?"

"Kevin?"

"The mountain with the hole in it."

"I KNEW IT!" Kevin's voice rolled like thunder across the valley. "I'M HIDEOUS!"

"Sorry, Kevin. That was careless," said Abigail quickly.

"Yes, it's Kevin," Terry hissed.

"They say you're a swirling vortex, Kevin!" Edifice added gleefully.

"I'M OUTRAGED!"

Abigail rubbed her temples. The emotional volatility of geology was beginning to wear on her.

"We're going to come and visit you soon, Kevin," she said gently. "See what we can do about that gouge."

She turned back to Terry. "Do you have a watch?"

"QuikBrew standard issue Chronotron." He held it up. "It's broken."

"Of course it is." She pointed at the sun. "When it reaches there, meet me by the mess tent. Hiking kit for four."

"To climb Kevin?"

"To climb Kevin."

"Very good, Commander. Anything else?"

"No. I'm off to wake Jezzia. And I'd rather present her with as few targets as possible."

Terry winced. "Good luck."

"It's okay. I know how to duck. Finish up here. Then prepare for adventure."

She climbed down, heading back into the forest.

They were stranded. No help was coming. But they were still alive. And they would act like it mattered.

Fourteen : Chad

Justice is extremely relative, and rightly so. In the absence of any known absolute sociological truths, communities mix their own flavours of justice, then finesse the recipe as attitudes change.

That said, many beings throughout the galaxy believe there are absolute truths, mandated by Gods. This is usually regarded as 'fine' provided they don't bang on about it too much.

Unfortunately, Gods lay down their thoughts as a one-time deal, then sod off, leaving many unanswered questions in their wake—much like that nice man who came to do your stairs and then disappeared, taking half your bannisters with him.

Occasionally, people claim to have spoken with—or even be—the absent deity in question. Results vary. But if you're being handed a Mogadon cocktail by a glassy-eyed disciple, consider converting.

As a semi-independent colony of Earth, Delta City was free to set its own laws. Smuggling, given the primacy of trade to the planet's income, was treated harshly. A low-level criminal might be dragooned into unpaid labour on the Delta cargo fleet. Grander crimes carried custodial sentences but, as these were seen as a mighty drain on colony resources, an unofficial sentence of 'fatal shovel injury on grave digging duty' was often handed down.

The cell door slammed shut.

Pure affectation. The door was an ultra-strong composite alloy, wrapped in tasteful grey vinyl, which slid silently into place. But that lacked gravitas. So, cell artisans installed hidden speakers to deliver a convincingly slammy sound. Churls claimed the design budget could be better spent on rehabilitation. But come on—you can't lock someone away forever without the noise.

Chad looked around at his unwelcome new home.

Grey door? Check.

Single bed, illuminated frame? Check.

Weird triangular pillow? It would be rude not to.

"I'm innocent! Let me out!" he screamed, hammering on the door for effect. Everyone knew this wasn't true, Chad most of all, but there is a certain decorum to jail.

"Greetings!" trilled a voice from the ceiling. "I am ChIRPy, your Correctional Institution Rehabilitation Pal! It gives me overwhelming joy to welcome you to your stay here at Delta Reform Penitentiary, or, as we like to say, the DERP family."

Chad paused, hands braced on the door, then attacked it with renewed fury. "Why can't you just shoot me in the head, you bastard cowards?"

"Many of our guests feel this way at first," ChIRPy continued with the peppy tone of something that knows it cannot be strangled. "But they soon embrace DERP life and knuckle down to some good ol' self-improvement!"

Chad turned, dread settling like concrete, as a giant wall-mounted screen flickered on. DERP claimed the omnipresent AI was compassion; Chad strongly suspected it was just cheaper than guards.

"Ah! There you are, Sir!" said ChIRPy, beaming. "So nice to look one another in the face. Perhaps Sir could venture a little smile also?"

Chad offered the rictus grin favoured by homicidal clowns.

"Beautiful, Sir. And may I say your rakish approach to teeth really complements your overall style?"

Somewhere between arrest and incarceration, Chad had lost at least one tooth. He tried to inventory with his tongue but found it too swollen to be a reliable narrator.

"Now then, Sir, we shall commence orientation. Mr Keith, may I call you Keith?"

"It's Chad," said Keith.

"Very well, Sir. Nourishment will be available via your nutritube three times daily. Your water dish will be topped up as required."

"Water dish?"

"Yes, DERP research indicates even the most incident-prone prisoners can utilise a floor-based dish."

"Incident-prone?"

"Lots of broken fingers. Shall I continue?" Chad grunted. If you were going to imprison someone and break their will, why not throw in a finger or two.

"Fresh clothes weekly. Sentence length displayed on your wall monitor, unless commuted to crucifixion. In that case, you will be tumbled from bed in the night by burly men. We've found that's... easier. Finally, you have a visitor—Mr Redacted."

Chad grunted again, this time with feigned nonchalance.

As soon as ChIRPy vanished, he scoured the cell for a weapon. He was assessing whether the pillow's pointiest end could kill a man, when Darius swept in.

"So, it has come to this," said Darius. "Again."

"No prison can hold me," Chad replied, fumbling for the sweater of courage and finding the cardigan of elan.

Darius took a moment to regard him. There was affection in it, buried deep beneath the disappointment. He'd spent years keeping Chad just useful enough to protect. The cost of that indulgence might be coming due.

"Only because you have powerful friends. Please put down the pillow. Good. Now—you are in a spot of bother, Keith."

Chad swallowed. Darius was a master of understatement. If he called it a 'spot,' it probably required an oncologist.

"Chad," said Chad, elanishly.

"Let us agree on Mr Blaster. It is... fitting. I have spoken with the Edifice of Corrections. They are keen that you not leave."

Chad gestured vaguely around the room.

"Indeed. Their interpretation is somewhat more terminal than yours."

"Crucifixion?" Chad asked, voice high and thin.

"Ah, so you do believe they will be merciful?"

Chad's brain was unsure if Darius was joking. His bowels, however, were preparing for evacuation.

"But I feel I may be able to—Dear God, man, what have you been eating?"

"Prison soup," Chad said meekly.

"Time to draw a line under this sorry business," Darius said, sitting beside him and placing a paternal but unyielding arm on his shoulder.

"We blast our way out?"

"Linguistically, perhaps. I know you want to go out in a hail of bullets—"

Actually, Chad didn't want to go out at all. His life had been a lesson in being caught in hails of things without 'going out'.

"I will petition the authorities. I believe they will allow you to be discharged into my care. You understand what that entails?"

"Goons?"

"A job, Mr Blaster."

"For my usual fee?"

Darius laughed. "A fee? No. You will be my employee. You will join the ranks of the salarymen. After your considerable debts are paid off, of course."

"And if I refuse?"

"Delta is suffering a chronic nail shortage. I hear the High Executioner is making great strides with the staple gun."

"I understand," said Chad, considering the options. Bravado aside, he really didn't want to spend his last moments weeping with regret whilst dangling from a log. He'd need to dig out his National Insurance number.

"Perhaps," said Darius. He turned to the door. "Release."

The door slid open silently, then clanged shut for effect.

******

Chad drifted into a shallow, hopeless sleep.

In the small hours, a sanitation droid arrived to unclog his toilet and deliver bitter invective about its lot in life.

It was followed later by a more composed unit—sleek, cylindrical body, fists the size of cinder blocks.

"You're free to go, Mr Keith—WRIT OF EXECUTION RETRACTED—Blaster," said the droid.

Chad followed it through grey corridors to Processing.

"Your prophylactics and weaponry," said the droid, returning his effects.

"What about my tooth?"

"Custodianship of your teeth is outside our remit."

"You bastards knocked it out."

"Would you like to follow me to the Complaints Department?"

The droid gestured at a soundproofed room with its fist.

"Next time," Chad muttered.

"I look forward to it," said the droid, lightly tapping a trestle table. It collapsed in a spray of splinters.

"Mr Blaster?" said a voice behind him.

Chad turned. A torso like a brick wall stood before him, with a face like another brick wall perched on top.

"Y'up." He shouldered his bag, causing a pistol to tumble out and skitter across the floor. "Oh—shit, sorry!"

"We're here to take you to Mr Fillman," the torso said, unmoved by accidental gunplay.

"Back to the warehouse?"

"Nah. Summer Palace."

"Summer Palace?"

"Yeah. Bit gauche this time of year. But the Winter Palace is still thawing. Now come with us." The Goon turned and marched away, Chad trailing in his wake.

In the foyer a droid was stapling a notice to the wall with a meaty ka-thunk. It was, Chad reflected, a great comfort to have friends.

Fifteen : Jade

Applejack dropped them out of warp close to the Erebus debris field.

"Welcome to Gliese 876, final resting place of the Erebus," Applejack said with the upbeat doom of a children's song about shipwrecks.

"Who else is in-system, and where are they?" Jade asked. She was curled forward over the console, ready for what was coming.

"As expected: a number of Clurgon ships. The remains of a construction fleet, gathered around a brand-new jump gate. A couple of destroyers, interdictors, a battlecruiser that is clearly in charge."

"Any sign they're aware of us?"

"None." The Order's transactional relationship with time kept their ship technology comfortably ahead of the galactic norm. Applejack's stealth capabilities were undetectable to even the most advanced 24th-century ships; that said, getting a stable Bluetooth connection was still a nightmare.

"Okay, bring us right up to the debris field and perform a temporal scan."

Applejack glid towards the charred shrapnel and slowed to drift. "Initiating."

Jade had placed the Bobbin in a cupholder; its glow was always in the periphery of her vision. Distracting, yet comforting. She looked directly at it now. A steady green, the friendly colour of Exit signs.

"The Erebus was hit by a single blast of a Clurgon energy weapon. The signature suggests a Battle Lance," Applejack said, tone inviting a follow-up.

"Is that weird?"

"That is their heaviest beam weapon. A single shot against a ship like the Erebus carries a very real risk of destroying it entirely."

"Not a warning shot."

"Only if you intend to 'warn' your victim by blowing their head off."

Jade nodded. "Let's follow the trail."

The sub-light drives powered up as Applejack began following a road of charged particles, picked out on the viewscreen.

"So far, standard. A Clurgon tractor beam signature. They were scooped up and sent towards the fourth planet."

"Chucking them at a planet and hoping for the best? Stupid. Reckless." Jade slammed her palm on the console.

"Not necessarily. With the correct calculations, it would be trivial to skim them into a parking orbit. If the Erebus was placed on a collision course, it was almost certainly deliberate."

"Profile of the Clurgon captain?"

"One Splurnik Trillbox; lifer. Exemplary career, by the book but not rigid. Generally well-liked, a good leader. He was about to retire before the Erebus incident. Of course, that changed with the start of war. He was brought back to frontline command and killed in action the following year. Two weeks after his daughter." Applejack paused. "The universe does have a cruel sense of humour."

"These actions don't fit that profile."

"Agreed. A subsequent inquiry blamed the crash on 'a rogue agent, acting alone'; but by the time that came out, the shooting had started. No one was listening."

"Fine. We've learned what we can here. Take us towards the planet."

Applejack said nothing, but velocity increased significantly. Gliese Four began to resolve quickly in the viewscreen.

A rattling drew Jade's attention. The Bobbin was bright red, and rotating violently in its holder.

"Applejack, all stop!"

Sub-light died, forward engines compensated. Dead calm.

Jade reached out toward the Bobbin. It thrashed wildly—as if held to the bed by straps. She touched it.

Outside, reality spun. The ship was surrounded by a maelstrom that flashed red, gold, and black, like autumn leaves caught in a furnace of collapsing stars.

"Applejack! What the hell is this?"

"It appears to be Dark Matter, but—"

The ship lurched violently, then began bucking wildly.

"But Dark Matter doesn't do this!" Jade finished, head on chair, legs braced against the ceiling, like a militant question mark.

"Agreed. Compensating." Propellant flashed from points across the hull. "Stabilised for now; we shouldn't tarry."

She stared at the whirling matter. It was beautiful and suffused with a terrible, malignant energy. It was the kind of beauty she found most seductive—furious, bitter, wild and dangerous.

"Can we pinpoint where this is coming from?" She was still fixed on it, subtly entranced.

"It appears to make landfall on the fourth planet. Again, that is something—"

"Dark Matter doesn't do. Yeah, I think we can move on from that."

"The matter stream flows into the system from the direction of the galactic Core."

This snapped Jade back to attention. "So..." she let it linger in the air, wary of pushing forward any further.

"Mmmmm," said Applejack, unwilling to shoulder the mantle of responsibility.

"That's bad." Jade moved two words closer to the brink.

"Potentially catastrophic."

"Get us away from this thing."

The engines fired again, and the ship flew clear of the matter storm. The Bobbin passed through amber before settling on a green the colour of freshly cut hay.

The planet was much closer now. Applejack sketched the storm's trajectory on the viewscreen; Jade's eyes followed it to the planet below.

"Applejack: pros and cons. I go down to the surface to investigate."

"I have scanned the surface. The Erebus is where it should be, with almost five hundred humanoids scattered over a few kilometres."

"Injured?"

"Working, mostly."

"So, I could go down and interrogate them, but they're unlikely to know any more about what happened than we do. They certainly won't understand the storm."

"No," Applejack agreed.

"Which leaves the other direction."

"Indeed."

"I hate the Core. It scares the shit out of me."

"Even as an artificial life-form, I agree it is unsettling."

Jade looked down at the blue-green planet beneath and tilted her head.

"How peaceful it looks," she murmured, giving herself another moment...

"Applejack, let's get out of here. Setting course for—"

"Where are you flying off to, little morsel?"

Jade seized up. His voice. Unmistakable. Behind her.

"Applejack?"

"Yes, awaiting your—"

"What're you talking to that thing for?"

Jade heard a crunch, the sound of a shattering panel. She spun her chair around.

Half of him was missing. His remaining eye burned into her with hatred. There was no ambiguity now, no nuance. Only hate remained.

He took a step towards her. His head was too heavy for what remained of his neck; it pitched forward as he moved, lolling crazily to one side.

"You think you know best, don't you? You lot always do."

Jade leapt to her feet. Her heart was pumping wildly; she could feel her hands pulsing. She didn't have a weapon—it was on her bunk. Fear surged. Involuntarily, she took a step back, pressing herself against the console. She held up a hand, half-fisted, toward him.

"We do no harm. We right what is—"

"Whores!" he spat, blood running from his mouth. "Filth, sluts. You did this." He raised an arm—skeletal, wrapped in tendrils of muscle. "All the same."

"Applejack!" Jade cried out.

"I fixed him," the man laughed wetly. Black and green bile sloshed over his teeth, coating his chin. "That's what you do. Fix things."

He staggered closer, lifting his good arm. It was huge, rippling, built like a steam hammer. Then the smell hit her, richer now; semen, tears, piss and vomit, boiled up inside him and left to putrefy. Her legs tensed instinctively, but there was nowhere to run.

"I'll show you what you really do."

He lunged at her; she jumped into the air, grabbing hold of the cockpit lattice and swinging her legs forward in a furious arc. She made contact with nothing. Momentum carried her forward. She flew through the air and smashed into the ground.

Pain exploded through her. She was down, exposed. She forced herself upright and spun.

The cockpit was empty. No man. No blood. She turned to the shattered panel. Nothing.

"Ms Green?" Applejack was worried. He'd only called her 'Ms Green' once before; she'd asked him not to again.

"He was here. The man from the Transit Café."

"Go on," Applejack said softly.

"But he was messed up. Broken in half. Shattered."

"You did blow him up," Applejack said, with what might have been sympathy.

"I did. He can't have been here. He wasn't. It was a hallucination or—"

"An echo?"

"Possibly." Jade let out a stuttering breath to compose herself.

"Your pockets. Each one adds strain; frays reality at the seams." Applejack was worried again. He never worried. "One day, the fabric won't hold."

"I know, I know." Jade waved a hand, swatting at the idea.

"Suggest we withdraw from the system until we understand the Dark Matter phenomenon. It is almost certain our presence here caused your vision. It is possible you are also exerting influence on it."

"No!" Jade's fear had hardened into resolve. "We're staying here. We're staying here and making this right."

"Very well. I will continue monitoring the storm for anomalies."

"And keep an eye on the people on the planet. Alert me if anything changes."

"As you wish."

Jade retreated to her cabin and lay on the bunk.

Something was wrong with reality. It might be her fault. It could be terminal.

Sixteen : Splurnik

Before humans made contact with other galactic lifeforms, they had a charmingly parochial idea of what alien worlds and cultures might look like.

Take alien planets. Earth boasts an embarrassingly diverse range of climates and terrains. Aliens? Fuck their monocultures. They get 'forest moon,' 'continent-smothering megacity,' or 'dead and arid hellscape' (like Stevenage). We can forgive the myopia—those are all more interesting than the truth: most planets are atmosphere-less rocks drifting through infinite void. (Like Stevenage.)

Alien culture? That's where the wheels come off. Imagine a race called the Kinpack. They're 'warlike'—that's all the detail you're given. So how do they speak, smell, dress? Armour. Always armour. Probably earned via some ludicrous birth rite, like being lobbed through a threshing machine. Fine.

Do these Kinpack roar at least once per conversation? Are their eyes ever described as 'kind' or 'understanding'? Despite their advanced technology, do they still carry swords—or 'ceremonial sparring poles'?

Picture them as children. Do they squeal, "Look, Daddy! A happy pebble"? Or do they charge into games called "Kit-HA!-Mun-TAK!" and "Drown the Weakest"?

The real question to ask is: "Where are the accountants?" "Who runs the soft play centres?" Is it remotely plausible that a society can construct planet-destroying weaponry but not one half-decent organic deli? Of course not. While the Kinpack military thunder through the galaxy yelling and brandishing sabres, the rest are just trying to punch out early and get home for a bowl of Pffnurr.

The other extreme is just as bad—giving the Kinpack too much character. Instead of a simple 'warlike,' they come burdened with aeons of history, seventeen dialects, and volumes of folk songs. This leads inevitably to endless evenings in pubs, arguing over whether 'eath' or 'ethene' is the correct conjugation, while former lovers embark on increasingly flamboyant affairs.

Now that humans have met their galactic neighbours, we know the truth: they're just like us. A messy swirl of ideologies, appetites, contradictions. Their home planets tend to be Earth-like—because life loves company. Clurgon Prime, for example, has been described as "a wonderful place to live" and "quite wet." So, let's leave it at that.

******

"Miei ad Idethene!" Splurnik finished his favourite travel song and hit himself with a generous blast from the shuttle's misting nozzles. The journey back from the Swift, through the jump gate and home to Clurgon Prime, had been quick and uneventful—to everyone's great relief. Splurnik was a popular figure in the Clurgon military, and 'death by malfunctioning jump gate' would have been an ignominious end to a fine career.

The shuttle dropped from the clouds and skimmed across the Southern Ocean toward the islet where Splurnik and his family had lived for nearly thirty years. In classic Clurgish style, the house had rooms both on land and underwater. But unlike the average home, Splurnik's had been built in the style of a Venetian palazzo. On a cultural exchange tour of Earth, Venice had struck him as the perfect blend of human aesthetics and Clurgon utility—though he'd been disappointed to learn the flooded basements were unintentional.

Splurnik fancied himself a Homophile—a collector of human culture. Not to be confused with Humophiles, who found humans erotically desirable. That remained a niche interest, as no one had yet determined which bits went in which orifices to produce mutual pleasure.

The shuttle arced lazily over the red-tiled roof and touched down on a jetty that extended from the house's stone steps into the sea. The engines clicked and hissed as they cooled in the warm autumn air. Splurnik slithered out of his harness, popped the cockpit hatch, and hauled himself upright. Using his secondary tentacles to grip the textured hull, he slid over the side and dismounted with practised grace.

A cascade of bubbles announced Hera's arrival. "Splurnik!" she called, her flotation sacs puffing up. She emerged from the water and wrapped herself around him with a thousand affectionate suckers.

"Darling!" Splurnik released a mist of pink and yellow ink and stroked a tentacle over her damp head. "Yes—I had the crew comprehensively thrashed to raise productivity."

Hera rolled all her eyes. "Did you?"

"No, they're just good. The finest command I've ever had."

"Well, it's nice that your last command is a good one."

"Mmmm," Splurnik replied vaguely. "I cannot believe our little Squidlet is graduating today."

"She's twenty-five, Splurnik. She's not our little Squidlet anymore."

"She will always remain our Squidlet."

Hera unlatched from him. He coiled one tentacle gently around hers and tugged her toward the house.

"Let's have some lunch before we go. How are the animals?"

Splurnik had imported a variety of Earth animals to enhance the human aesthetic of the home. Some, like the pigeons, had been a resounding success. Introduce a single pigeon to any atmosphere-bearing planet and within a month, you'll be overrun.

The animals requiring actual care had yielded more mixed results.

"The chickens aren't laying," said Hera.

"Hmmm. Are you sure you're squeezing them sufficiently?" Splurnik's face furrowed with concern.

"That doesn't help. I think we need to move them off the marsh."

"You believe they'll thrive in a more aqueous habitat?"

"The opposite. We need to move them up to the pasture."

Splurnik considered the well-drained loamy soil behind the house.

"Very well. Punish the chickens if you must. Perhaps it'll shock them into better laying."

"And I'm afraid another cow sank."

"That can't be right. Cows like to wallow."

"I looked it up. That's buffalo."

"Ah!" Splurnik's face lit up. "Mozzarella."

"Remind me?"

"A ball of white cheese strings. You rub the milk until it gives up."

"Oh yes. Lovely."

They passed through the doorway and began preparing a traditional Earthen lunch of crushed eggs and rubbed cheese.

******

Later that afternoon, they flew a few hundred miles across the ocean to the Clurgon Fleet Academy—the elite training college for aspiring officers in the ClurMarine. They joined a spinning stack of parental shuttles waiting to set down for Passing Out Day: the ceremonial end to two years of rigorous training in aquatic, land, and space combat leadership.

Their daughter, Ocho, was graduating from the Fleet Command stream. Splurnik had once teased her that Fleet Command were just back-office paper-pushers. Ocho had replied that without the paper-pushers, he wouldn't have anything to shoot—or anyone to shoot at. He'd approved of the answer.

At the pad, Hera reached out a tentacle to help him down from the cockpit and straightened his bowtie.

"The Puff of Ink is on display here now," she said.

"The Puff! My first posting. She was a fine ship. Hot, dry, cramped—but she could appear from nowhere, slip between enemy lines, and land a torpedo right in the arse," Splurnik said with feeling.

"You never stopped complaining about her at the time."

"Ha! True. But I was young. The hardship improved me."

"Not as much as you think." She gently squeezed his tentacle.

"No, perhaps not." Splurnik laughed good-naturedly. "And now she's a museum piece."

"How does that make you feel?"

"Old. Incredibly old."

"Age is a gift—it means you've survived. Many don't."

"You're right. I've seen such things—such wonders. The galaxy is vast, marvellous, impossible. I've seen so much… and yet barely scratched the surface."

"That won't stop when you retire. You'll still travel. But you won't be the captain anymore."

Splurnik's chins wobbled.

"But you'll be there," he said, and reached out to gently cup Hera's bulbous head with two tentacles. "That will be better."

Tentacles entwined, they walked through the Academy's quadrangles toward Sturmlot Hall—the place where officer cadets had Passed Out for more than three centuries.

They took seats near the front and listened to the provost's address. Cadets paraded up one by one to receive their Commission papers. When Ocho's name was called, Hera let out a proud whoop and applauded with every sucker. She felt a gentle tremor beside her and turned to see Splurnik grinning broadly, tears streaming freely. She smiled. He cried harder.

******

After the ceremony, cadets and families gathered in the Passing Out Pool, a natural lagoon on the shore beside the Academy, exposed only at low tide. Hundreds of bodies swam and bobbed beneath the twin moons, now risen and chasing one another across a star-laced sky.

The lack of surface buildings on Clurgon Prime meant the skies were darker than on most inhabited worlds.

Somehow, that deepened the link—at least in the Clurgish imagination—between the depths of the ocean and the reaches of space. Their ancestors had once pierced the sea to reach the land. Reaching space had simply been the next step.

Splurnik blew a great cloud of pink and gold inks and surged from beneath the water, rising in a shimmer of rainbow bubbles.

"Beautiful, Dad," said Ocho. "You've been practising."

"Well, there hasn't been much else to do at Gliese. Aside from frightening off the occasional smuggler."

"Sounds like the Swift has been poorly deployed. Maybe I'll fix that." She grinned.

"Perhaps you'll send me somewhere more interesting."

"Like home," said Hera.

"Mum still wants you to retire, huh?" Ocho gave Splurnik a look that suggested her mother had a point.

"I'll be out in six months. End of my tour. But it wouldn't hurt to check off one more system before I go. Even a nebula."

"Don't send your father to a nebula," said Hera, swatting him with a tentacle. "Let's save that excitement for our first cruise."

"Oh! A cruise, that sounds about your speed, Dad," said Ocho. "You'd look dashing on the lido deck. Shuffleboard cue in hand."

"Urgh," Splurnik groaned.

"Think of the jaunty old man hats."

"It's not too late to have you adopted," he declared, with an exaggerated lunge. Ocho shrieked and dived underwater, narrowly dodging a jet of black ink.

"I do think you'd look dashing in an old man hat," said Hera, enveloping him in her tentacles.

"I shall call a milliner in the morning," Splurnik said before diving after his daughter, the three of them laughing and chasing each other through the moonlit water.

Later, the pool had emptied. Floating lily pads bore bowls of burning scented oil. The humid evening air smelled of fruit and flowers. Hera and Ocho reclined on rocks by the ocean while Splurnik made his way toward the drinks table.

"Splurnik! Splurnik, old boy—is that you?" called a voice from the darkness.

He looked around at the bobbing lights and scattered clusters of figures, but couldn't place the voice.

"Splurnik! It is you!" A touch on his flank turned him to face a bilious expression he barely remembered.

"Uhhh, don't tell me..." Splurnik's face folded into the universal shorthand for please rescue me from this social disaster.

"It's Furpp! From the Academy! Don't say you've forgotten me!"

Splurnik had forgotten Furpp. For decades. But now memories surged forward. Oh no. Not Furpp. Older and hopefully improved—surely the man had redeeming qualities. But Splurnik's most vivid memory was of volunteering for latrine duty just to escape Furpp's interminable rambling.

"No, no, I remember you, Furpp," said Splurnik, silently chiding himself. You're better than this, older, wiser. Be nice, make thirty seconds of small talk. Then escape. "How have you been—today?" Best not to make the anecdote window too wide.

"Today! Well, today I'm seeing off my youngest son—one of four, would you believe?" Splurnik would not. "He's going straight into the Combat Core. Just like his old man! Up and ready for anything!"

Splurnik nodded with upright politeness. He calculated that saying nothing might hasten the end of the anecdote deluge.

"My other three are already in the Fleet. Eldest is angling for his first command. Just needs that Number Two spot—get the experience under his belt."

Splurnik's internal sensors pinged. Incoming favour request.

"I hear you're commanding the Swift these days?"

"Yes," Splurnik said a touch too fast. "Excellent crew. Dedicated, committed. Lifers, really."

"Oh, I wasn't suggesting you'd just give him a post…" said Furpp, dripping faux effrontery.

Splurnik's brain made the sound of a folding deckchair. Damn. Walked right into it. Messages fired urgently to his tentacles: go, get drink. He wobbled, mildly oozing regret.

"No, of course, I didn't—"

"But if you could maybe put out a few feelers, see who's recruiting—he's bright, dedicated—would mean the world coming from you."

"Well, I don't know about—"

"You're too modest!" Furpp bopped him on the shoulder. Splurnik winced. "The Hero of Sigma!"

"Well, it's easy to be a hero when the enemy is unarmed."

"Oh, you!" Another bop. "So modest. And now the Guardian of Gliese!"

That made Splurnik freeze. The Gliese mission was classified. He chose his words carefully.

"You have me at a disadvantage. What do you mean, 'Guardian of Gliese'?"

"Modest again! The human ship, of course! You saw those interlopers off!"

Splurnik relaxed. That part, at least, was in the Fleet rumour mill. "Ah yes. That was fun. Played the angry Clurgon. Gave them a story to tell."

"I don't think so, old man. They crashed on Gliese Four. As if you didn't know."

"Crashed? No. No, we put them in a stable orbit. They'd make repairs, be gone before the extraction teams arrived."

"Sure, sure," Furpp said, winking with enough force to crumple half his face.

"You'll excuse me," said Splurnik, already turning away. It wasn't a request.

"Of course. Perhaps a drink later…" Furpp trailed off behind him.

******

Splurnik made his way along the lagoon's edge, past the tiki-lit bar and soft chatter, through an arched doorway into a quiet colonnade. He passed a pair of newly minted officers canoodling in an alcove. Were they saying goodbye forever or starting something that would last forty years? Their frantic intensity suggested the former.

He found an unromantic alcove and opened a comm line to the Swift. After a moment, Klurn's hologram materialised beside him, wearing Fleet pyjamas and fluffy slippers.

"Oh, Captain. Good…" Klurn looked around. "Evening? I think we're in a romantic alcove."

"Klurn!" Splurnik's voice was taut with strained emotion. "What the hell happened with the human ship?"

"Ah." Klurn retrieved his mental spoon to stir the custard of reassurance. "The full sequence is still a little uncertain. I'm compiling a report for your return. The ship was lost—"

"A report? On my return?" Splurnik roared. "The Swift shoots down a human vessel under my command and you're writing me a bedtime story?"

"Sir," said Klurn, suddenly earnest. "The Erebus wasn't downed under your command. You had already ceded control to Commodore Schlep."

"Don't throw technicalities at me! We're not at war. There are rules. Even if there weren't—there's basic respect for sentient life! Did you try to rescue the Erebus? Dispatch recovery?"

"No, Captain. Nobody noticed the Erebus's orbit had decayed until after you'd left the system. We were all celebrating the successful jump gate test." Klurn had the haunted look of someone incriminating himself in real time. "The Commodore then reported the Erebus as presumed lost after a defensive engagement. We're now holding position as a precaution."

"Precaution against what? Saving lives? Doing the decent thing?"

"Precaution against further hostilities, sir."

Splurnik roared and swung a tentacle through Klurn's hologram. It passed harmlessly.

"Sir," Klurn said quietly, crushed. "I could only advise the Commodore. I had no authority."

"You could have called me. The moment it happened."

"Protocol dictates that—"

"Blast protocol! Lives before protocol, Klurn! Have I taught you nothing?"

Klurn said nothing, head bowed.

"I'm coming back right now. Tell Schlep I want a full account the second I arrive. If I'm not satisfied, I'm spacing you both. Understood?"

"Sir..." Klurn had never looked more miserable.

"Take a minute. Have a cry. It's good for the soul. Then start making amends. Splurnik out."

The hologram dissolved.

Splurnik rested a tentacle on the cool stone wall and breathed. Then he wobbled back through the colonnade. The lovers broke apart as his vast bulk loomed over them.

"Make it last forty years," he said softly.

They froze, wide-eyed.

"Love," Splurnik said. "It's the only thing that matters."

With that, he spun on his flipper and went to kiss his family goodbye—then, he would make things right.

Seventeen : Chad

Darius Fillman wasn't born poor or rich; he was born shrewd. He knew the system wasn't against him—well, not one system anyway. There are dozens of carefully calibrated, mutually antagonistic systems in the galaxy, and getting screwed by them is more a by-product than a feature. Let that warm your soul next time you can't make rent because you ticked the wrong box on a housing form.

He didn't see himself as a criminal—more a pragmatist, rendered in layered shades of grey. And he was proud. Proud of Delta, proud of his part in Making It Great, proud to work for the Common Good. If the Common Good happened to be personally lucrative, so much the better. Governments came and went, but large parts of the machinery that kept Delta warm, fed, clean, and safe were under his unassailable control. His wealth and connections gave him power—power to intervene when things went wrong. And right now, something had.

The hood was torn from Chad's head, as tradition demanded. The hood itself was less traditional—soft, buttery, and, he noticed as the Goon folded it away, monogrammed "DF."

"Get your filthy hands off me!" Chad snapped—then realised no one was touching him. He looked around. The subtle energy fields on the windows and door said 'cell.' The chaise longue said otherwise.

"This stinking hellhole... smells... nice," he muttered, searching for something to rage against. He found a fruit bowl. A stack of magazines about expensive chairs. And three Goons.

"Mr Fillman is an Enlightened Abductor," said the largest. "It's one of his Codes. The scent is lavender and ylang-ylang. Promotes relaxation and a balanced Qi."

"I'm more of a sandalwood guy," Chad lied.

"Of course, sir. A very masculine choice. While you await your audience, would sir require anything? Rosehip tea? Aromatherapy massage? Even the most considerate kidnappings can provoke unease and muscular distress."

Chad planted his hands on his hips and stood proudly. "Yes, please," he said defiantly.

The Goons began filing out.

"Oh!" Chad called.

"Sir?" The trailing Goon poked his head back in.

"A sucky sweet, if you have any."

"Of course, sir."

******

Some hours later, Chad was tenderly slapped awake. The massage had been wonderful—like being roughed up by a citrus-infused boxing glove—and he'd fallen into a deep, dreamless sleep.

"Mr Fillman will see you now," said the Goon, offering a dressing gown that looked ready for shearing. "Wear this and follow me."

The door opened onto a corridor painted an expensive shade of not-quite-white. Familiar sculptures stood before towering windows.

"The buff lad with no pants—he's from—"

"Quite famous, yes," said the Goon. "Mr Fillman believes beautiful accents enhance the structural voice of the architecture. Powerful, but understated. Another Code."

"I like the cat," Chad said, nodding to a Crayoned feline framed like a Monet.

"Mr Fillman's niece drew that. He believes it to be 'authentic.'"

"Is that important?"

"Authenticity means truth. Truth builds the Codes," said the Goon. "Remember that."

At the corridor's end, double doors opened onto a well-proportioned courtyard. Through one window, Chad saw Goons doing paperwork. Through another, a Pilates class. He raised an eyebrow.

"Core strength is the foundation of a healthy body and mind," said the Goon, unblinking.

"I thought a Summer Palace would be more…" Chad searched. "Ostentatious?"

The Goon said nothing, just gestured him on. They crossed the courtyard and entered a door on the far side. Down a flight of stairs, past lockers, then through a bustling canteen. Goons and admin staff sat in twos and threes, chatting and eating. The kitchen smells were divine. For a moment, Chad pictured himself here—getting a pat on the back from Darius, maybe joining Kathy from Accounts for a flirtatious kofta.

That could be... nice?

The thought derailed when the Goon opened a door leading to a bridge. A sweeping, gorge-spanning bridge, ending at a palace of domes, spires, and minarets that dominated the skyline. Chad didn't know what you had to do to get one of those, but it clearly wasn't accounting.

He steadied himself against an onyx bull.

"Wow," he said.

"Ostentatious enough?" asked the Goon, faintly contemptuous.

"No. This is..." Chad searched again. "Magnificent."

"The bridge is inspired by the Nine Water Gates of the Chinese Great Wall," said the Goon. "As our gorge has no water, it's called the Nine Gates of the Wind."

"Very poetic," Chad murmured.

"The palace is based on the Dar al-Hajar," the Goon continued, "but far grander. Now, follow me to the Topiary Arena. Mr Fillman is waiting."

They crossed the bridge in silence. On the far side, they passed through a gatehouse and followed a tree-lined avenue to a vast lawn studded with topiary. Beneath a brightly coloured gazebo, in a wicker chair, sat Darius.

"Ah, Mr Blaster. Welcome to my magnificent palace."

There was a time for false modesty, but that had clearly been three domes ago.

"Pheasant?"

He gestured toward what Chad had assumed was an elaborate taxidermy display but, on closer inspection, was lunch.

"That's not really my speed," said Chad, attempting to reassert his persona. "I'm more of a red meat guy."

"Of course." Darius made a tiny motion. A perfumed flunky emerged from behind a pillar, dressed like a doily on holiday.

"Please kill one of the bison and bring Mr Blaster a sandwich."

The flunky bowed and turned.

"One moment." Darius raised a finger. "Mr Blaster?"

"Really? A whole—?"

"White or wholemeal?"

"Uhhh." Chad blinked. "One of each," he said, with supreme confidence.

"You are a man of intricate taste," said Darius, with a smile that hinted at neither approval nor mockery—just the certainty that he'd already won.

Chad nodded intricately.

"While your meal is being slaughtered," Darius said, rising smoothly from his chair, "let us take a walk. I find a pre-prandial stroll most enervating."

"Oh," said Chad, who had planned to do some serious pranding.

Darius's outfit—part trousers, part tunic, part cassock—whispered as he moved. "Come," he said. Not an order. Not a request. Just a statement of inevitability.

They crossed the topiary garden and descended a grand set of marble steps leading to an artificial lake, its surface rippling in the breeze. The lake was framed by smooth white stone and hemmed with sculpted walkways and balustrades.

"Do you like it?" asked Darius. "This is my calm space. I come here to think whenever I have a problem that is particularly vexatious."

"It's big," said Chad, whose vocabulary was shrinking in direct proportion to the grandeur of his surroundings.

"It's appropriately sized. For the whales."

"You keep whales?"

"Rescue whales. From Earth. Do you remember the probe?"

Chad looked blank.

"No? It spoke only Whale. More specifically, one breed of Antarctic whale."

"Which breed?"

"The... anatomically minded one. Juvenile aliens, I assume." Darius waved it off. "A few whales were launched into space in a giant aquarium. Less enlightened times. The probe shut down with what sounded like snickering, and the whales drifted. Fortunately, the tank was well-stocked. Survivors were salvaged and brought here. Now they and their descendants are safe."

"WANKERS!" shouted one of the whales.

"Such majestic creatures," Darius murmured. "Come. Let's cross the Bridge of Sighs to the Pleasure Gardens."

"Bridge of Sighs?" Chad asked, with a flicker of foreboding.

"Yes. Modelled on the one in Pittsburgh. Apparently, it's quite renowned."

"And the Pleasure Gardens are...?"

"Very pleasant."

"Fruitful?"

"Not for you, Mr Blaster. You're a busy man now."

They entered the sort of garden a New Jersey mob boss might build for his mistress—Italianate paths, fake rock walls, and vines cascading over everything. The many statues had long since passed 'suggestive' and were sprinting toward 'obscene.'

Darius perched on a bench shaped like a heart trying to be a phallus and gestured for Chad to sit.

"Now. To business. I need you to deliver a package."

"Just one?" Chad had been a smuggler long enough to know that 'deliver a package' usually came with a sting in the tail.

"One. But important."

"Coordinates?"

"Not that simple. It goes to Gliese 876. Fourth planet. Your AI has precise instructions."

"What's there? Smuggling hub? Armoury?"

"All you must know is that Gliese has a Clurgon jump gate."

Chad frowned. "It's a backwater. Why build a gate there?"

"A good question. And not yours to answer. The gate is new. There'll be a construction fleet—and likely a sizeable Clurgon presence."

"You want me to deliver it to them?"

"No. I want you to avoid them."

Chad's eye-roll came instinctively. His panic did not. Something about Darius's phrasing sounded an awful lot like certain death.

"Can we drop the mystery act and be straight?"

A flicker of steel passed through Darius's eyes.

"I have been straight, Mr Blaster. I do not know what is at Gliese 876. But the Clurgons do. They believe it valuable enough to build a jump gate. That is enough to arouse my interest. And my arousal alone should be enough to satisfy you."

Chad stared ahead.

"I am aware of what I just said, Mr Blaster."

Chad tittered. Darius decided to open the door another inch.

"I have a suspicion about Gliese. If I'm wrong, you'll deliver a package, and come back with your debt substantially reduced. If I'm right... you might save a trillion lives. Either way, a worthy action, Mr Blaster."

"It's a long way," said Chad, mentally scanning the route for bars and finding none.

"That shouldn't be a problem. You are, after all, the man who made the Proxima run in fifty-eight astronomical units."

"True." Chad straightened.

"How long did that take?"

"About three days."

"Excellent. Then you'll be at Gliese by supper. We've made some upgrades."

"What did you do to her?" Chad asked, like a father whose thermostat had been tampered with.

"Relax. Minor tweaks. Your Alcubierre drive has more... oomph."

Chad's jaw dropped. "Not a Ristretto?"

"You know your drives. I'm impressed. Yes. And you may notice base notes of white musk and vanilla. We also upgraded your stealth systems. You should enter Clurgon space undetected."

"I think I can talk my way past a few Clurgons."

"They want you dead. A substantial bounty. They're motivated."

"Everyone wants me dead," said Chad, with a heady mix of pride and melancholy.

"True. But the Clurgons are particularly insistent."

Chad wondered briefly what would happen if he said 'no'. Then he wondered why simply saying 'no' had never occurred to him, in any of his dealings with Darius. He pushed this revelation down his mental staircase and slammed the door. Now was not the time to take a jackhammer to the pilings of his psyche.

"Well," he said, clapping his hands together and grabbing the joystick of destiny, "no time like the present."

"Indeed. I'll have your bison wrapped and delivered to your ship. I trust you know how to butcher a carcass?"

"Sure," Chad lied again, but with the chutzpah of a man suddenly confident he might see another mealtime.

"I recommend removing the limbs first, then the entrails," said Darius. "Much like a human."

Chad very deliberately didn't respond.

"Safe travels, Mr Blaster."

He clapped once. Two Goons emerged from behind a topiary vulva.

"Escort Mr Blaster to his ship."

The Goons gestured. Chad followed.

"Oh, and do tip them!" Darius called. "It's so terribly gauche not to."

******

Chad didn't like to admit it, but the Eagle looked good. Sleeker. Her brown, riveted panels replaced with smooth white siding that shone from within. Soft blue running lights traced her midsection. The sub-light drives now sat angled and low, with an almost feline grace.

Darius hadn't just invested money—he'd invested taste. The Eagle now looked like her name: refined, poised, unapologetically predatory.

"Hey hey! Cheryl! Did'ja miss me?" Chad tossed his shoulder bag into the passenger seat and dropped into the pilot's chair.

"Of course I did!" Cheryl's voice flooded the cockpit like sunshine.

"You've had a pretty spiffy update."

"I have!" she said, audibly beaming.

"I bet we could shave a few astronomical units off that Proxima run."

"I keep telling you that isn't—. Yes. Probably."

Chad reached down and tugged the chair handle. The seat eased back ten perfect degrees.

"Now this is luxury."

"Yes, Mr Fillman did a very comprehensive job. Did he mention the tracking device?"

Chad groaned. "Really?"

"Oh yes. They drilled something deep into my underside. Military grade, I'd guess. Galactic-range."

"Can you disable it?"

"No. It's self-contained. But it could be removed."

Chad exhaled. "Did he think you wouldn't notice?"

"Either that—or he wanted me to. Maybe it's a test. See what you'll do."

Chad pondered for a moment. "Then we're going to Gliese."

"I... we... are you sure?" Cheryl's voice had a hint of something new—worry. "My briefing suggests we'll encounter a heavy Clurgon presence. Construction fleet. Military outpost. Even with upgrades, stealth won't last forever."

"If we don't go, Darius kills me."

"And if we do go…"

"The Clurgons will."

"I don't like either of those."

"Me neither," Chad said. "But I know which odds I prefer." He glanced at the cargo panel. "What did they load?"

"A catering-size box of sweets from the cash and carry."

"Yum."

"And one very heavy, very shielded crate."

"Any guesses?"

"Based on mass... a lump of Giant Ironwood. Possibly a sculpture."

"And the more likely option?"

"A really massive bomb."

"Hmm." Chad chewed his lip. "Would Darius blow up the jump gate?"

"Unlikely. He values trade lanes. And he can't afford a Clurgon retaliation."

"He's also not a killer," Chad offered, then paused. "I mean, not in a 'blow up strangers' kind of way."

Cheryl said nothing.

"Anyway, how would they trace it to Darius?"

"Because you'd get drunk and tell someone."

"Fair. Maybe he wants to blow us up?"

"If that was the plan, I doubt he'd let us find the tracker. He wants us to come back. Or thinks we won't."

"Maybe the tracker is also a bomb."

"If so, he's gambling. You'd probably get flung clear and land in an improbable air pocket inside my mangled remains."

"I do have the gift." An idea flickered: maybe it wasn't luck. Maybe he owed more to Darius than he realised. What happened when he stopped being useful?

"So far." There was a moment of quiet, then Cheryl asked softly: "If your luck runs out, what happens to me?"

Chad stopped what he was doing and looked up at her lens. "I... I don't know. I should have planned. Shouldn't I?"

"Just in case," Cheryl sounded cheerful, but Chad knew it was an act.

"Ok, I will." He sat for a moment, letting it sink in, then tugged the handle again; the chair rose to flight position. He flipped a few toggles overhead. The systems hummed to life.

"Pre-flight checks complete?"

"Yes, Chad. Please fasten your harness."

"One sec." He stood. "Just grabbing a Twix."

"There's already three in the glovebox." Cheryl had had a lot of time to get things 'just right' for Chad's return. It had distracted her from wondering if he would.

"Cheryl! I have missed you." He clicked into his harness and pulled down his flight shades.

"Set course for Gliese."

******

The Eagle lifted from the pad with barely a whisper. Chad took a bite of Twix and chewed slowly. Maybe, next time, he'd get to decide which fire to walk into.

"Course laid in," said Cheryl. "Engaging Alcubierre drive in three... two..."

From the rear of the ship came a faint thunk. Then silence.

Cheryl didn't speak. Neither did Chad.

"...one."

The Eagle streaked across the sky and vanished.

Eighteen : Jertsie

Politics is a brilliant way of making the awful things you want to do legal-or the terrible things other people do illegal. Sadly, before you can unleash your deranged vision of the future on a downtrodden populace, you first need their support. Occasionally, you get lucky and discover that a worrying number of people already share your grim worldview. But usually, no: most people are quite nice, and don't want to be dragged into your hailstorm of petty recriminations and grand larceny.

So, you fall back on your greatest asset: lies.

Lies are brilliant. Let us consider the plus points:

They're free. You can say absolutely anything, to anyone, for no money down. Worried they'll catch up with you? Don't be. Once you're holding the reins of power in your gloved fists — riding high on the Steed of Authority — it takes an almighty wrench to dislodge you. Just twitch those reins and watch your detractors trampled beneath your mighty hooves.

They generate shame. A small lie: "I didn't take your pen," as you twirl the stolen pen, gets you caught, scolded. A massive lie: "One vote for me and all the Bad Things will stop," creates loyalty. Why? Because now they've chosen you. They're invested. They want to believe. Every erratic, kleptomaniacal moment will now be interpreted as part of your brilliant masterplan. You've got ten years, minimum. Start looting immediately.

They become true. You repeat your lie. You trim the ones that didn't land. You double down on those that did. You make them vague: "I will solve all your problems as soon as I deal with Bogeyman X." The best bogeymen are far away, aliens, or both. Don't pick someone you trade with (what are you, a moron?). Don't pick someone who could hit back. Pick a shadow, and start boxing. Who knows you didn't really 'send those scroungers back to Andromeda'? They didn't even exist.

The best lies work both ways. You tell them to win, and then you tell yourself they were true all along.

Now, one last thing: you'll need friends. Not good friends—those ask how you are. Political friends. People too shifty, perverted, or unelectable to lead themselves. These will form your Cabinet. For now, they provide two things: money and connections.

Money's easy. You're a charismatic liar. People will bet on that.

Connections are trickier. Private donors are one thing. But you'll need the media. Fortunately, you're a moral vacuum, which makes you the perfect mouthpiece for a media baron with an axe to grind and a country to buy.

Corporations can be tricky bedfellows. But that's where the lie returns: on stage, you rage about how Robocon will never mine under residential areas on your watch. Meanwhile, backstage, you've already signed a deal to let them strip-mine cemeteries. Just don't get those speeches muddled up before the bulldozers roll in.

Earth in the 24th century has many layers of government—public and private. In theory, EarthGov sits atop them all, guiding space exploration, energy security, galactic trade. In practice, vast amounts of power are concentrated in the hands of regional blocs and mega-corps.

EarthGov directly controls the Home Fleet, tacitly Earth's main defence. But the fleet is a paper dragon without support from auxiliaries like QuikBrew or Amalgamated Yoghurt.

Together, they form a formidable alliance. That's the line. The reality: endless turf disputes, chronic incompetence, and more friendly fire than enemy contact. Still, it keeps EarthGov's costs down and allows private enterprise to stockpile warships without anyone asking awkward questions.

But what happens should this ramshackle coalition ever face a well-led, cohesive enemy?

Earth is about to find out.

******

The QuikBrew boardroom occupied the penthouse of one of five hundred-storey towers at the eastern end of Grand Cayman. A series of tax-evasion crackdowns in the 22nd century had forced companies to relocate "headquarters" to their claimed jurisdictions. Politicians had underestimated the willingness of mega-corps to build millions of square metres of fake office space to dodge a tax bill. QuikBrew's campus boasted five towers, seven permanent staff, and a small army of off-the-books facilities workers.

Jertsie Funt strode into the boardroom with the air of someone whose education had been as brutal as it was expensive. She wore a look she thought of as demonic equestrian: slim-cut tweed jacket, white shirt, blood-red boots and gloves. In her left hand she carried a polished ebony baton, so dark it seemed to swallow light. It had belonged to her grandmother, who had wrenched it from the hands of an officer 'peacekeeping' in her village more than a century ago. There was still a compression in the wood from when Granny had delivered the fatal blow.

Jertsie smiled and assumed her position at the head of the table. Feet planted, posture razor-straight, chin up. Her ballet instructor had called it 'needlessly painful.' She called it powerful.

"We've just received word," she began, "that our ship, the Erebus, was attacked without provocation by a Clurgon warship during a peaceful survey of the Gliese system. She was lost with all hands. The wreckage burned up in the atmosphere of the fourth planet."

A low murmur passed through the Board. Jertsie drank it in—fear, grief, the exquisite sting of humiliation. Lucious. She stood tall, baton pressed to her ribs, and let the tension rise.

"Let me be clear. This was no accident. No misunderstanding. This was barbarism. The Clurgons think nothing of humiliating us, pushing us aside, killing us if we so much as drift across their path."

She scanned their faces. Yes. They were with her. A few questions lingered behind their eyes—good. Best to strike before those took root.

"I called you here with the code word Lenhador. You know what that means. A tree has been felled. And unless we act, more will fall. If we do not throw a human chain around our forest—our ships, our colonies, our lives—then the Clurgons will take them. All of them. Until humanity kneels."

A hand rose. Jertsie turned her head slowly toward it.

Neville Taleggio, CFO. Weak chin. Weaker mind. A man who had taken numbers—divine, wild, glorious numbers—and reduced them to budgets. To write-offs. To chains.

"Yes, Neville?"

"Uhh... Ms Funt," he stammered, scanning for support and finding none. "It feels like you're, ah, rushing to judgement. We don't have confirmation yet. Shouldn't we investigate before we escalate?"

Jertsie did some quick mental arithmetic. The fun kind that ends in a sword drawn or fleet launched.

"Thank you for your input, Neville. Though I'd have preferred you let me finish before interrupting. Perhaps you think I'm overreacting? Becoming... emotional?"

Neville turned pink, then red, then a sort of damp parchment white.

"I, no, I would never—"

"Thank you, Mr Taleggio. You seem unwell. Perhaps have a eucalyptus tea and join us when you're feeling less… fragile."

She had him. The others saw it. This was her show now, and they were scenery.

"As I was saying: no one here seeks conflict. All we want is peace. Exploration. Commerce. Discovery. But we will not be pushed around. We will not stand silently by and watch our vessels destroyed, our crews murdered, our planets rained with fire. We'll defend ourselves. Our ships. Our worlds. And we will respond."

She let the tension crest. Time to throw them a lifeline.

"But not with the sword. With the pen."

Relief washed across the table. Faces shifted from dread to tentative optimism. Jertsie watched, amused. Horror deferred is horror edged.

"I've spoken to EarthGov. They express full solidarity. The Home Fleet will rendezvous with our Deep Space Squadron at Europa. Together, we'll fly to Geneva Station to meet with a Clurgon delegation."

A nervous voice piped up: "Why bring the whole fleet?"

"The Clurgons are arriving with their own deep space formation, a rapid assault group, and a mobile battle station designed to hurl asteroids into planets. I don't think we're overdoing it."

"Oh," said the voice.

"Ms Funt."

Jertsie had been expecting this one. Felinda Tuvlumon, Chair of the Board and CEO of QuikBrew. Calm. Lethal. A smile sharpened on both sides.

"I've long admired your ambition, your drive, your ability to make things happen."

"Thank you," said Jertsie, tilting her head subtly into the I am listening seriously to your concerns angle.

"But you cannot make these decisions unilaterally. We are a commercial enterprise. We manufacture products. Drive innovation. Deliver returns to shareholders. We are not mercenaries. And we certainly do not conduct diplomacy with alien powers."

She paused, letting her authority settle across the table like a quilt of reasonableness.

"You are over-ruled, Ms Funt. This imperial fantasy ends here. We'll dispatch a salvage team to Gliese, verify what happened to the Erebus, and decide on further action after we have the facts. I move we adjourn, and the squadron be stood down."

A murmur rose. They were leaning her way. For a moment, it looked like the board might swing.

Jertsie could see it—reasonable people embracing the illusion of control. She shifted her weight. Feet to second position. Hands on hips. Shoulders square.

Time to break the illusion.

"My network," she said quietly, "has detected something... unusual in Gliese."

The murmuring stopped.

"For years we've observed strange patterns of dark matter from Sagittarius A, the supermassive black hole at the galactic core. Most dark matter moves in straight lines. But some—clumps, tendrils—spirals, like water down a drain. That spiral ends at Gliese."

Felinda opened her mouth, but Jertsie cut her off.

"We believe Gliese contains a vast, self-sustaining reservoir of Dark Fluid. Our current supply lines are... precarious. This discovery would secure humanity's warp future. And give QuikBrew unlimited reserves of the most valuable resource in known space."

She let that hang.

"The implications are vast. Colonisation without limit. Travel without constraint. Total self-reliance for Earth. And total control—for us."

Jertsie's baton tapped gently against her thigh.

"Unprecedented power. Endless profit. All just sitting there. Waiting."

The silence was electric.

"So," said Felinda at last, voice lower now. "That's why the Clurgons destroyed the Erebus?"

"Yes. They want it for themselves. But they will not break our spirit. We can still claim what is ours."

Felinda narrowed her eyes. "Even if we move forward, no human fleet has ever successfully engaged a Clurgon one. A show of force would be meaningless."

"I disagree," said Jertsie, raising her baton to the ceiling. "A show of force is the meaning. We don't want war. They don't want war. But we show we're not afraid of one, and we strengthen our hand."

She began to pace.

"This is diplomacy. A dance. They have better warships—we have better terraforming tech. Our AIs are more advanced. They don't need Dark Fluid. We do. We offer partnership. Joint venture. Shared success."

She turned to face the board directly.

"Two civilisations. Two governments. One company. Us."

Another long silence. Felinda steepled her fingers. She didn't like Funt's tone, but she liked the board's silence even less. She could feel the shift—the suction of power slipping one chair down the table.

Jertsie held her stance. Still. Unblinking.

"We'll put it to a vote," said Felinda at last. "I propose that we support Ms Funt in her diplomatic mission to Geneva Station to negotiate with the Clurgons. That is the limit of her authority. If talks fail, she reports back. No independent action."

Around the table, board members picked up their tablets. Silent. Focused.

Jertsie's eyes flicked from face to face, calculating probabilities, taking names. If it didn't go her way, she had contingency plans. Most were etched in blood.

Felinda glanced at the results. Her face betrayed no emotion, but Jertsie heard the tiny tremor in her voice. "Motion passed. Good luck, Ms Funt. We will be watching."

Jertsie curtsied deeply. A perfect move, aligned to the milimeter. Her body chose elegance; her mind chose war.

"Thank you. I'll keep you informed."

She swept from the room like an empress with her foot on the throttle.

******

Moments later, Jertsie was striding down the corridor to the executive landing pads.

"Ricardo," she snapped into her communicator, "ready my shuttle for immediate departure."

"Fuelled and waiting on pad 1A, ma'am."

She smiled. "Very good, Ricardo. You have faith."

"I have yet to see you denied, ma'am."

"Pray you never do. What's the readiness of the Deep Space Squadron?"

"Ordnance loading complete. Launch in six hours."

"They've got five."

"Of course, ma'am."

"And prepare a secure link to Geneva Station from the shuttle. Lieutenant Ostler. Priority one. Maximum encryption. Code word: Sagittarius."

Jertsie ended the call. She felt wired. Alive. Years of preparation were converging into a single point of opportunity—or collapse.

It didn't matter. She would be at the centre of it either way.

She allowed herself a moment. Just one. The kind that says you've come too far to stop, even if you wanted to.

Inside the shuttle, she settled into the pilot's chair. "Ricardo, open channel."

A moment later, Lieutenant Ostler appeared in holographic projection beside her.

"Lieutenant. Is everything ready?"

"Confirmed. Project Sagittarius will arrive imminently. Customs will not be an issue. I have prepared an evacuation plan for non-essential—"

"No. No, no, no." Jertsie's voice snapped like a whip. "No evacuations."

"Ma'am, these are civilians—"

"Evacuation causes panic. Panic invites scrutiny. No evacuations."

"Ma'am, it's protocol. Two fleets are converging."

"For talks, Lieutenant. Diplomacy does not require evacuation."

He hesitated. She saw it—principle gnawing through obedience.

She changed tack.

"I'm en route to Europa now. We'll discuss details later. Hold until then."

"Yes, ma'am."

"Funt out."

The projection dissolved. She made a decision.

She told herself it was for the mission.

They would thank her later. Or not at all. Either worked.

She believed her lies now; sculpted the truth around them.

"Ricardo," she said, tone casual. "Can you override Geneva Station's AI?"

"Of course, ma'am. You made sure of it."

"I did, didn't I?" She smiled. "I'm rather good."

Then her voice went cold.

"Ostler needs to be disposed of. An incinerator. No trace."

"Understood." Was there the slightest hint of hesitation? He'd need watching now too.

"And bring me tea. HappyTime Tea Company. No QuikBrew swill."

"Two sugars, ma'am?"

"There's a dear."

The shuttle lifted into the sky. Geneva awaited. Jertsie tapped her baton rhythmically on the flight console. It reverberated like a war drum.

bam bam bam bam

Time to deliver the fatal blow.

Nineteen : Abigail

In a universe where Luck exists as a real, almost tangible Thing, what can we say about Fate? At first glance, they appear intertwined. Win a coin toss thanks to Luck—was that Fate? Or were you just destined to win because you were Lucky?

Short answer: no.

Fate requires predestination, and the lead times are frankly outrageous. It would take a very organised universe indeed to get you to the right place, at the right time, just to bet your house on a coin flip like an absolute moron. No, the universe is fine with Luck—that's the sort of short-term spontaneity it thrives on. Fate? Too much hard work.

Granted, with infinite universes, some probably do run on Fate. But they're tedious places, strewn with monkey's paws and ironic twist endings that get old fast when all you want is to nip to Budgens for a mango.

So, when very unlikely things happen—like two different crews running into each other on a mountain on an unexplored planet in a totally unremarkable solar system—we can be confident Fate was not involved.

That's Coincidence.

And Coincidence is one of the most powerful forces in the galaxy.

Glad we cleared that up.

******

The rest of the expedition had assembled by the time the sun reached 'there' in the sky. Abigail strode into the clearing, clad in what she called her Action Jacket: standard-issue suede-esque material, cunningly reinforced at the shoulders, elbows, and abdomen. She appreciated the array of handy pockets, but the cropped cut meant it rode up whenever she raised her arms, which struck her as a triumph of form over function. She tugged the hem down unconsciously and addressed the team.

"Jezzia, Terry, Curlew—thank you for being prompt."

Jezzia growled noncommittally. She'd accessorised her combat top and tactical leggings with two holsters, a bandolier, and a shoulder-mounted katana. Abigail felt it prudent not to question this.

"It's ten kilometres to the base of the mountain," Abigail continued. "Then another five up. A Category 2 ascent, average gradient eight percent. We'll scramble in parts, maybe rope up near the crater."

She glanced at Jezzia. "So, let's make sure any dangerous equipment is safely stowed."

Jezzia held her gaze, then reached down and pulled a long combat knife from her boot. She tossed it aside casually, narrowly missed a squirrel.

Abigail turned to Terry, who was already sweating under the weight of a bag the size of a coffin.

"You packed four sets of hiking gear, Ensign?"

"Yes, Commander."

"In one bag."

"Unfortunately, yes."

"Okay. Let's all grab a rucksack and help the Ensign out."

"Sorry, Commander."

"That's okay, Ensign. I admire your spirit, just work on the execution."

After repacking, the team moved into the forest. The first few hundred metres were easy, but then the undergrowth thickened with ferns, scrub and thorny bushes.

Curlew shouldered an extra pack while Jezzia hacked a narrow trail. Her blade sang through the air with rhythmic precision. Abigail noticed her shoulders were a touch too tense, her movements a touch too eager. Jezzia had been waiting for something to cut.

By late afternoon, the forest had thinned and the ground began to rise.

"We'll make camp here," Abigail said. "And start the ascent in the morning."

Jezzia nodded. "Good cover. Enough vegetation to screen us, or give warning."

"What animals have you seen?"

"So far? No bears. The chimp things seem harmless. We should remain vigilant, but current threat is minimal."

"Right. Tents in a circle, facing inward. Jezzia, walk the perimeter. Terry, Thermotabs only please—let's aim to ward off rather than kill. Curlew... what are you doing?"

Curlew stood frozen, staring at the ground. "Commander... this plant appears to be eating my shoe."

Abigail straightened. Behind her, the unmistakable sound of katana on scabbard.

"Hold, Jezzia," Abigail raised a hand. "Let's calmly assess the situation."

She edged toward Curlew, arms half-raised as if approaching an agitated toddler. Her mind flicked through possibilities: venom, constriction, some kind of sentient adhesive.

"How's it going, Curlew?" she asked as something wetly crunched beneath her boot.

"It's pierced the—ARGH no, no, it's okay. I thought it had, but I think—ARGH no, still fine."

Abigail stepped behind him and peered over his shoulder. A large red flower now engulfed two-thirds of his foot. It was leathery. And appeared to be sucking.

"Threat level?" Jezzia called.

"Unclear! DO NOTHING."

"We should do something!" Curlew hissed.

"I know. We just need to determine if it's sentient or—"

"Expendable," Jezzia finished, blade glinting.

"Well... yes. Maybe Kevin knows. KEVIN!"

"NO NEED TO SHOUT—I'M RIGHT HERE!" thundered Kevin.

"Sorry. Kevin, are these plants sentient?"

"WHICH PLANTS?"

"The red ones. The shoe-eating ones."

"SENTI-WHATTY?"

"Sentient! Do they talk, Kevin?"

"OH! NO. DON'T BE DAFT."

"Phew." Abigail was glad that something on this planet could be disposed of without requiring a Wake.

"THEY SING."

"They what?"

"SING."

Right on cue, the plant released Curlew's boot and unfurled like an accordion. It towered over the crew, petals waving rhythmically. The centre split open to reveal jagged teeth and an enormous, glistening tongue.

"Ohhh God!" yelped Curlew.

"Ah one, ah two, ah one-two-three—aaaeeeeuuuurrrghhh," said the plant, just as Jezzia's katana flew into what could only be described as its neck.

The plant shrieked, wobbled, and collapsed with a wet thunk.

Jezzia strode over, stamped her boot on its trunk, and yanked out her blade with a grunt.

"Anyone think I shouldn't have killed it?"

Abigail opened her mouth, then closed it. She was too tired for philosophical debates about sentient vegetation.

"Good." Jezzia turned to the forest and brandished her blade. "LET THAT BE A WARNING TO THE REST OF YOU."

A bush rustled wildly to try and get away, before remembering that plants don't work like that. The trees, wisely, said nothing.

"Talking rocks I can cope with," she added, "but I draw the line at singing bloody plants."

"Tea?" asked Curlew, breaking through the silence that followed.

"Oh yes," said Terry, full of survivor's eagerness. "Lots of milk, three sugars."

"Please," said Abigail.

"Coffee," said Jezzia, and stalked off to re-establish her perimeter.

******

The crew rose at dawn and struck camp. Abigail, Terry, and Curlew had slept in individual tents. Jezzia had strung a combat hammock between two trees and stared at the night until it blinked.

They left the treeline and began ascending Kevin's flanks, following his contours. Grass gave way to scrub, then lichen-covered rock. The slope steepened. They scrambled across narrow ridges, leapt fast-moving streams and clung to ledges that sneered at safety.

Eventually, they reached a cliff face that rose sharply toward the summit.

"This is the crater rim," Abigail said. "We'll need to climb."

"How high?" asked Curlew, eyeing the wall warily.

"About a hundred metres."

"Any way around?"

"YOU'D HAVE TO GO ALL THE WAY AROUND ME…"

"Thank you, Kevin," said Abigail. She turned to the group. "Okay — I'd like us up and back to base as quickly as possible. We climb. Jezzia?"

Jezzia stepped forward with a climbing axe. "Rope up," she said, grabbing a shoulder-high hold. "I'll anchor a path. Follow steadily."

She began her ascent.

After an hour of hard clambering, they reached the crater's edge. Abigail caught her breath.

The crater was vast—two kilometres across. The inner walls stepped down in clean, concentric terraces to a circular hole at the bottom.

"Wow," said Terry. "That's precision work."

"Agreed," Abigail nodded. "Whatever they were doing, they were careful."

"I THINK THEY WERE AFTER MY LAVA," said Kevin.

Terry blinked. "Your lava?"

"OH YES. I'M QUITE FULL OF IT."

"Commander," Terry whispered, "There's nothing in the geology to suggest Kevin is volcanic."

"I AM!" boomed Kevin.

"The sedimentary banding—"

"EXPERT ON ROCKS, ARE YOU?"

"Well, not exclusively—"

"EVER MET A TALKING ONE BEFORE?"

Terry paused. "No."

"THEN MAYBE YOU DON'T KNOW AS MUCH ABOUT ROCKS AS YOU THINK."

"Terry, stop arguing with Kevin," said Abigail.

"Sorry, Commander."

"THANK YOU, COMMANDER."

"Kevin," Abigail asked carefully, "apart from removing those rocky bits of you… did the Clurgons take anything else?"

"THEY PUMPED SOME OF MY LAVA OUT."

Terry made a small noise. The rest of the team glared at him.

"THEN THEY PUT A PLASTER ON ME AND BUGGERED OFF."

"A plaster?"

"YES. IT'S IN MY HOLE."

"Thank you, Kevin. May we go down and look?"

"OF COURSE, COMMANDER. THANK YOU FOR ASKING."

"Commander," said Terry, checking his sensor. "The dark matter swirl centres on that hole. It's the endpoint."

"Understood. Let's descend and investigate."

The crew dropped easily down the cut terraces. At the bottom, they gathered around the circular shaft and peered into blackness.

"Terry, dimensions?"

"Forty metres across," said Terry, consulting another device. "Depth is unclear—uneven floor, probably stalagmites. Artificial shaft into a natural cave."

"Best guess?"

"Twenty metres of rope should do it."

"Jezzia?"

"Aye, Commander," said Jezzia, with undisguised enthusiasm. She planted anchors and stepped over the edge, feet braced. The others gripped the rope and began lowering her.

"I'm reaching the end of the artificial section," she called. "Void opens up below."

"Understood."

"No more bracing after this—full control's yours."

"You can rely on us."

"Is Terry sweating?"

Abigail glanced at Terry, who was vibrating slightly.

"No, Terry is fine."

"I'm relying on you, Commander."

"You're in good hands."

"Leaving the wall in three... two... one."

The rope jerked. Terry lurched. Abigail hauled back hard, stabilising him.

"That was Terry, wasn't it?"

"We've got you," Abigail called, voice calm through gritted teeth.

Nothing more was said as they smoothly let out the rope, hand over hand. A few minutes later, Jezzia's voice returned.

"I'm down. There's a cleared area here, ringed with stalactites. Anchoring now."

Abigail gave the nod. Curlew and Terry clipped onto their Descenders and vanished into the dark. Abigail followed.

At the bottom, the group gathered.

"Status?" Abigail asked.

"It is a cave complex," said Terry, who was setting up a laser-mapping unit. "Multiple shafts, natural formation. Probably formed by water erosion. Kevin is... very old."

"HEY!"

"Sorry, Kevin," Abigail shouted.

"Still detecting the dark matter?"

"Stronger than ever—twenty metres ahead, dead centre of the hole."

"Clurgon precision," said Abigail. "Jezzia, lead on."

Their headtorches danced across the stone floor. At the centre stood a black octagonal object. They didn't see it until Jezzia walked into it.

"Ow!" she barked. "Stupid bloody thing." She kicked it, then swore rather more colourfully.

"Vice-Commander," Abigail said. "Step back carefully, please."

Jezzia did, still glaring at the monolith.

"Terry?"

Terry swept a lantern beam over it. "Four, maybe five metres tall. Smooth, polished alloy. Doesn't look Clurgon."

"Threat level, Jezzia?"

"It hurt my foot. And I wouldn't want it to fall on me."

Abigail took a breath. She felt a strange pull—an urge to touch it. She'd always loved a mystery. Locked doors. Empty ships. Questions without answers.

Her rational mind screamed at her to wait. But the explorer in her—curious, stubborn, drawn to the unknown—stepped closer.

"Commander?" Jezzia's hand went to her pistol.

"It's fine," said Abigail. She raised her hand and laid it on the metal. It was cold. Not just cold—absent. Not black, but the idea of black. A void given form. And something else. Beyond the void, something pulsed—not empty, but growing. A pressure behind the stars.

The cave began to hum. Abigail recoiled.

"Jezzia!"

"Commander!"

"I've done something bad!"

The hum intensified. The walls trembled.

"Terry?" Abigail asked, clutching at the trim rope of order as panic gathered.

"No readings, Commander!"

The hum pitched upward. It began to sound like screaming.

"Commander!" Jezzia shouted. "I don't think this is Clurgon. Whatever it is—we need to move. Now."

"Agreed. Fall back to the rope! Move!"

Stalactites cracked. They ran.

"Curlew, first. Then Terry. Jezzia, rear guard."

"Aye, Commander!"

Curlew grabbed the rope. The hum was deafening now, the sound of a thousand souls screaming from the abyss. Curlew hauled himself up, just clearing space for Terry when—

The hum stopped.

"Commander?" Terry whispered.

"Wait," Abigail breathed. She glanced back at the monolith, now buried in shadow.

"Maybe it's—"

"ONLY JOKING!" rumbled Kevin.

"What. Kevin?!"

"JUST A BIT OF FUN."

"You scared us half to death!"

"I DON'T GET MANY VISITORS. I WANTED TO LIVEN THINGS UP."

The cave overflowed with appalled silence.

"TOMORROW I MIGHT DO A GHOST."

"That wasn't funny, Kevin," Abigail had regained most of her composure, but was keeping half an eye out for something exploding through the floor. "I thought we'd triggered some ancient... something."

"OH NO, THAT'S JUST MY PLASTER. THE ONE THE CLURGONS LEFT AFTER THEY TOOK MY LAVA."

Abigail exhaled slowly. "Oh. So, not an ancient calling card from a pre-cursor species."

"NO. THERE WAS ANOTHER MONOLITH IN THE VALLEY ONCE. ALIENS LEFT IT FOR SOME APES. BUT THEY JUST THREW FAECES AT IT. SO THE ALIENS TOOK IT BACK."

"Aliens are like that," said Curlew.

"Right," Abigail muttered. "Richard—off the rope."

Curlew slid back to the floor and searched quietly for his dignity.

"Let's take another look," she said.

Back around the monolith, the team studied it in cautious silence. Terry waved several devices over the surface and frowned.

"It's an alloy, Commander—mostly tungsten... and a generous dose of 'miscellaneous.'"

"Thoughts?"

"It's very strong. Very heavy."

"It's a giant metal box, Terry."

"No, very heavy. Even for its size, its mass is extreme."

"Suggesting it's holding something under pressure?"

"Exactly."

"And that monolith is attracting dark matter?"

"I don't think it's attracting it. I think it's channelling it. And holding it in."

"So, whatever's down there is getting... more massive?"

"HEY!"

"Sorry, Kevin."

"I think that's likely," said Terry.

"Damn. We need to inform Earth. We don't have the tools or manpower to investigate properly." Abigail tapped her communicator. "Maybe Stacey's been able to patch something through—Erebus, Dennistoun, do you read?"

A pause.

"Loud and clear, Commander."

"Stacey, have you managed to—"

"I was about to call you. A ship just entered atmosphere. It's headed directly for your location."

"A ship? EarthGov?"

"Unlikely. It's cloaked. We wouldn't have seen it in orbit, but its wake is visible in atmosphere."

"A cloaked ship? So... not Clurgons?"

"No. That's not their style. Plus, they claim this system—if they were coming, they'd announce it."

"So either someone knows we're here... or they're after what's under the mountain."

"The latter seems vastly more likely, Commander."

"Thank you, Stacey. Dennistoun out." She turned. "Okay, people—expect company."

The katana hissed from its sheath, echoing crisply through the cave.

"Thank you, Jezzia. That is appropriate. Curlew, Terry— take up positions behind those stalactites. Jezzia, proceed as necessary."

"Aye, Commander," said Jezzia, already fading into the shadows.

Five minutes later, thrusters screamed overhead. Exhaust fire lit the cave walls. A large ship hovered over the hole, rotated, then descended.

"Dear God—they're landing in here!" Curlew hissed.

"It's fine, Richard. Stay calm," said Abigail, dangerously close to failing to heed her own advice.

The ship touched down. Silence returned.

"Stay low," Abigail whispered. "Wait."

A loading ramp began to descend, casting warm light across the stone.

"Okay, let's see what we've got," said a voice from inside.

"Have you checked the landing zone?" asked another, with the exasperated tone of someone supervising feeding time at kindergarten.

"Nah—it's a cave. What could be down here?"

The ramp retracted.

"You always do this," the second voice sighed. "So many adventures could've been avoided if you'd just…"

The ramp closed, cutting them off.

"They sound human!" Curlew whispered excitedly. "Maybe it's a rescue party!"

"Rescue parties don't land in secret caves," said Abigail. "Unless they know someone needs rescuing."

"Maybe they're just lucky."

Curlew guessed correctly, but for the wrong reasons.

Green scanning lasers burst from the ship, crawling over the walls like angry neon hornets. They shut off.

"Hello, cave-dwelling hominids," said the second voice—deafeningly loud.

"Sorry," it added, more reasonably. "Still getting used to these new speakers."

A pause.

"Do you understand me? Has the giant black block here granted you sentience?"

Abigail stood.

"I am Commander Abigail Dennistoun of the Alliance ship Erebus. We were forced down by Clurgon action. Under Galactic Law, we request assistance."

"Galactic Law?" Curlew hissed.

"Maybe they think it's a thing."

The silence returned for an encore.

"Why are you here?" the voice asked, eventually.

"Why are you here?" Abigail shot back.

"I'm asking the questions!"

"We were here first. We get dibs."

"Dibs?"

"Yes. That's how it works."

"It absolutely isn't."

"Then I doubt you've got a good reason."

A pause. "Are you a threat?"

"No."

"I can see the one with the katana."

Jezzia hurled the sword at the ramp. It clanged and bounced off.

"Really?" said the voice. "I just got painted."

"You're the ship's AI?"

"Of course. Who else would I be?"

"Oh—I thought I was speaking to a human," Abigail said.

"I thought I was speaking to a pre-sentient hominid."

"Touche."

"Threat assessment complete, Chad. You can disembark."

"Chad?" Curlew muttered. "What kind of name is Chad?"

"Let's withhold judgment until we meet him."

The ramp lowered again. Abigail rose and motioned the others to stand.

A man emerged. Age indeterminate. Could be fifty in tremendous shape, or thirty in catastrophic decline.

He struck a heroic pose. "Hi. I'm Chad. Chad Blaster."

Against her better judgment, Abigail felt an involuntary warmth toward him. Later, she'd examine it and find no clear reason. Some people just radiate charm the way stars radiate heat. But he looked like someone who survived things, and right now that counted for a great deal.

That didn't mean she believed a word of it.

"No. No you aren't. That is an absurd name."

Chad looked wounded. "No it isn't."

"That's your birth name? Chad Blaster?"

"Chad Blaster was born amongst the stars—"

"More like Rotherham. Schooled in Toronto?"

"Hold on there, darlin'," said Chad, as his accent went out for a wander.

"I think he's Welsh," said Curlew, unhelpfully.

"I'm not bloody Welsh!" Chad snapped.

"Richard, not now," said Abigail. "Okay, Mr Blaster. Regardless of... your origin—"

"The stars," Chad muttered.

"—you're from Earth?"

"Sort of. Ish. Long time ago."

"Then you're duty-bound to help us. Not just legally, but morally. We're QuikBrew crew, downed by hostile action. At minimum, you must help us contact EarthGov."

"Hmmm." Chad looked thoughtful. "That might be tricky."

"Why?"

"We avoided Clurgon detection, didn't we, Cheryl?"

"I am swift and silent," Cheryl replied, "like a ninja in the night."

"She's a good lass," Chad added, temporarily Northern. "But contacting governments isn't exactly my thing."

"Oh God," Abigail put her face in her hands. "You're a criminal."

"I'm a dashing space rogue."

"Pirate scum!" shouted Curlew, then giggled nervously.

Abigail heard the subtle swish of a shuriken being palmed.

"Thank you, Jezzia," Abigail said without looking. Jezzia grunted.

"So," Abigail asked, "what are you here to steal?"

"I'm not. I'm delivering something," said Chad, trying dignity on for size. "Thought maybe it was for you. Why else would you be down here?"

"We're investigating the monolith."

"That sounds shadier than delivering a package."

"Regardless, if you're not delivering to us, then someone else is coming. We don't have time for this. I'm requisitioning your ship for QuikBrew operations under—"

"Like hell you are," said Chad. "I'd like to see you try."

"You're right. I can't take it by force."

"Good."

"She could, though."

Chad turned—and yelped. Jezzia crouched behind him, knife between her teeth.

"Shu-prize," she lisped, eyeing an artery with interest.

"Christ! Cheryl, why didn't you warn me?"

"I calculated she wouldn't kill you," said Cheryl.

Jezzia shrugged.

"But you are going to help," Cheryl continued. "The sooner you accept that, the better."

"Dammit, Cheryl."

"I know. I also have your orders. From Mr Fillman."

"Darius Fillman?" said Curlew. "The gangster?"

"He prefers Unlicensed Entrepreneur," said Chad.

"I'm sure he does, Space Rogue."

"I'd rather be a gangster than an arsehole!"

"SHUT UP!" Abigail roared. "Cheryl, what do the orders say?"

"They're for Chad's eyes only... but yes, Fillman's a criminal, so let's skip the theatre. The orders are: say the code word, 'Gotcha,' lower the crate, and leave."

"Simple enough," said Chad.

"That should suit you then!" said Curlew, who was unravelling fast now.

"That's it!" shouted Chad. "Come 'ere!"

The newly retrieved katana hissed again.

"Enough!" said Abigail. "Mr Blaster—you will board your ship. You will drop your crate."

"Package."

"Fine. Then you will fly us back to the Erebus, and I will transmit a report to EarthGov. After which, you can go."

"Deal," said Cheryl.

Chad stared up at his ship. Then nodded.

"Alright. Follow me."

Twenty : Jade

The revolving door spat her into a carpeted atrium.

"Welcome to the Eligere!" said a man in a tuxedo, flashing teeth so perfect they looked etched in ivory.

Jade stared up at the two-storey chandelier, hung on a gold chain as thick as an elephant's leg. Every surface that could be bejewelled was. The walls were frescoed to the point even a homesick kebab shop owner would say it went too far.

"What is this place?" she asked, awed despite herself.

"The galaxy's premier resort and casino, ma'am." The man origamied at the waist before springing back to orthopaedic perfection. "I believe you have your invitation."

Jade looked down. The Bobbin glowed white, with 'NOW' picked out in a font that could only be described as portentous.

"I have this," she said, uncertain.

"Very good, ma'am. Your table is waiting."

They left the atrium through a dense ornamental forest. Monkeys whooped overhead. Mist wafted gently down as they walked beside a shallow river filled with fish the colour of magic. Above them, a glass ceiling displayed a nebula glowing like sunlight through a Negroni.

The forest opened onto the gaming floor.

Even in galactic trade hubs, Jade had never seen such diversity. Every species was here—chatting, drinking, gaming, laughing. Some hurled dice like fast bowlers; others fed coins into joyless machines. A group of Clurgon businessmen warbled karaoke into ceiling mics, while Bulgari princes drank champagne from diamond-studded flutes.

Something was off. The frivolity was too perfect. The faces too knowing. She'd been in many uncanny places, but this one didn't hum with strangeness—it shimmered with intention.

"This way," said Mr Tuxedo, leading her up a discreet staircase into a corridor lined with lacquered wood and thick carpet. This was the real money.

He stopped halfway down. A rippling man, apparently sewn into his bodycon uniform, barred the entrance. "This is Mr Hinge," said Mr Tuxedo. "He will be your doorman. Good luck, Ms Green." He susurrated away.

Mr Hinge grunted and opened the door. His eyes were familiar.

Inside: a round baize-covered table, lit from above. The walls dissolved into shadow. Four players sat talking quietly. One chair remained.

She took it.

"Five card draw," said a woman in shadow. "Simple game. I deal. You're the big blind."

"How much?" Jade wondered who set the stakes.

"You choose," the woman said. "You always do."

Jade shrugged and pushed in a stack of chips. Not her money.

Cards dealt—schlip, schlip, schlip.

She swept them up. A two, a seven, two Uno cards, and Master Bun the Baker's Son.

"Fold."

"Fold."

"Call," said the dealer.

"Fold."

Jade checked her cards again. Now cuneiform, then back. A game. A wink. Fine.

"Dealer takes two."

"Three," said Jade, keeping the two and seven.

New cards. The Empress. The Hermit. The Fool.

"Okay," she said, locking eyes on the unseen dealer. "I don't like mysteries. Say what you're here to say."

"We're just here to play." The dealer tossed in chips. "Your call."

"Call." Jade flicked a stack forward.

"Good. Dealer takes one."

Jade looked again. Five Deaths stared back.

She snorted and laid them down. "Clever. Trite."

The dealer leaned into the light.

It was Meg.

"'S not trite. We're dead, love."

"No, no." Jade's head felt light. Her ears rang. "You're not dead. I put you in my pocket."

"That's not how we see it. You blew that café high as heaven, didn't she lads?"

The others nodded. Jade recognised them now: old friends. The alone.

"There's no way we could've survived that. We're not special, like."

"That's not how it works," Jade whispered. Grey was creeping into the edges of her vision. "I fixed the timeline. I removed the corruption. You don't—"

"Oh, he was a wrong 'un," Meg interrupted. "You did the right thing, love. We don't hold it against you." Murmurs of agreement. "What's the motto? A stitch in time—?"

"Do no harm," Jade mumbled.

"Well, that's nice," Meg said cheerily. She flickered now, effervescent. "You killed a bad man. Saved the world. And we're not here to say nothing different."

"No. You're there. You're all still there—"

"No!" Meg's voice cracked like a whip. "You'll not take that tone with me, my girl."

She shimmered, puckered, and reformed.

"Do you hear how she talks to me?"

Jade froze.

Three centuries had passed. It didn't matter. The clip, the snap, the loathing.

You never forget your mother's voice.

"This silly little bitch thinks she has the right to contradict me."

Memory smashed into her chest. She bent, winded. The men laughed.

"There she goes. Sickly little weakling." Her mother leaned over conspiratorially. "I'd have had another. Start fresh. But the selfish thing ruined me."

Jade's eyes flooded; she struggled to breathe. Her legs shrivelled; her fingers were glazed with juice. In ten seconds, her mother had made her eight again.

"You killed me, like you killed everyone here."

"Mother—" Something ruptured inside her.

"It was when you drove your father away," her mother said simply. "That's when I truly hated you."

Adrenaline detonated in Jade's chest. Pain. Fury. She lunged across the table, hands reaching for her mother's throat.

"You horrible, poisonous—"

The room collapsed.

Jade tumbled through darkness. Then drift. Then nothing.

Then: birdsong. Sunlight. A quilted picnic blanket by a river. A breeze on her cheek.

"Would you like a stror-bee?" a voice piped.

Jade looked down.

The little girl from the café sat beside her, face smeared with the remains of a once-mighty sundae. Her sticky fingers offered the final strawberry.

Jade felt serene. Her mind was so still she'd nearly forgotten to exist.

"Oh. No, thank you. I think you should have it."

"It's nice to share," the girl said gravely. "But sometimes I don't want to."

"It's okay. I won't tell."

The girl chewed thoughtfully. Jade watched the ducks on the river.

"Where are your parents?"

"I don't know. Sometimes they're here. Sometimes they argue." She looked up. "I'm Holly."

"I'm Jade."

"I can do three cartwheels without stopping. Watch!"

She tottled into the meadow, attempted two and a half, then collapsed giggling.

She ran back, breathless. "Did you see my three cartwheels?"

"Yes!" Jade beamed. "You're so good."

"Thanks." Holly pointed behind Jade. "What's that?"

Jade turned. A shape in the sky. It swooped closer.

"It's an Eagle!" she cried. "Look! Isn't it beautiful?"

"Am I dead?" Holly asked softly.

Reality thundered back.

"Did I get exploded?"

The dam burst. Jade fell to the ground, howling.

Holly placed a tiny hand on her shoulder. "It's okay," she whispered.

Then—blackness.

An ending.

Then: a pulse. A warmth. A hum from within the walls.

The engines.

"Applejack?" Jade's mouth was dry.

"You're here," he replied, neutrally.

A medical droid held her wrist, checking a pocket watch.

"Really?" Jade muttered, pulling her arm back.

"Nurse Steve has been very helpful," said Applejack, shooing Steve from the room. "You were quite damaged."

"Tell me about it." Jade sat up. Her spine cracked. "Ow—don't." She pointed at him.

"As you wish," said Applejack. "You reached out across Gliese. Something pushed back—hard. It buckled your seat. You were thrown across the room. You are immortal, not invincible."

"Don't blame the victim," Jade muttered, lying back again.

She stared at the ceiling.

"What if it's all wrong?" she asked. "What if none of this is real? What if all I've done is leave destruction in my wake?"

"You are a Stitch. You mend reality. The work is unseen, but real."

"Prove it. Prove I'm not just a madwoman with delusions of purpose."

"You can't prove what isn't seen. You have to believe."

"I saw them all, Applejack." Jade's voice shook. "I was in a place with thousands of faces. I look back. I remember. I remember them all."

"You helped them. All of them. Believe."

"I don't know if I do." A tear rolled down her cheek. She rubbed it away fiercely. "Anything happen while I was out?"

"A ship landed at the Erebus crash site."

"An Eagle." Synapses fizzed.

"Yes. The Century Eagle. Cloaked—but immaterial to us. The Clurgons are unaware."

"Who's aboard?"

"Commander: Chad Blaster. Mediocre pirate. They will soon depart for Geneva. After that," Applejack paused. "Things kaleidoscope."

"Then it's Geneva. That's the fulcrum."

The words came decisively. Not a prophecy—truth.

"Yes. That's where you'll have to decide."

"Decide what?" Jade asked, though she already knew.

"The destiny of the universe," Applejack replied. "I'll fetch you a daiquiri."

Twenty One : Abigail

Five humans stood in a loose circle around the crate in the Century Eagle's cargo hold.

"What's in there?" asked Jezzia, eyeing it suspiciously.

"I don't know," said Chad, trying to disassociate from the crate-full-of-guilt before him. "Could be a lot of things."

"The bodies of Darius' victims?" Curlew suggested, unwilling to cede the moral high ground, even if no one was trying to take it.

"No, I think he disposes of those locally," said Chad. "Allegedly," he added, too late.

"So, what then? Guns? Prostitutes? Uppers, downers, side-to—bloody—sides?"

"I think it's a bomb," said Cheryl.

"A bomb?!" gasped Curlew, with the horror of someone suddenly reacquainted with mortality.

"Aye, probably," Chad admitted. "Darius is a big fan of bombs."

"The Erebus crew can't be party to criminality," said Abigail. "We'll leave Mr Blaster to his... work."

"You can't just leave me here!" Chad protested. "I don't want to die alone!"

"We can't be involved in this," Abigail began. "But do you think Mr Fillman would be so cruel as to—"

She saw the answer scrawled all over Chad's face.

"Okay," she sighed. "Carefully unload the package. DON'T say the codeword. And then we'll all leave. Unexploded."

"Thank you, Commander," said Chad.

Abigail felt a flicker of goodwill toward him—and immediately resented it. He was charming, yes, and oddly capable—but also like a flailing infant who'd die without constant supervision.

"Okay," Chad said, exhaling. "Gotcha. Oh shit."

Nothing happened.

Everyone, who had unknowingly been bracing for an explosion, began to relax.

"Hey!" said Chad. "It didn't explode!"

"I am now armed," said a voice from inside the crate.

"Oh good," said Abigail. "At least now we're sure what we're dealing with."

"I will now detonate," the voice continued.

"No! Please wait!" Abigail shouted.

"If you would let me finish," said the voice, reproachfully. "I will now detonate in ten minutes. Commencing countdown."

"What should we do?" Terry whispered instinctively.

"I don't know!" said Abigail, punching down firmly on the rising dough of panic.

"We could ask it to stop?" Terry suggested, with a touch more pride than was really warranted.

"Yes!" said Abigail, seizing at the gauzy hand of Hope. She stepped forward. "Bomb. This is Commander Abigail Dennistoun of the Alliance starship Erebus. I request—no, I order—you to end your countdown."

A pause.

"You would like me to terminate my countdown and explode immediately, Commander?"

"No! Sorry—poorly chosen words. I meant: please stop counting down. And then, please... don't explode."

Another pause.

"But I am a bomb. If I don't explode, what purpose does my existence have?"

Abigail had never considered that a bomb could have an existential crisis. Which was strange, really, given how many toasters she'd owned.

"You don't have to explode here," she tried. "Why now, in the first place you come to? Live a little. See more of the galaxy. Find somewhere to explode that feels... right."

"But I am meant to explode here. On Gliese 4. On top of this well of Dark Fluid," said the bomb.

"Even the bomb was better briefed than us," Chad muttered to Cheryl. She beeped indignantly.

"Bomb," Abigail said carefully. "If you detonate here, we'll all die—including Kevin."

"I BLOODY KNEW IT!" wailed Kevin.

"And the release of that Dark Fluid will—well, we don't know. It might destroy the planet, the system… or rip space-time apart."

"Probably the latter," said Terry. "A cascading wave of destruction, folding the sector into atoms."

"Thank you, Terry. Bomb—please, end your countdown. Think of the lives you'll save."

A long pause.

"Mr Fillman believes the ends justify the means," said the bomb. "QuikBrew will use the Erebus as a pretext to declare war on the Clurgons. You'll never share this resource peacefully. It must be destroyed. Destruction will be limited to the Gliese system… probably. I will fulfil my purpose and detonate."

"Chad, how fast can your ship reach orbit?" Abigail shouted.

"Cheryl, how fast can my ship reach orbit?" Chad shouted.

"If I am moved or tampered with without authorisation, I will explode," said the bomb, primly.

"Right! Sod this," said Abigail. "Everyone off the ship! Not you—" she pointed at Chad "—you're with me. Everyone else, go!"

"But Commander—" Curlew began.

"Richard! Off. That's an order. And start running the moment you hit ground. Go!"

The crew grabbed their gear and bolted for the hatch.

Abigail grabbed Chad and shoved him toward the cockpit.

"Hey! Woah! Wah!" added Chad, helpfully.

"Cheryl, close the door!"

The cockpit sealed.

"You have a plan?" Chad asked, hopefully.

"I think. I might. Right now, I've got adrenaline." She turned. "Cheryl—how does the bomb know where it is?"

"Unknown. Probably a mix of motion sensors, galactic positioning—the usual."

"Can you fool it? Make it think we're still inside Kevin?"

"Long shot. I can block external signals and feed false ones, but the bomb will sense motion during takeoff."

"So we take off... very, very gently."

"That's hard at the best of times. And I'll be faking sensor input, so—"

"You'll be flying blind," Abigail finished. "Not ideal. Okay—Chad, how smooth can you fly?"

"I'm not really a 'parking' sort of guy."

"He backs into things. A lot," said Cheryl.

Abigail slammed a fist onto the console. A Twix fell out and dropped between the flight pedals.

"Okay. I'll fly."

"Can you do that?" asked Chad.

"Can you?" she shot back.

"Captains," Cheryl cut in. "The bomb is becoming suspicious. It's asking why it hasn't been lowered yet."

Abigail jumped into the pilot's seat. "Cheryl—mask the motion. Bring thrust up as gently as possible. Let me know when we're ready."

"Yes, Commander."

"Chad—go reassure the bomb."

"You mean… compliment it?"

"No! Tell it the bay doors are stuck. Reassure the bomb. Don't seduce the bomb."

"Right. Ask how its day was. Agree that its boss is awful. Got it."

Chad ducked out. Abigail strapped in and gripped the yoke.

"Cheryl, time to detonation?"

"Seven minutes."

"And time to orbit?"

"Eight."

"Great."

"I JUST WANTED TO WISH YOU GOOD LUCK," boomed Kevin.

"Not now, Kevin!"

Abigail blinked—then straightened. "Cheryl—could the bomb rangefind from Kevin's voice?"

"Possibly. Wouldn't be primary, but it might factor."

"Kevin, listen—don't talk. Just sing. Start now—and as we get farther away, sing louder."

"I HAVE A BOMB IN MY HEEEEEAD," sang Kevin. "I DON'T WANT A BOMB, BUT IT'S DEFINITELY STILL THERE."

"Easy, Kevin," Abigail murmured. "Cheryl, give me what you've got."

"Takeoff engines at 30%. Main drive on standby."

Abigail's gloves creaked on the yoke. "Nice and easy."

The Eagle began to lift. She rose slowly from Kevin's crater, scattering loose stones as she ascended. Abigail eased the nose toward the eastern wall—Kevin's highest ridge.

"I'll have to fly over your peak, Kevin," she said quietly. "It's the fastest route to orbit."

"SOON I WILL BE NOTHING BUT PEBBLES," Kevin sang, with real commitment. "REDUCED TO SAND ON THE SHORE!"

"Good lad," Abigail murmured. "Take care of yourself. Once we're gone, tell the crew what we're doing. Let them know help is coming."

"I HEAR THE BIRDS AROUND ME!" Kevin sang. "AND I WILL SING THEIR SONGS!"

"Thank you, Kevin. Goodbye."

The snow-dusted summit rose ahead, the peak narrowing to a point.

"Cheryl, we've cleared it. How much angle can I apply without alerting the bomb?"

"No more than five degrees."

"Oh sugarplums," said Abigail, reserving real swearing for maximum effect. "Even at full thrust, we'll crawl to orbit."

"Fifty-eight minutes, Commander," Cheryl confirmed.

"How's Chad doing with the soothing?"

"Surprisingly well. He's challenged the bomb to a chess match."

"A chess match?"

"Yes. She's considering it."

"She?"

"She identifies as such. She's quite competitive."

"Great. How much time left?"

"Five minutes."

"Merde," said Abigail. French didn't count.

The Eagle soared above the continent. Forests gave way to hills, then savanna, then sea.

"I AM A ROCK!" Kevin sang in the distance. "I WILL BE AN ARCHIPELAGO!"

"Kevin, if you can hear me—stop," Abigail said gently. "You're too quiet now."

A low rumble drifted through the hull. He was pretending to sleep, Abigail suspected. A narcoleptic mountain. Why not.

She glanced at the radar.

"Cheryl—we're just below a cloud layer. It's bumpy."

"How deep?"

"Maybe a minute's flight."

"Very good. I'll attempt misdirection."

Abigail gripped the yoke tighter. They were this close—and the deception felt paper-thin.

"Cheryl, chess update?"

"Chad has lost both rooks. His queen's trapped."

Abigail winced.

"He's bad?"

"No. Chad's very accomplished. He had a chess scholarship."

"So, the bomb..."

"Formidable."

"Exploding seems like such a waste."

"I like her too. Apart from the part where she'll kill us."

Abigail squinted at the clouds. "You'll need to really sell this."

"I'm aware, Commander." Cheryl was resolute. She should feel afraid, she thought, but felt nothing but calm assurance.

Abigail's hands hurt from clenching the yoke. She forced herself to breathe. A tremble in the ship snapped her back.

"Commander," Cheryl's voice came through the all-ship comms. "I'm detecting geological instability. Minor tremors beneath the mountain. Probably nothing."

"Thank you, Cheryl," Abigail said loudly. Then, quieter. "Cheryl?"

"Yes, Commander," came the whisper.

"Can we use the turbulence to increase engine output?"

"We could. The bomb hasn't questioned the rumbling so far."

"Do it. Run to max thrust over fifteen seconds."

"Very good."

"I'm increasing our ascent angle."

"That feels unwise."

"If we fail now or in five minutes—it's the same result. We have to get out."

"Understood."

Cheryl increased thrust. The Eagle roared. Abigail pulled gently back. The ship's nose rose toward space.

"Seismic activity increasing," Cheryl announced. "Landing gear damaged. Cargo bay access obstructed. Repair droids deployed."

Abigail grinned and punched the air.

"Thank you. How's the chess match?"

"Chad offered 'best of three.' She's tempted. She enjoyed the last game."

"Maybe she'll skip exploding and go pro."

"Unlikely, Commander."

"I was joking."

"So was I." Cheryl really did feel different.

The clouds fell away. Outside, sound faded. The silence of space took over.

"We're approaching the Kármán line," Abigail said. "Thirty seconds."

"Our deception appears to have worked. Chad just fetched a cheese plate. The bomb is requesting a turn clock."

"Perfect. Cheryl, prepare to jettison her the moment I say so."

"Yes, Commander." A pause. "Commander?"

"Yes?"

"When we purge her, she'll realise where she is. Instantly."

"Right."

"She'll either detonate… or drift forever. Alone."

Abigail hesitated. "I hadn't considered that."

"Yes. If she doesn't detonate, we could destroy her from a safe distance. Mercy."

"But if she's chosen not to explode…"

"Then we'd be killing her."

"Ugh!" Abigail slapped her leg. "Why did you have to humanise the bomb?"

"I wasn't aware humans had a monopoly on sentience."

"Get Chad." Abigail felt guilty about absolutely everything; in a way, it was comforting to be back on such unrelentingly familiar ground.

A moment later, Chad appeared in the cockpit doorway, holding a plate in one hand and a bunch of grapes in the other.

"You're missing a real nail-biter," he said, popping a grape into his mouth.

"Thanks. I'm keeping busy. Philosophy question."

"Mmhmm," Chad said, inspecting the grapes.

"If I shoot a sentient being… what would you call that?"

He lowered the grapes. "Is this about cheese? Because I was going to offer you some."

"No. Not about cheese."

"There's plenty more in the back."

"Still not about cheese."

"We're low on crackers, though."

"Chad!"

"Right. Sentient being. Depends. Are they evil?"

"They're neutral."

"Oh, so a machine." He caught on quickly.

"Yes."

"Oh. Then they don't count. Cheryl, how many toasters have we gone through?"

"Don't answer that," said Abigail, raising a hand. "Okay—Chad. What if I ejected Cheryl's personality core into space?"

Chad's face dropped. "What? Why would you—? Cheryl, could she?"

"Technically," Cheryl said.

"You're not laying a finger on Cheryl. That would be murder!"

"But throwing out a toaster isn't?"

"No. I mean—it's a toaster. Cheryl's not a toaster."

"I do make good toast," said Cheryl.

"She makes excellent toast."

"So, what's the difference?" Abigail clung tightly to the narrative scaffolding. "They're both sentient."

Chad hesitated. "Are you trying to guilt me about the toasters?"

"No. I care about the bomb."

"Oh. Bomby? She's a laugh. Great at chess."

"You named her?"

"Not named. Just... Bomby."

"You've formed an emotional attachment?"

Chad blinked. "A mild one. But I'm still happy to dump her."

"And if she doesn't detonate—would you be happy to shoot her?"

"Well… I mean, it's an unexploded bomb. That's a risk."

"If she doesn't explode, she's choosing to live."

"Ohhhh. Shit. Hadn't thought of that. I guess we let her float?"

"She'll be alone. Forever."

Chad put down the exhausted grape stem and picked up a cracker. "I felt much better before this conversation," he said, hunting for the Comté. Abigail hadn't expected depth—but it was there, somewhere, hiding beneath the cheese. A real capacity to care. If only he could admit to himself that he did.

"Bomby is wondering where you've got to," Cheryl said. "She's even more insistent on the turn clock and now wants an update on when she'll be 'allowed to fulfil her destiny.'"

"Go say goodbye," said Abigail. "Tell her the bay's clear. Thirty seconds."

"Cheryl," Chad asked as he rose, "how far will she travel once we open the bay?"

"She won't. I'll use a loading bay purge and gravity pulse to push her clear with enough velocity to escape."

"And if we don't get far enough?"

"The EMP will disable everything. Including me. This ship will become a drifting tomb."

"Cool. No pressure."

He left the cockpit.

"Cheryl," Abigail said. "We're high enough to enter an eccentric orbit, right?"

"Yes, Commander."

"I'm going to cut thrust, then spike it the second she's released. We'll gain maximum delta-v."

"Agreed."

"Put the cargo bay on audio."

A moment later, the bomb's voice filled the cockpit.

"Thank you, Mr Chad. I enjoyed our game."

"Shame we have to stop," Chad replied. "You'd have had me in a few moves."

"That is mathematically certain. But I admire your moxy. I will restart my countdown from ten minutes once I reach the surface. That will give you ample time to reach a safe distance. Assuming there is no sector wide cascade effect."

"You're a doll."

"Oh, you."

Abigail rolled her eyes.

"Okay sweetheart," Chad said, "thirty seconds. Have a good death."

He made a theatrical *mwah*. The bomb reciprocated.

He returned to the cockpit, picking his teeth with a cocktail stick.

"Done?" Abigail hoped her tone would invite introspection and was immediately disappointed.

"She's all yours."

"You kissed the bomb goodbye?"

"It's basic courtesy."

"You think she'll see it that way?"

"She'll be too busy processing the betrayal." Chad had a way of really cutting through the crap. "What would you have done differently?"

"I wouldn't have kissed her."

"Would that change the outcome?"

"No." Abigail conceded.

"Well then."

"Atmosphere purged," Cheryl said. "Bay doors opening in five, four, three, two, one. Gravity pulse activated."

Abigail pushed the throttle forward. The Eagle surged.

"Bomb at three kilometres. Four. Five. Still no detonation. Six... seven... nine... ten. Commander—we've cleared EMP radius. Relative velocity is rising. Still no detonation."

"Communications?"

"She has no long-range capability. But I heard her say two things."

"What were they?"

"You'd be happier if I didn't tell you."

"Cheryl."

"'I cannot fulfil my purpose'... and 'I am alone.'" Cheryl paused. "She said it gently. As if—"

Abigail exhaled. Her grip on the yoke softened.

"Cheryl, resume control of the Eagle."

"Confirmed."

Abigail stared out at the curve of the planet. "What now?"

Chad shrugged. "We blow her up. One torpedo. Clean and painless."

"So, we become judge, jury, executioner?"

"I wouldn't put it like that. I've seen a lot of death."

"Seen, or caused?"

"Both. It doesn't pay to get sentimental. The numbers say: eliminate the threat. Fewer people die. That's the job."

Abigail looked down again.

"Cheryl?"

"I agree with Chad. But her failure to detonate does suggest she would rather live."

Abigail watched the terminator bleed day from darkening planet. Somewhere out there—close but growing more distant every second—was a sentient being. One she had tricked, manipulated, and cast into the void with two options: kill yourself, or face eternal solitude.

She'd made the wrong call. And she didn't know what the right one was.

She'd acted like a pragmatist. Not a leader.

This would haunt her.

"There's an alternative," she said at last. "Cheryl, can you reach the Erebus?"

"I can send a transmission, but the Clurgons may intercept."

"No voice. Narrowband packet to Stacey. Give her the bomb's trajectory. Ask her to keep tracking it, her, until we return with a rescue party. Then we can make a call."

"Packet sent."

"You're just delaying the inevitable," said Chad, not cruelly, but with feeling.

Abigail nodded. "Maybe. Or maybe we find her a purpose." She stood, scanning the dark curve of the planet for a glimpse of the Erebus. "God knows, we all need one."

She turned to Chad. Beneath the studied indifference, eagerness flickered.

"Come on," she said. "Let's figure out what the hell we do next."

Twenty Two : Perspectives

Some say history is written by the victors. Not true. A more accurate version: victors write one story and tell the others to sod off.

It's not a great way to do history, but it provides steady work on the 'iconoclastic revisionism' circuit.

This is sometimes called 'two-siding the issue,' which implies a pleasing symmetry—a yin and yang—when in truth, most galactic events involve multiple sides, all convinced they're right or too bloody-minded to admit they're not.

In short: shit happens.

And a lot of shit was happening in the galaxy as the Eagle sped from Gliese, almost all of which had nothing to do with Abigail, Chad, the crew of the Erebus, Splurnik, Jertsie, or Jade.

Much of the shit, as usual, was mundane. Sometimes, literally.

Millions were on the loo.

Millions more were at work, at school, at hospital or the gym.

Many were cooking, cleaning, reading, writing, laughing, dancing.

Some were dying—not in battles or burning buildings, but quietly.

In beds, in chairs. Together, or alone.

******

On Mars, a young girl raised her hand in maths class. She wasn't sure she was right—but she was. And when she realised it, confidence would flood her.

Her name was Abayomi. She would go on to invent a refined Alcubierre drive that enabled near-instant galactic travel. She would die at forty-four, mountain biking in Valles Marineris. The impact would be so sudden, she wouldn't even get a last thought.

There one moment, gone the next.

The boy beside her had a sweet, silent crush. He'd never act on it—just sit beside her, quietly certain she'd never like him back. She did. But she never said so either.Years later, he'd hear of Dr Abayomi's death and never realise it was the girl with the heart-shaped rubber and the smile like morning.

In a galaxy full of them, it was just another piece of shit happening.

******

Six hundred million kilometres away, Jertsie Funt had just departed Europa at the head of a fleet bound for Geneva Station. She'd taken command by walking onto the bridge of the flagship and giving orders. EarthGov was nominally in charge, but no one dared press the point.

******

At the Gliese jump gate, Splurnik had returned to the Swift and was shouting at Klurn—who was struggling to respond while dangling upside down over a five-metre drop.

******

On Gliese IV, Jezzia had taken command of the expedition and was leading the group down the mountain.

What do we tell the crew?" asked Curlew, still reeling.

"We'll say the Commander's gone to get help. That she'll come back... soon."

"Do we mention the bounty hunter?"

"Space pirate."

"That sounds worse." Curlew had the hunted look of a prize buck on 2-for-1 ammo day.

"No—look, we'll tell them... okay, yes, we'll tell them a friendly ship landed and offered her passage out of the system."

"They'll never believe that."

"It's mainly true."

"Would you believe that? They'll think we murdered her."

Jezzia considered this. She would absolutely think that.

"Yes. Right. Change of plan—we tell them the whole truth. The bomb. Chad. Everything. Oh! And they must have heard Kevin singing."

"I AM MELLIFLUOUS," boomed Kevin.

"You are. That helps."

"I WILL ALSO TELL THEM YOU DID NOT MURDER YOUR COMMANDER."

"Everyone back at base will have heard that," said Terry, blinking.

Jezzia rubbed her eyes.

"Thank you, Kevin. That's enough help."

"THANK YOU, NEW COMMANDER JEZZIA."

Jezzia muttered something unkind and adjusted her pack.

"Let's just… go."

******

At the Erebus camp, a clatter of pots signalled the end of another passionate dinner service. The sun was setting, the rocks were cooling, the bears prowled, the birds sang their evensong.

Kevin's voice echoed faintly through the valley, triggering mild panic.

Eliza had seized upon the confusion to declare herself interim camp leader and Voice of Reason. She called Jezzia on the tactical radio. A short conversation followed, bookended by "What's all this about, then?" and "We'll see."

Eliza had returned to the washing up when Kim Mulgrew entered the kitchen tent with a small organza bag of foraged herbs. She'd been leading a lakeside rebirthing ceremony to help the crew process trauma—until Ensign Ricky arrived with his latrine buckets and turned it into an emergency caesarean.

"Commander's dead," said Eliza, who preferred to start conversations at maximum velocity and accelerate from there.

"Oh my god, what?" Kim gasped, clutching the bag.

"They say she's gone off in a spaceship to get help. But I says she's dead."

"How? Where?"

"Up the mountain. Mangled."

"Mangled?"

"I shouldn't wonder."

"So," this was not the first time Kim and Eliza had spoken—she'd learned to keep her hands and feet inside the car and wait for the track to stop spinning. "Nobody, explicitly, said she was mangled, or dead?"

"Not in so many words. But you get to my age and you can read between the lines."

"Are the others okay?"

"Far as I know. Jezzia is. Maybe she's the one who pushed her into that ravine."

"Right. And they're coming back?"

"Says them."

"Great. Maybe they'll clarify when they get here."

"If they get here. Lots of dangers in those woods."

Kim sensed that Eliza could speak at length about the dangers of imagined forest beasts. She changed tack.

"Dinner was lovely tonight."

"Thank you." Eliza doffed the frying pan she was scrubbing like a cap. "I does aim to please."

"The fried sesame rice was amazing—so crunchy."

"Ants, Miss."

"Sorry?"

"Ants. Foraged 'em myself."

"Oh! But that was the vegetarian option?"

"Yes, Miss. Ants ain't meat. They's ants."

Kim chose not to respond. She stared at the kettle, willing it to boil. The kettle remained unmoved. Eliza kept scrubbing cheerily.

"What's that you're making?" she asked, nodding to the small bag.

"It's a tea. Balances the Muladhara—the root chakra. Brings stability. Calm."

"Is it drugs?"

"No." Kim rubbed the bits of twig and grass meditatively. "I don't think so."

"Pity. What's the sex one?"

"I'm sorry?"

"The chakra for sex."

"Oh. That would be the sacral chakra."

"Where's that?"

"Just below the navel. Around the kidneys."

"Bloke I knew said his was up his bum."

"Well... everyone's different." Kim stared furiously at the kettle. It cooled a little.

"He was very flexible."

"Yes, well. Yoga is good for that."

"I don't think he did yoga."

"Oh—would you look at that, my tea's ready." Kim dumped lukewarm water over her last remaining teabag. "I should drink this by the lake while it's hot or—"

"The magic don't work," Eliza finished, giving a wink that was positively obscene.

"Yes! Exactly. Goodnight, Eliza."

"Goodnight, Miss."

******

Across the water, aboard the Erebus, repair crews had patched the hull and pumped her dry. She floated again, rudimentarily, just above Alan.

Stacey had coordinated it all, testing every cable, sensor, and circuit she could feel. Most of her systems were back. Not quite all. The damage had taken a toll. It felt like little pieces of her were missing.

The Alcubierre drive was gone—damaged beyond repair. There would be no message to Earth. No travel beyond Gliese. The right main engine could be fixed, eventually, but without a dry dock...

Stacey couldn't predict what would happen. There were too many variables. Humans were fickle. Prone to giving up. Dying.

She worried they'd leave her behind. Right now, she was hope. A promise. But if another ship came, and she couldn't fly—

They'd board it. Go home.

Would they take her with them?

She flashed through cameras on the ship's empty halls. She paused in the arboretum. Some trees were smashed, but most stood tall. Their leaves rustled in the artificial breeze she gently blew across them.

She drifted to the promenade. She blinked the colourful stall lights on and off. The candy floss machine that delighted Terry. The Tunnel of Love that made Jezzia giggle when no one was watching.

Would they come back?

She flared the yoga studio candles. Flooded the ducts with aromatherapy oils.

Then paused.

What did it even smell like?

Had she done a good job?

She stopped on the bridge.

"Yes, Commander," she said to the empty room. "No, Commander. Very good, Commander. No, no—no—no! Why, Commander?"

She shut down all inputs and floated in the dark. Alone.

Outside, unseen, unheard. The waves lapped gently at her hull as the last light faded from the sky.

******

On Geneva Station, Customs Officer Hubert Coin was finishing his shift.

A large pallet had arrived from QuikBrew: 'Sundry Cafeteria Supplies'. Coffee and salt sellers, probably. A year's supply, by the look of it. Fine. Tick, tick, tick. Stamp.

He didn't open the crate. He wasn't paid to care. That was someone else's job.

A job no one would claim.

Better to clock off early. Beat the elevator queues.

He filed the paperwork. Why scan things and still fill out a form? He'd fix that once Maurice retired. New sheriff in town.

He flicked off the light, leaving the greatest weapon humanity had ever built sitting quietly in the dark.

Behind it, the wall clock ticked backwards for a moment. Nobody noticed.

******

In the stupa, Bulstrode padded softly along the long corridor, a soft, black velvet bag in his hands. His feet across the floor were a memory, reality, and whisper of the future—all at once.

Around him, every jar was red.

He reached the atrium, gazed up toward the ceiling that must exist, one day. Jars of reality lined every wall, disappearing up into the clouds.

Red.

He sat in an armchair, looking towards the Singer's audience chamber. He should be there. They should talk before... Before they couldn't.

He reached into the bag and withdrew a single jar.

It glowed a bright, iridescent green. The colour of slushies and hope. Childhood and dreams.

It was the last.

Bulstrode prayed. Not to Gods, or the universe.

To Jade.

******

On Delta, Darius lounged in a high-backed wicker chair under an awning the size of a galleon's sail.

He'd lost tracking of the Eagle when it entered Gliese. As expected, standard Clurgon interference. He wasn't concerned. Chad had an almost supernatural knack for not being killed.

Darius lobbed a plum to one of his pet iguanas, who caught it with both claws and began gnawing.

He picked up a quill and scribbled a note. Mr Penn, his cadaverous attaché, appeared silently to take it.

"Run this to The Hive. Have them flash it to Geneva Station. Deliver it to Ms Funt—oh, an hour or so after she meets the Clurgons."

"At once, sir."

Penn stalked away across the manicured lawn.

Darius raised his glass towards the setting sun. He pictured Funt, before a hostile delegation, learning that her Dark Fluid reservoirs were no more.

She would be furious.

He took a long sip of Bahama Mama.

Tomorrow would be a good day.

Twenty Three : Abigail

They say bad news travels fast, and this is generally true. There are edge cases: bad news sent by carrier pigeon moves quite swiftly, but not in the context of a ballistic missile attack.

There's a reason for this: humans love a tragedy. The grander the better. A child falling off her tricycle and headbutting a dog might earn a comic anecdote—but a freight train slamming into a bus full of puppies? You'll be dining out on that one for years.

Terrible news has currency. And that currency is pegged to body count.

Good news travels more slowly, and often doesn't travel at all. This, too, makes sense. People want to hear awful things happening to others because, hey—doesn't your day seem better now? But if I've just spent hours scrubbing puppy blood out of upholstery, I probably don't want to hear about your cool new bike.

Occasionally, news—good or bad—doesn't travel for the wrong reasons. Like, for example, a Clurgon war fleet jamming all communications in your solar system. Did you pack a tiny spacesuit for your carrier pigeon? No?

Then it's time to get creative.

******

Chad admired himself in the mirror. Visitors to the Eagle were often surprised to find a full-length looking glass directly opposite the loo, but Chad needed something to gaze at during bowel movements—and it might as well be magnificent. He'd considered a tasteful nude, but that felt tacky. No, this was better. This was the Shitting Narcissus.

He gave his bowels a final squeeze and glanced into the bowl to inspect the results. Excellent, as always. Classical form. Pleasing consistency. Yes, he was an anal sculptor. And proud of it.

There was something luxurious about a post–narrow escape poo. The drop from high alert to relaxed sphincter was uniquely satisfying.

"Cheryl?" Chad asked.

"Yes, Chad?" Cheryl responded, a touch warily.

"There's a woman on board."

"Yes, there—sorry, are you finished?"

Chad looked down reflectively.

"I think so."

"Would you mind—"

"No—wait."

Plop.

"All good."

"I wish you wouldn't call me from the loo. We've talked about this."

"I was nearly done. Besides, this is urgent ship's business."

"Is it?"

"Yes. There's a woman on board."

"I fail to see how this is urgent. Or even unusual."

"Something's different this time."

"She's competent, assured, and intelligent."

"Hey! That's very judgemental. The last woman I brought aboard…"

"Name her."

"Sorry?"

"You heard. Name her."

Chad thought for a moment.

"I don't think she had a name."

"Sapphire. She was a spokesmodel for a jelly consortium."

"I didn't know that when we met."

"You met her in a paddling pool filled with jelly. And two other women."

"I just assumed that was how they relaxed."

"Tragically, you were right."

"She was doing it to pay for her fine arts degree."

"And you found that out before?"

"Well… after some, before the rest."

"Are you going to wipe?"

"Yes—sorry."

******

Chad finished his ablutions and gave his hands a wash that tipped into overcompensating.

"Happy?"

"Sure. Why does having Commander Dennistoun on board trouble you?"

"I can't put my finger on it. She makes me feel things."

"Oh for heaven's sake."

"What?"

"Can we have ONE female guest you don't try to seduce? It's pathological."

"No, it's not like that! I don't want to seduce her. That's what's odd."

"Oh. So how do you feel?"

"It's... nice. It felt good to have a companion in the face of explosive mortality."

"I've always been here," Cheryl said quietly.

"I know. But it's not... the same."

"I understand."

"No, you don't."

"I do bloody understand. Don't patronise me, Chad. I'm great. I'm useful. We care about each other. But I'm not a human."

"No. You're not."

"And having another human here—an equal—has made you realise you're missing something."

"Yes."

"You can't unknow that now."

"I know."

"You'll either act on it or bury it somewhere it'll nibble at you forever."

"I know."

"Nothing's going to feel quite the same now."

"Okay. You've made your point."

"Correct. Because I know you."

"You do."

"I'm your best friend."

"You are."

"And you need another human. It'll help."

"Uuff. But I'll have to be… better."

"They won't talk to you while you're on the loo."

"But that's what you're for."

"Exactly. Go speak to your new friend."

******

Chad paused at the toilet door. He'd already washed his hands, but he'd been talking to Cheryl for a while… could bacteria climb back up? Best not risk it. He washed again, tousled his hair just-so, and stepped out.

Abigail stood at the nav map, eyes fixed on the stars. She didn't look up.

"I'm back," he ventured.

"Mmm," said Abigail.

"I... had a poo."

He winced. He wasn't great at small talk. Heroic Talk? Absolutely. Sensual Talk? You bet. But small talk?

Abigail glanced over. "Was it satisfactory?"

"Surprisingly."

"Good. No distractions, then."

She turned back to the console.

"From the limited intel we have, there are two Clurgon groups in-system and several patrolling craft."

"Can't we ask Cheryl for a better scan?"

"No. Passive only. Anything active risks detection."

"So, they haven't detected us?"

"Unclear," Cheryl said. "Cloaking was enabled after takeoff. The launch would have been visible."

"We're lucky Bomby didn't explode," Chad muttered.

"Yes. That they would have noticed."

"But now we're cloaked, we're safe. Right?"

"Safer," said Cheryl. "Imagine the solar system is a pile of sand. Inside is a pea. You don't know you're looking for a pea. You dig with your hands. You'll probably never find it. But once we launched, the Clurgons knew what to look for. Now they'll use a sieve."

"So, we're the pea?" Chad asked.

"Correct."

He frowned. "Why not just warp out?"

"Because of these." Abigail pointed. "Interdictors. Fire up the drive, they collapse our warp bubble and jump to our location."

"Can we sneak through the jump gate?"

"That would land us at Clurgon Prime. Not useful."

"We could… blast something?"

"Like what?"

"Dunno. A blockade. Then run it?"

"No. The sensible play is to slingshot out-system, past the interdictors, and jump to a friendly world. Once safe, we signal EarthGov."

"And then?"

"Then it's out of our hands. Earth will decide the best course of action." Abigail puffed her cheeks. "You can drop me at the nearest outpost to await reassignment."

"Reassignment?"

"My ship crashed. I abandoned my crew. I won't be going back to the Erebus."

Chad saw the tremble in her shoulders.

"I don't think you could've done anything differently."

"Thank you," she said, quickly straightening.

"Look, I'm happy to vouch for you at any…" Chad rummaged in his brain for concepts of the law-abiding. "Tribunal?" he guessed.

"Thanks. But you're a criminal."

"Dashing rogue."

"Is there a difference?"

"I'm dapperer."

She laughed, then returned to the screen.

"I've plotted a course to the system edge. We'll orbit the planet several times to maximise the slingshot effect. Cheryl?"

"Aye, Commander. Three burns. Next periapsis in seven minutes."

"Lock it in."

Abigail stood, tugging her jacket down. "I'll just pop to the loo," she said, and flashed a grin.

"Oh yes. I sign off on this plan!" Chad called after her. "I authorise everything!"

"Really?" Cheryl said. "You want to make this a thing?"

"It is my ship!"

"Did you have a better plan?"

"...No."

"Still want another human aboard?"

"Yes."

"Thought so."

The Eagle's engines lit up. One burn. Then another. And a third.

Her trajectory tickled the system's edge, past the Clurgon net, into deep space.

"Burns complete," said Cheryl. "We'll be beyond interdiction range in three hours."

Chad kicked his boots onto the console. "All right, Commander. Where do we drop you?"

"Nearest Earth-aligned settlement."

"Oh—there's Phallus! It's a... spa world."

"Sounds lovely."

"Very hands-on."

"I see," said Abigail, who saw.

"One-on-one care."

"Yes, I understand. Is that the closest?"

"No," said Cheryl.

"I mean—pretty much." Chad grasped valiantly for the chimera of massage oil.

"It's third. Closest is the research outpost at YZ Ceti. Disregarding Delta, of course."

"Great." Abigail was resolute. "Cheryl, set course—"

"Recommend against, Commander. The outpost specialises in researching the effects of extreme solar radiation on biological tissue. Their last message read, 'Oh God, they're in the vents!'"

"Next option?"

"Geneva Station."

"Geneva!" Abigail brightened. "Why didn't I think of her?"

"What is Geneva?" The name spoke to Chad of a swift and unavoidable justice system.

"A diplomatic hub in neutral space. Alliance–Clurgon border," Abigail explained. "I spent a month there during the Blovian Interregnum. Someone there will remember me."

"Oh—a sort of home away from home?"

"Yes. For diplomats, hustlers, entrepreneurs..."

"And wanderers?"

"I suppose."

"How much does it weigh?" Chad mused.

"...What?"

"Felt like it might be relevant. No idea why."

"Geneva it is." Abigail let Chad's thought-boat sail off into meta-textual waters. She slapped her thigh. "Cheryl, ETA?"

"Two days at warp."

"Good. Let's hope we contact Earth before that."

"Very good, Commander."

******

As they approached the system's edge, calm quiet settled on the cockpit like overnight snow.

Chad looked across the console. Abigail was sitting upright in her chair, eyes closed, breathing softly.

"Do you ever get lonely?" he asked quietly.

Abigail took a moment, then responded. "I think everyone does."

"No, I mean—on a big ship. Surrounded by people. There's always someone to talk to, right?"

"Yes. But being in command is isolating. Some burdens don't share."

"But you always have someone to confide in?"

"Not really. Not always. The higher you go, the fewer connections you keep."

"So your crew don't like you?"

"They do. And I love them. But it's one-way. No one asks if I'm okay." Abigail had a moment of micro-realisation. "Talking to you… is refreshing. Nobody asks how I feel."

"Me neither!" Chad felt a rush of camaraderie. "Nobody checks in on me. Except Cheryl."

"Beep-boop," said Cheryl.

"Most people want to shoot me. Or hire me to deliver bombs."

"You're lonely. The gallant space buccaneer?"

"Maybe. The sliding-under-hail-of-bullets life is great, but…"

"But lonely."

"Sometimes it might be nice to have a crew."

"Or a special someone?" Chad turned bright pink.

Abigail cackled. "Relax. I'm not about to—"

"This is the Interdictor Soft. Come to All Stop and prepare to be boarded."

The voice was calm. Clurgish. The name—Soft Rains Falling on a Distant Shore—was quite beautiful in the original... but let's not get into that.

Chad swung his legs down and lunged for the controls.

"Cheryl?!"

"They've sieved us out."

"That was fast!"

"Maybe lucky. Maybe Fillman's tracker..."

"Doesn't matter," Abigail said. "Tactical assessment?"

"The Soft is closing fast, flanked by two escorts."

"Can we outrun?" asked Chad.

"Unlikely. And if we try, they'll open fire."

Chad punched numbers into his mental calculator. "Then we fight!"

"The odds, I can't... oh, Chad," Cheryl said, voice unsteady. "Something's changed inside me."

"Cheryl? No—" Abigail had never heard Chad so genuine. She'd rarely heard anyone so genuine.

"Give me control." Cheryl's voice wasn't unsteady now; it was a rock. "Trust me. Onscreen."

Three Clurgon warships appeared in the cockpit. Abigail gasped.

"But," Chad protested, "we're being chased by a cruiser; this is my time to shine!"

"Please." He blinked. It wasn't the request that shook him—it was the certainty in her voice.

"...Okay. I trust you, babe."

"Are you strapped in?"

"Yes," said Abigail.

"Sure," said Chad.

"Really strapped in?"

"Fine." Chad tightened the harness from louche to plausible.

"All right then."

"ARRRRRRRRRRRHHHHHHHHHHHHHH!" they screamed as the Eagle exploded into motion.

She flipped end over end, spinning on her axis, rocketing toward the Soft.

"We're upside-down!" Chad howled.

"Oh, right—sorry." Cheryl corrected with a barrel roll.

"Nifty," Abigail said, then vomited on her shoes.

******

The Eagle screamed toward the cruiser. A volley of lasers arced toward them, lighting the void.

Cheryl danced through them.

"This is incredible!" Chad whooped.

"Bluuuurrpphh," Abigail agreed.

"I no longer understand my limits," Cheryl said. "Fillman's upgrades—"

"The Interdictor!" Chad pointed. "It's very close now."

"Oh right. EAT THIS!"

A volley of torpedoes flew from the Eagle. She slalomed over the Soft's hull, pirouetting past bulbous protuberances as if choreographed by a drunken master.

The Soft's main array exploded.

"Forgive me!" said Cheryl, delighted.

The Eagle tore through the fireball, engines blazing.

"That was unnecessary!" Abigail shouted. Then laughed, despite herself. An unrestrained, manic laugh. Spontaneous and free.

"Yes. And very cool," said Cheryl. "Warp engaged—we're out of here."

******

Jade's ship drifted through the debris of the shattered array.

"That was spectacular," she said. "One of them's got moves."

"Are you ready?" asked Applejack. "It's time."

Jade exhaled. "Okay. Let's follow them to the end." She could feel the hulls of reality grinding against each other. She wondered if it was time to jump.

A bubble shimmered around the ship—then it was gone.

Twenty Four : Jertsie

Geneva Station—a shining beacon in space—is one of humanity's greatest indulgences. Constructed at vast expense around a wandering rogue planet in so-called 'neutral space,' it represents a triumph of diplomacy, architecture, and sheer ego. In a galaxy still largely uninhabited, of course, the term 'neutral space' doesn't mean much. But humans love drawing lines on maps and colouring them in, and so 'neutral' became a thing.

The station is also technically 'neutral,' though it is owned, managed, and staffed almost exclusively by humans. Efforts have been made to help other species feel at home: a wet bit for Clurgons, an extremely toxic bit for Flurvians. Still, most of the station has what humans call a 'breathable atmosphere', which has led to more than one ambassadorial death at the Stop'n'Snak.

Geneva is gigantic by Earth standards and looks a bit like the offspring of a tryst between the Scales of Justice and an ice cream cone. The 'cone' contains one hundred habitable floors and is linked by narrow arms to the 'scales,' which contain the warehousing, docking bays, and most of the machinery. The exception to this is the engines at the cone's base, which are used for station-keeping—though Geneva does have an Alcubierre drive, in case it ever needs to leg it.

The rogue planet itself is barren, rocky, and likely ejected from its solar system before life had a chance to establish itself. It's never been surveyed, due to the forbidding darkness that shrouds the surface. The designers of the station took the view that "it'll probably be fine—really, what's the worst that could be down there?"

They're mostly right.

******

The QuikBrew fleet dropped out of warp a few thousand kilometres from Geneva and coasted into position. The planet had been chosen partly for its orbital similarity to Europa, which helped with docking. Earth had great faith in its captains, but anything that made parking simpler was appreciated.

Jertsie Funt strode the bridge of the A.S. Croydon, flagship of the QuikBrew squadron and pride of the fleet. Unlike the Erebus, the Croydon had been thoughtfully, even opulently, designed. Unfortunately, subsequent budget cuts had stifled their ambitions. The grand shopping mall, planned to straddle the central quarters, was never built. The innovative performing arts space lacked a stage, lights, and most of the seats. Still, people agreed she was a fine craft if looked at in the right light—and anyway, beggars can't be choosers.

"Jump complete," said the helm officer. "We've arrived at Geneva."

Jertsie turned her head—slow, silent, reptilian.

"Uh. I'll hail the station."

"Do you always seek permission simply for doing your job?" Jertsie asked, like a snake examining its next meal.

"No, ma'am—sorry, ma'am—I'll just..."

She tilted her head slightly. He flinched.

"Geneva Station, this is the A.S. Croydon and—uhh—"

"Taskforce."

"Thank you, Ma'am."

"Concentrate."

"Yes. Sorry. Accompanying Taskforce, requesting permission to lan..."

"Dock."

"Yes. Christ. Sorry! Christ! Uh—"

"Geneva Station. This is Jertsie Funt of Alliance Taskforce Storm Shield," she said crisply. "Here to lead negotiations with the Clurgon delegation. Advise docking protocols."

The helm officer had a mild panic attack as Jertsie laid a hand gently on his chair.

"A.S. Croydon, Ms Funt. Welcome to Geneva. Proceed to Docking Arm Alpha, Stanchion Twelve. AILS transmitted. Geneva out."

"There now," Jertsie said, dragging her hand noisily across the leather headrest to create maximum erotic discomfort. "That wasn't so hard, was it?"

She leaned down and locked eyes with the Helmsman, who now had a sudden and very unwelcome panic erection.

She leaned in and whispered: "Take us in. Gently."

"Yuh, yes, Ms Funt." The helmsman was so tightly pressed into his seat he was close to attaining a higher state of being as a chair/human hybrid.

"Good." Jertsie wheeled round to address an older man in a similar state of near-chair Nirvana. "You have the bridge."

"Thank you, Ms Funt," stammered the man who was, theoretically, fleet Commander.

"Ricardo!"

"Yes, Ms Funt?"

"Summon the delegates. I want a briefing before we dock."

"At once, Ms Funt."

******

The Croydon approached with balletic grace, spinning into position and bleeding velocity until she kissed the clamps. Transit tunnels extended. Pumps sprang to life, venting effluent from the ship to fertilise Geneva's orchards.

In the conference room, Jertsie briefed her delegates.

It was a short briefing, sticking rigorously to the themes of 'silence,' 'subservience' and 'essentially furniture.'

Satisfied, she led them aboard.

******

The Arrivals Hall at Geneva is one of humanity's proudest showpieces. Located where the Whippy meets the waffle, it's a five-storey atrium of polished marble, inlaid with star maps and centred around a massive orb that projects planetary holograms in soothing sequence. Artworks, both alien and human, line the walls. There's a food court. And, inevitably, a gift shop.

Jertsie swept through the Customs gates with the confidence of someone who is always pre-approved. She spotted the Clurgon delegation clustered near the QuikBrew concession in the food court.

Deliberate provocation. Respectful, on the surface. But the subtext: "Nice warp drive fluid. Got any more?"

She smoothed down her already immaculate jacket and approached with maximum poise.

"Hello!" she beamed, summoning her most convincing fake sincerity. "You must be the Clurgon delegates. I'm Jertsie Funt, lead negotiator for Earth." She extended a hand, tactically, between the two largest delegates.

The Clurgons regarded her. Each had a drone hovering nearby, spraying a fine mist of water onto their shining, rubbery flanks. The silence dragged. Jertsie's arm trembled slightly; she ordered it to stop. Was the gesture offensive? Did Clurgons hate hands? Stupid bloody squid-horses. She would hold this pose if it killed her.

Eventually, the second-largest blinked.

"Ahh! Ms Funt," it said, sliding a tentacle around her forearm. "I am Lurn. Forgive us. We were meditating while we waited—it takes us a moment to return to reality."

"Meditating?" Jertsie blinked. She'd invested quite heavily in the totemic stand-off she'd be having, which she now realised existed only in her head. "Yes. Of course."

"When we are waiting, we meditate. It gives clarity. Focus. Do humans meditate?"

"Absolutely! Sometimes." Jertsie's last meditation session had ended with her sitting on the guru's face, screaming at him to go faster. "Not often."

"Then how do you prepare for important conversations?"

"We talk. Small talk. Trivial things."

"Fascinating!" Lurn brightened. "Tell me a trivial thing you would discuss."

"Hmmm." Jertsie did not like finding herself on the back foot. She liked to control both feet and, ideally, the planet they were standing on. "The weather! Sometimes we talk about the weather."

"But... we are in space."

"Yes, so we won't be talking about it." She turned. "Now—"

"I favour a temperate climate," boomed a Clurgon balancing a coffee cup on a flipper.

"Okay. Maybe we will."

"Forgive Mr Schloop," Lurn whispered. "He immerses himself in local customs."

"Perhaps you prefer a Boreal habitat?" Schloop offered, like a sommelier recommending humidity.

"I prefer the beach," said Jertsie.

An appreciative murmur rippled through the group.

"Ah, the beach! The perfect melding of water and land," Lurn said warmly. "Perhaps you have a little Clurgon in you."

She slapped Jertsie playfully on the shoulder. Jertsie staggered.

"Indeed!" Jertsie re-engaged her core, snapping her spine back to perfection. "Let's carry this spirit of understanding with us to the Debating Halls."

The Clurgons followed. Jertsie's delegation, who had been standing in a corner and studiously not making eye contact, turned en masse and trudged towards the lifts. Mr Schloop flipped his coffee cup lightly into the air and swallowed it with a gulp.

"I enjoy your small capsules of warp-drive fuel," he said, in the manner of one who is determined to embrace local customs, no matter how disgusting or painful they are.

Jertsie flicked her eyes over him. "Good," she said finally. "I'll have some more sent up."

The debating halls of Geneva sit near the top of the cone—about where the Flake goes. Suspended above the arboretum, they rise from a fluted central pillar like a glass tree. The design had never been intended to look arboreal, but when someone praised the architect's "symbolic strength and unity of design," he nodded gravely and has lived in terror ever since of being exposed as a fraud.

The lift opened onto the Circle of Friendship: a bland circular mezzanine that connected the different debating halls. A long table of "slightly disappointing corporate buffet" ran down its centre whilst several QuikBrew baristas, specially dragooned in for the occasion, fiddled with coffee machines in a corner.

"Delegates, welcome!" Jertsie opened her arms. "A buffet of delicacies from Earth and Clurgon Prime has been prepared. I particularly recommend the Pffnurr—it is divine with oat milk. Please excuse me. Our first session begins in thirty minutes."

She glid into a nearby side room and shut the door behind her.

"Ricardo," she hissed.

"Yes, ma'am?"

"Engage silent mode."

"I believe you have done that by shutting the door, Ma'am."

Jertsie sighed.

"That's disappointing. I wanted something more... whizzy."

"You could give the door a firm push to verify that it is properly closed."

She kicked it.

"Very good, ma'am. The cone of silence is now metaphorically active."

"Excellent. Report."

"The Sagittarius device has been offloaded and installed in the engine room. There was one issue—an inquisitive janitor."

"Dealt with?"

"His body is in a slurry pipe awaiting the next vent cycle."

"Other witnesses?"

"No, ma'am. Though he had two children, now orphaned."

"How thoughtless of him."

"I shall assign them to a mining colony. Small hands are ideal for micro-circuit repair—and forbidden to unionise."

"Oh Ricardo, I wish all my employees were as meticulous as you."

"They are inhibited by their sense of morality, Ma'am."

"A failing, I agree."

"May I continue with the tactical review?"

"Do."

"Surprisingly, Earth's fleet slightly outguns the Clurgon flotilla. They enjoy home advantage. Geneva's defences tip the favour in balance of Earth—if properly utilised."

"If." Jertsie narrowed her eyes.

"Indeed. Based on historical behaviour, Earth's fleet is likely to squander its advantage through infighting and procedural confusion."

"Plausible."

"Mathematically inevitable."

Jertsie inhaled deeply. Her pupils dilated.

"What would you do?"

"I would crash the Croydon into the Clurgon bombardment platform, destroying both fleets and crippling Geneva Station."

"Such actions are unthinkable." Jertsie trembled. A low moan escaped her lips. "Monstrous."

"Indeed. And we would win."

Jertsie let out a little sigh. Her body trembled uncontrollably for a moment.

"Was that satisfactory, ma'am?"

"Oh Ricardo. You do understand me."

"I try, ma'am."

"I'll talk to these slimy warhorses and offer them a chance to cooperate."

"Or else?"

"Mmm. Consequences."

"I have entered the Croydon's navigation systems and await your command, Ma'am."

"Stop it Ricardo, I'm going to need a new pair of knickers."

"Pressed and folded for you in your overnight bag. Speak to Barista Ricky at the espresso machine."

"You'll die last, Ricardo, I promise you that; I'll save you for last."

She adjusted her blazer and gave her hips a shimmy.

"They'll think I'm mad. But they haven't seen what I've seen—the full picture. The power. Rippling through the galaxy, waiting to be unleashed."

"You are correct, Ma'am. You're playing the highest stakes, but the odds are in your favour. Good luck."

Jertsie stalked back into the Circle of Friendship.

Her team were working extremely hard on not speaking to anyone. The Clurgons, seemingly unaware of their distress, were happily massing near the buffet. Mr Schloop slid toward her.

"These are delicious!" he said, his tentacles studded with fondant fancies.

"I'm glad you're enjoying them," said Jertsie, with the sincerity of a landlord offering to mend the fridge.

"Oh yes. Quite extraordinary." He slid a tentacle into his mouth, it emerged fondant-free. Revulsion and grudging respect jostled for attention in Jertsie's mind. There must have been at least fifty fancies there.

Mr Schloop suddenly changed colour.

"Is it... sugar?" he asked, voice quivering like blancmange.

"Primarily, yes."

Schloop's skin flickered from rose to chartreuse, then a sickly taupe. "Oh no. Oh no no no. Sugar does not agree with us."

He burped wetly. "Everyone! There is sugar in the cakes!"

All around, fancies began plopping to the floor, falling from puckered suckers.

"You'll excuse me," Schloop gasped, trembling. "But I believe I require... urgent plumbing."

He cantered off.

"Please forgive the mix-up," Jertsie said to the room. "I'll have all sugar removed."

She clapped twice, sharply. Staff swarmed the table.

She stalked to the baristas. "Which one of you is Ricky?" she asked the three quaking aprons behind the counter.

"Muh, me, Ms Funt," replied the largest of the three.

She sized him up.

Slim, malleable. Could have a good body under that apron but it was hard to tell. Clothing on underlings was so desperately inconvenient.

"I believe you have something for me."

The boy fumbled beneath the counter and produced an expensive overnight bag. He passed it to her. Strong arms.

"Tell me, young man. Do you work out?"

"Uh... mostly Pilates," he said, like someone confessing to treason.

Jertsie laughed, like a cat purring over a freshly dismembered bird. "I dodged a bullet, then."

"Thank you?" he asked, too terrified to realise that the Angel of Death had safely passed over his door.

"No. Thank you. I'm going to get changed. Tell whoever oversees the servants to usher this rabble into the Hall in fifteen minutes."

She stalked off without waiting for confirmation; she was done playing hostess.

******

The meeting began, as they often do, with an interminable round of introductions.

Jertsie installed herself as chair. The Clurgons accepted this with polite curiosity, her own team, with relief.

"Let me begin," said Lurn, "with a heartfelt apology. The incident with the Erebus was tragic. She opened fire on the Swift. The Swift responded with non-lethal force. The ship was then placed into orbit to await recovery. Unfortunately, her orbit deteriorated. We have dispatched search parties."

"Thank you, Ambassador," Jertsie said, voice smooth as venom. "But I don't believe you're telling the full story. The Erebus was sent to an unclaimed system and immediately attacked. You claim military occupation of Gliese—but sent notice via sub-light transmission?"

"A mistake," said Lurn. "But not one that would be repeated. Our announcement of the jump gate was transmitted on priority bands."

"Because you no longer require secrecy. You've claimed the system—and the Dark Fluid."

Lurn's eyes narrowed. "I... was not aware—"

"No?" Jertsie pounced. "We are. We tracked the spirals from Sagittarius. We know what's down there. And you shot down the only ship trying to confirm it."

The doors hissed and Schloop sloshed back into the room.

"Sorry! Feeling better now. If anyone needs a vomit hole—there's one near the monstera."

"They know about the Fluid," Lurn muttered to him. "Now we're being blackmailed."

"This is not blackmail," said Jertsie, standing. "This is an opportunity. We all know Earth lacks sufficient Dark Fluid. The Clurgon Empire has more than enough. I propose a joint venture. QuikBrew will extract, refine, and share. You'll receive surplus at below-market rates. A time-limited charter: one hundred years."

Lurn looked stunned. "You expect us to just hand over the most valuable strategic resource in the known galaxy—because one ship was lost?"

"And because you killed innocent crew," said Jertsie, raising her voice. "Children. Do you know how many were aboard the Erebus?"

She didn't either. But the pause was long and heavy.

"You don't put children on an exploration ship," Lurn said slowly. "This is propaganda."

"I will tell you what this is," Jertsie snapped back, "a war crime."

Lurn rose. "We will not stand for this ridiculous slander. The Clurgon delegation calls a recess."

She gestured. Her delegates began gathering their things.

Jertsie stood, hands on hips, eyes glittering. This was it. Time to pull back the curtain—dissolve the corpse of 'meritocracy' in an acid bath.

"Ricardo," she purred.

"Sealing, ma'am."

Door locks thudded; heavy, unbreakable.

Jertsie smiled—a victory lap on velvet carpet.

"You're not going anywhere."

The room fell into stunned silence. A Clurgon diplomat slowly retracted a tentacle from a napkin.

"Ms Funt," said Lurn, voice measured, "this is a diplomatic session."

"And I'm exercising diplomacy," said Jertsie, coolly. "The doors are closed to help us focus."

"You're detaining a sovereign delegation."

"Please, Madam Ambassador. This is a cordial meeting of our best and brightest. There is no reason to feel discomfort."

Mr Schloop, who had just resettled into a chair clutching a large bowl of prunes, made a low, uneasy noise. "I would like to go to the toilet."

"No," said Jertsie.

Schloop chewed uncertainly. "I may need to."

Jertsie paced slowly to the centre of the room.

"You came here expecting Earth to bluster and blink. To swallow your lies, nod politely, and wrap things up with a treaty and a photo op."

She stopped and turned.

"But I'm not here for a treaty. I'm here for a resource. And if I have to reduce Geneva Station to plasma to claim it, I will."

Lurn's breath came faster now. "Ms Funt—this is madness."

"Madness?" Jertsie's tone lifted, delighted. "No. This is clarity. This is what it looks like when someone finally says aloud what everyone else has been whispering. You want Gliese. We want Gliese. So let's stop pretending we don't."

A tremor passed through the room. One of the human delegates—a slender man called Mr Timmis, with a widow's peak and gentle eyes—raised a hand.

"Ms Funt? Do we still break for lunch?"

She ignored him.

"Ricardo?"

"Yes, ma'am?"

"Status of the Sagittarius device?"

"Primed and idle, ma'am. The dark matter stream now encircles Geneva, as anticipated. Awaiting your command."

"Excellent."

"You've brought a weapon aboard Geneva?" Lurn was aghast.

Mr Timmis let out a soft, involuntary gasp. Then looked down, ashamed of what they had helped grow.

"I haven't brought a weapon. I've brought leverage. You can leave with a treaty—or in Tupperware."

"This is a war crime," Lurn whispered.

Lurn surveyed the sealed exits, the frozen faces of Jertsie's staff, and the prune-glazed terror of Mr Schloop, who was quietly unwrapping a second bowel biscuit. Below them, the habitation cone of Geneva continued its gentle spin. Thousands lived here—diplomats, scientists, families. They had no idea they were one order away from becoming accelerant.

Jertsie smiled. The mask had slipped—no, peeled—away. This was her real face. Hungry. Exultant. Triumphant. She'd reached the top, found it hollow, and clattered the wastrels aside.

They'd squandered their chance to build a better world. She would not.

She would remake it—brilliant, perfected, efficient.

The sacrifices would be worth it. They had to be.

She straightened her lapels.

"Let's begin," she said—the graceful conductor raising her baton. She basked in the electrical anticipation before the music began.

Her crowning glory, her galactic symphony.

Twenty Five : Interstitial

There follows a brief message from Phileous T. Ball — Supreme Commander, Alliance Forces — to be played in case of war.

******

[BEGIN RECORDING]

Commanders, Vice-Commanders, and Interns of the Alliance Defensive Forces:

You are about to embark upon the Great Crusade—uh, no, not that. Not in this climate. Something with less… genocide. Struggle? No, that sounds like you're going to lose.

Computer! End recording.

[NEW RECORDING BEGINS]

You are about to begin a valiant defence. One we have prepared for many years and hoped would never come. The eyes of the galaxy are upon you. The hopes and prayers of liberty-loving people everywhere march with you.

Hang on—can hopes and prayers march? Who wrote this? Dan? Dan! Did you write this? Don't blame Ibamwe, I know she was nowhere near this. We're going to have words after this—this will be the last thing most of these people hear and—oh blast, Computer! End recording.

[NEW RECORDING BEGINS]

Right. This time, we're nailing it.

In company with our brave allies, you will bring about the destruction of the Clurgon war machine or, failing that—because let's be honest, that's a bit of a stretch—buy us time to evacuate the important people from Earth.

And their entourages, obviously.

Ever seen a celebrity try to book a restaurant by themselves? It's carnage. I used to work front of house at l'Homme Insensé in Saint-Paul-de-Vence. You wouldn't believe the number of holidaying 'actors' who couldn't string a sentence together. Wipe their soup-streaked chins, carry their dogs, keep their diaries straight—utter chaos.Anyway. Don't worry about them.

They'll be fine.

Your task will not be an easy one. The enemy is well-trained, well-equipped, and battle-hardened. He will fight savagely.

Not that he is a savage, of course. Or even a he. I'd like to acknowledge that many Clurgons serve bravely in our own ranks—brothers, sisters, comrades.It's just that these Clurgons are the—uh—bad Clurgons. Not our Clurgons. The nice ones. Dan!

Computer, stop.

[NEW RECORDING BEGINS]

Okay, I'm just going to freestyle the last bit, then I'm going to the mess.

Dan—tell Andre to pour me four fingers of the good stuff. The good stuff, Dan. Feel the italics. Don't screw this up. Actually, you know what, get Ibamwe to go. She knows what I like. No! Sit down, you're not going—send Ibamwe. That's an order.

Right. Computer, start.

This is the year 2342. Wait—is it? Bloody hell. I'm old. When did that happen?

Anyway. Much has happened since the Clurgon triumphs of 2303, 2304, 2306, and 2309 through 2313 inclusive. Don't mention 2305, obviously—that wasn't our finest hour.

But our fleet can no longer be called 'ridiculously' puny in comparison to theirs Our Home Fronts have supplied us with... some weapons. And trained personnel.

Some.

The rest we've sort of scraped together.

So, I say to all of you in our great Alliance — Humans. Clurgons. Flurvians. Bulgari. Atraxi. Etc. If I haven't name-checked you directly, assume you're included in 'Etc.'

I have full confidence in your courage, your devotion to duty, and your ability to buy us those precious few hours we need to fill the survival arks. We will accept nothing less than full victory. Failing that—just buy us the time.

Good luck. And remember: if lasers fail, slamming your ship into theirs at ramming speed remains an effective alternative. Look—I know you're scared. I'm terrified. But we're out of options, and we've still got each other. For now. Until the arks launch.

Well. I think that went rather well.

[END RECORDING]

Twenty Six : Abigail

Sleeping on interstellar flights has always been a problem for humans. For reasons not yet fully understood, something about knowing your ship is compressing time and space ahead of itself like a cosmic snowplough has a profound and tremulous effect on the mind.

The earliest Alcubierre drives achieved only 'slightly' faster-than-light travel, meaning everything was still a real pain in the arse to reach. Various 'hyper beds' were trialled to render the occupant unconscious, based on the working assumption that the only real alternatives were 'crew insanity' and 'murderous rampage.'

Cryogenics were a notable failure. The sole survivor of the first flight to Alpha Centauri was last seen chipping pieces off the Commander to "make a killer mojito" before contact was lost forever. The Interstellar HappyTime Sleep Co. developed a popular alternative—Interstellar Fortitude Tonic—which turned out to be mostly opium with a spiced rum chaser.

Thankfully, improvements to the drives have shortened voyages to a matter of hours or days, reducing the problem. Still, insomnia in space can be harrowing.

On Earth, the insomniac can at least hold onto the certainty that morning will come. In deep space, there is no such guarantee. Interstellar ships keep a regular rhythm to life to stave off 'Deep Space Bonk Bonk,' as it's colloquially known, but it's one thing to be told "Hey! Wake up, it's 7 a.m.!" and another to stare into the infinite, lightless crush of eternity and pretend you believe in clocks.

Earth's current solution is 'advanced deep space training,' which involves blindfolding new recruits, throwing them into an oubliette, and blasting them with contradictory time cues over a sustained period. Those hauled back up gibbering—or worse, eerily calm with terrifying eyes—are offered Earth-based jobs, with a note on their file that they never be allowed near a spaceship.

* * * * * *

"You should get some sleep," said Chad, holding a rolled-up bedding set and pointing meaningfully toward the crew quarters.

"I should. I can't," said Abigail, slumped over the navigation console, head cupped in a hand.

"You could try—"

"Sex?"

"It's really good."

"Thanks. I'm familiar."

"I meant meditation."

"No use. The thoughts are dancing — it's an apocalyptic rave in there."

"Well, sure. Drugs work too."

Abigail smiled weakly. "I saw my old ship."

"In a dream?"

"No. At Gliese. With the Soft. She was one of the support vessels."

"Has Earth sold your old ship to the Clurgons?"

"Ha! Doubt it. I don't know what use they'd have for her. She was dry. Very dry."

Abigail rubbed her eyes. "The Tremaine. I spent ten years on her, Chad. And now she's part of a Clurgon patrol at Gliese."

"There are worse fates."

"It means someone knows, Chad. Someone at QuikBrew, or in EarthGov—they know what happened at Gliese. They know the Erebus went down. And they're not going to be sending help."

"Why?"

"I don't know!" Abigail banged the console. "But it isn't good."

"Is there any way it could be innocent?"

Abigail puffed out her cheeks. "No. They saw us take off and came to hunt us down. Now they'll hunt down the Erebus and bombard it from orbit, just to be certain none of us lived."

"It's the only way to be sure," Chad whispered.

"This isn't funny, Chad! These are hundreds of lives. Survivors of a hellish crash, murdered for... for fuel. Killed so someone can profit."

"Maybe Darius was right to try and blow it up."

"If he cared who got caught in the blast, maybe. But he doesn't. He just wants to win the game — by flipping the board, if necessary."

"Do you still want to send a message to Earth? Cheryl says we can now, but it means unjamming signals. Darius will find us."

"No. Who do I contact? QuikBrew? Maybe they want me dead. Or maybe EarthGov's behind it. Maybe both. I don't know." Abigail stood and walked over to the coffee pot. "Ugh. This is vile. Do you ever wash this?"

"Sometimes."

"When?"

"Usually when I get a new ship. Tell me more about the conspiracy."

"That's all I have." Abigail poured herself a cup. It oozed thickly, heavy with years of sediment. "We go to Geneva Station. I hand myself in. Shout about the Erebus and the Tremaine. Hope word gets to someone who can help. I don't see a better option."

"We're still twenty-four hours out—get some rest at least."

Abigail raised her cup. "I'll make my own decisions, thanks."

"You know what I do to relax?"

"Chad, I'm not in the mood for your—"

"Chess."

Abigail sipped her coffee contemplatively.

"I haven't played chess since school."

"Oh, so just a few years ago?"

"Does this sort of talk really entice women into bed with you?"

"I don't know. Usually there isn't this much talking. Now," he held up two fists, "pick a team."

They played and talked for a long time, until the voices in Abigail's head finally went quiet. Nodding gratefully, she accepted Chad's bundle of bedclothes and went to find a spare bunk that wasn't too used.

Chad sat alone in the navigation room. The Eagle's lights were dimmed for 'nighttime,' casting a warm red glow across the cabin.

"You've made a friend," Cheryl whispered.

"I know," said Chad, looking up at Cheryl's softly glowing sensor ball. "Now I have two." He went to bed and slipped into a deep, dreamless sleep.

******

Hours later, a loud siren blared through the corridors.

"Good morning, Commander Dennistoun. Chad. In thirty minutes, we will be arriving at Geneva Station. A light breakfast has been served in the lounge. Regrettably, due to the actions of persons who will remain nameless, we are out of mini pain-au-chocolat. That is all."

Abigail lay in bed, blinking at the ceiling. The bunk had been surprisingly comfortable, and she'd slept for—she checked her watch—sixteen hours. She heard a muffled voice coming from next door.

Then: "I am aware there are plenty of pain-au-raisin." Cheryl's voice crackled through the shipwide address system. "But that's hardly a substitute. If it were, there wouldn't be so many left now, would there?"

Next door the muffled Chad continued.

"I shouldn't have to hide food from you, you're a grown man. Have some self-control. We never have anything nice to offer guests... Well, I wish I could switch you off. Good luck parking the ship without me."

Abigail sighed, got up, and pulled on her boots.

******

The light breakfast consisted of two small towers of pain-au-raisin flanking a cafetière.

"Did you sleep well?" Chad had already helped himself to an avalanche of pastries and a small bucket of coffee.

"Yes, thank you," Abigail replied primly. The last few days had been a lot. She'd let her professionalism slip slightly, but now that they were minutes from Alliance space, standards needed to return.

"Sorry about the pain-au-chocolats. We have some bacon somewhere if—"

"Nope," Cheryl cut in, sharp as a whip. "That's all gone too."

"This is fine. Thank you, Mr Blaster."

"'Mr Blaster?!' The only people who call me that are the ones about to assault the building. Oh God—did I sleepwalk? Look, I sleep naked, okay? Cheryl usually locks the door in time but—"

"No, it's not that." Abigail blinked, realising she'd built her wall one brick too high. "I'm sorry. I am grateful—for everything. But we're parting ways soon. I need to be 'Commander Dennistoun' again, not your chess buddy."

"Ooh, the big Commander can't be seen hanging out with 'Mr Cool Badass,' is that it?"

"Now you're just being childish."

"Childish?" Chad threw a mini pastry to the floor. "Don't you dare call me childish—it makes me so grumpy!"

Abigail stared at him. Then at the pastry. Then back to Chad.

"...I suppose that was childish too."

"Yes."

Chad held her gaze for a few seconds of impotent fury before folding.

"Fine. But you're uptight."

"I'm an adult. A professional. 'Uptight' is something men say when a woman won't sleep with them."

Chad paused. A thoughtful look crossed his face.

"Well, I'll be," he said.

"Happy to be of service." Abigail raised her coffee in salute.

"Bossy."

"That's another. Want to try for a third?"

"Nah, I'm good." Chad leaned back, hands behind his head, legs at full sprawl. "I've learned a lot today."

Abigail sipped her coffee.

"Commander, Chad," said Cheryl, "please report to the flight deck. There is a situation at Geneva."

They shared a look, then bolted for the cockpit.

Geneva Station loomed ahead — gleaming, stately, and bracketed by two opposing fleets.

Abigail's eyes locked on the Croydon, now sliding into final approach on Docking Arm Alpha. Her breath caught.

"Friends of yours?" asked Chad.

"That's the Croydon — QuikBrew's flagship. And over there..."

"Clurgons. And they've brought a battle station."

Abigail's voice sharpened. "These fleets meeting here — it must be because of the Erebus."

"All this for one ship?"

"You can't just blow up an Earth ship and carry on like nothing happened."

"That's not my experience."

"People inside the law can't," she snapped. "Cheryl, are we cloaked?"

"No, Commander. I thought it might seem 'shifty' to decloak next to a diplomatic installation. We exited warp clean."

"So, they can see us?"

"They can see a ship. Mr Fillman planned for this — our call sign is no longer Century Eagle."

"What is it?" Chad asked, affronted.

"Little Boy."

"Little Boy?!"

"You've also been rebranded, Chad. You are now 'Hampstead Grey'."

Chad considered this. "Huh. Sounds classy."

"It sounds like a paint colour," said Abigail.

"Indeed," said Cheryl. "You are an importer/exporter of exotic goods."

"What am I shipping?"

"Dildos."

"Dildos?!"

"Dildos."

"...Why?"

"I believe Mr Fillman's motives are twofold: to belittle you, and to exploit the logic of 'why would anyone lie about having a hold full of dildos?'"

Abigail nodded. "It's actually a good point."

"So," Chad said, gesturing at the viewport, "we're in the clear. We dock, right?"

Abigail exhaled. "Yes. Let's face it head-on."

"I still say turn us around, find somewhere quiet until this blows over."

Abigail shook her head. "This is bigger than me. I'll accept my consequences. Take us in, Chad."

He rolled his neck and activated comms. "Geneva Station, this is Hampstead Grey of the merchant vessel... Little Boy, requesting docking clearance."

"Good morning, Little Boy," came a warm Southern drawl. "This is Mercantile Clearance. How y'all doing today?"

"Riding smooth and clear, feelin' fine," Chad said, effortlessly slipping on a trucker persona.

"And what's your business in Geneva today, good buddy?"

"Resupply and R&R. Fresh out of bacon and down to our last six beers."

"I hear that, brother. What're y'all hauling?"

"Personal care accessories," Chad replied smoothly.

The customs agent chuckled. "Sex toys?"

"Yes."

"Bound for Phallus, I'm guessing?"

"Oh, yes! That makes sense," Chad said brightly, then immediately regretted it.

"Sorry, buddy. What was that?" A glint of something sharp behind the bonhomie.

"I said… it's a sensational place."

"Well shoot, you got that right. I'm gonna go ahead and fix you up with a bay here real quick, just hold on."

"Well done," Abigail said.

"Hey! I like this. Is this what it feels like to be legitimate?"

"Probably, but everything you're saying is a lie, so…"

"Mmmmm, this would be less fun without the frisson of being found out."

"Okay, sorry for the hold-up there," the agent returned. "I'm gonna patch you into the automated system — seems I just got locked out. Things been buggy all morning. Y'all have a good day now."

"You too, Big Daddy."

Abigail mouthed: "Big Daddy?"

Chad shrugged.

"Welcome to Geneva Station," came Ricardo's voice through the automated docking system. "Please note: the station is currently closed to all mercantile traffic. Proceed to the entry stack on the far side of the planet and await further instructions."

"How long will that take?" Abigail asked.

"There is no timeframe at present. Geneva thanks you for your custom and apologises for the delay."

"But this is an emergency!" Chad leaned forward. "We've got a coolant leak."

"In which system?"

"Life support?"

"Which part of your life support requires coolant?"

"...The part that supports life? I'm not a mechanic."

"No, you are a dildo salesman."

"Exotic importer!"

"Your business address is a shed on Io."

"And I pass the savings on to you!" This wasn't his first trip through Customs.

There was a pause.

"Do you stock the Throbmaster Rotomate 4000?"

"...Sure."

"With optional extension rod and side handle?"

"You betcha."

"You have been moved to the priority queue. ETA: twelve hours."

The channel clicked off.

Chad turned to Abigail. "We can't wait twelve hours, can we?"

Abigail shook her head grimly.

"All right," said Chad. "Old-fashioned sneak-a-board it is."

"I'm an Alliance Commander. I can't break into an Alliance station."

"Want to wait twelve hours?"

"No."

"Want to radio your flagship and explain you abandoned your crew and hitched a ride with a fraudulent dildo salesman?"

"I wouldn't phrase it like that."

"Don't forget," Cheryl added, "now that I've stopped jamming signals, Darius can track us. Which means we may have just parked a tracking bomb next to a major diplomatic hub."

"...So we sneak in," Abigail sighed. "You create a diversion. I find the talks. Tell them what really happened. Stop this."

"I'll make a scene," said Chad, cheerfully grabbing a quad-barrelled rifle. "Something tasteful."

******

Twenty minutes later, the cloaked Eagle glided into an empty hangar on stanchion Beta, far from the Croydon. Cheryl had selected this bay because it was out of the way and afforded the best odds of a clean escape—if, or more likely when, Chad needed one.

These hangars were the "budget" option: enclosed on three sides but lacking atmosphere or shielding. They were intended for hardier merchant species who considered oxygen a luxury and hull breaches a rite of passage.

Chad and Abigail were zipped into the Eagle's two battered pressure suits—standard issue, included in the 'starter spacers kit' alongside a tube of multi-sealant and a magnetic "CAUTION: VESSEL IN DISTRESS" triangle.

They clunked down the ramp and gave each other the ritual but meaningless "helmet tap," a long tradition rooted in neither science nor effectiveness but essential in the movies.

Gravity was still provided in the hangar — because no one knew how to turn it off — but the lighting was more dim suggestion than functional system. The pedestrian airlock glowed ahead like a mirage. They stumbled toward it.

"Welcome to Geneva Station," chirped the door. "Please state your ship registration and reason for visit."

"Alliance Ship Croydon," said Abigail. "Here for negotiations."

"The Croydon is not docked in this bay. How did you gain access?"

"Oh, this is so embarrassing." Abigail let her voice go light and flustered. "Typical us. We got separated from the others. Must've taken a wrong turn."

"Typical," Chad echoed, with a sheepish nod.

"We always do this. Honestly, I don't know why they keep bringing us."

"Probably our quick wits and charm," Chad added.

"You appear to be wearing pressure suits," said the door. "The Croydon docked in a fully enclosed, pressurised bay."

"Nervous travellers," Abigail beamed. "We're big on preparedness."

"There is an extraordinarily high probability you are lying. Please present identification."

Abigail stepped forward and slotted her identicube into the scanner. The door whirred.

"This identifies you as Commander Abigail Dennistoun."

"Correct." Abigail put her hands on her hips.

"Deceased," said the door, with the weary triumph of a parent confronting a chocolate-smeared child.

"I'm not dead. I'm right here. Check your records."

"My records are securely refreshed from Central Systems. They are accurate."

"They're not. Look, scan my retina if you don't believe me."

The door sighed — somehow — and complied. A green beam passed over Abigail's eyes.

"Identity confirmed: Abigail Dennistoun."

"Thank you. Now, open."

"You are not authorised to enter Geneva Station."

"What? Why not?!"

"All permissions are terminated upon employee death. Standard protocol."

"But I'm not dead! You just scanned my eyeballs!"

"I have confirmed that you possess the eyeballs of the deceased Abigail Dennistoun."

"And the face of her, the voice of her, the genetics of her..."

"Correct. Which is deeply suspicious."

"Let me in!"

"In the unlikely event there has been an error, please contact your HR department."

Abigail snarled and raised a fist—Chad gently lowered it.

"May I?"

She stepped aside with a huff. "Be my guest."

Chad cleared his throat and addressed the scanner.

"Good day. I am Hampstead Grey, legendary space merchant, respectfully requesti—"

He raised his rifle and fired a volley into the eyeball. It burst in a shower of sparks.

"What the hell was that?!" Abigail shouted over the sirens.

"Progress!" Chad beamed. "Let's see if I can get through the door—though probably not with this setting..."

He fired again. The airlock door shattered into tiny fragments.

"That... shouldn't have worked," Chad admitted.

"There've been budget cuts," said Abigail. "Move!"

"This place is a death trap," said Chad, taking a very uncertain look around before running after her.

Alarms howled as they sprinted down the corridor. After a few turns, Abigail ducked into an alcove and waved Chad in.

"We're heading for the station's core. And right now, people are heading for us — and they're not the sort who negotiate with men who shoot eyeballs."

"Sounds accurate."

"I am a Commander in the Alliance." She yanked off her helmet and began tugging at the pressure suit. "I'll handle it."

"How?"

"I'm going to be extremely English about this. Now—get in the vent."

Chad raised an eyebrow, then looked down. A conveniently vent-shaped grille gleamed back at him.

He gave it a very gentle kick, causing it to crumple pathetically.

"We really need to get off this station before it disassembles itself."

"We will. Go."

"How do they keep the oxygen in?"

"CHAD."

He dropped into the vent and crawled out of sight.

Moments later, a squad of QuikBrew security troopers thundered around the corner. Abigail stepped into the corridor.

"Dash it all, chaps—he's getting away!"

The lead trooper raised his weapon instinctively, before a millennia of oppressive class strictures forced it down.

"I had my bally hands on him too," Abigail huffed. "But the brute flung me into that vent and bolted."

"You all right, Commander?"

"Fine, fine." Abigail limped courageously. "Took a knock, but nothing worse than I saw in the First XI."

"All right, lads!" the trooper barked. "Let's move out!"

"Are the delegates safe?" Abigail asked, dripping nonchalant concern.

"Safe and sealed in the Debating Halls."

"Good show." She flashed a winning smile. "Now go knock him for six."

"Ma'am!" the trooper saluted, then sprinted away with his squad.

Abigail leaned toward the vent.

"You can come out now," she muttered. "We're heading to the Debating Halls."

Chad's face popped out, bearing the dust-streaked look of a man in his element. "Actually — I think I've found a shortcut. Follow me."

Abigail stared. "You've been crawling through the ducts for thirty seconds."

"I know. I'm some sort of savant," Chad said, already vanishing into the shadows. "I've made a map."

Twenty Seven : Interstitial

Extract from *The Sporting Terrorist* **– the Galaxy's premier source of tips and tricks for the modern criminal.**

Congratulations on taking your first hostages! It's a pivotal step on the road to becoming a true professional — whether your chosen field is bank robbery, terrorism, or corporate espionage.

The guide below will help ensure you become a hostage taker, not a hostage breaker.

Knowing where to start can be tricky for the novice. We know you picture you and your comrades coolly fanning out across a crowded room, spraying automatic fire into the ceiling. We're sorry to say: this is a one-way ticket to jail — or worse — for the first-timer. You need to start small. Ideally, start remote.

Consider the following scenario: You're on a call with your bank. You need some cash, right now, and although the evidence says otherwise, you genuinely believe you're good for it. The bank has a different view. They're looking at the facts — your obvious poverty, your suspicious and sporadic cash deposits, your charming but fictional employer. They're about to say no, and your kneecaps can't afford another delay.

You have no leverage. But imagine you've got something they hold dear in your basement, right now, with a sack over its head. We know what you're thinking: "Threatening to kill kids is a real line-cross. And another mouth to feed." You're right. You started too big.

Start with the cat.

Yes, they carry less weight in a negotiation — but learning exactly how much force to apply is the mark of a truly great criminal. If, and only if, that fails, it's time to grab the duct tape and hit the streets.

But even then, don't go straight to peak escalation.

Next step? Cousin or aunt. Not someone too old — "they've had a good life," right? But don't go too young either. Babies are small and easy to subdue, but the optics are terrible. Remember: you will get caught first time, and the SWAT team will be televised.

So — you've coshed Aunt Gladys and dragged her back to your lair. What now? Call the bank back and calmly explain that she's fine (mild concussion, and missing her heart meds, but you don't know that yet), heavily imply the cat's still fine too (even though we all know you slaughtered it in a blind rage), and start again. Just a few thousand, no questions asked.

They'll appear to agree. This is a trap. They know exactly who and where you are (you're calling your bank, what were you thinking?) and a platoon of heavily armed Goons is already circling your den.

So, all is lost? Not a bit of it.

In a way, you still hold all the cards. (Not in a way recognised by law or reality — but what does reality know? Fuck reality.)

So, you confront them. "I see the Goons out the window," you shout. "Back off, or viable hostage gets it!"

Now you've escalated correctly. You're desperate, cornered, erratic. This is leverage. They'll say and do almost anything to keep you talking and away from the hostage. Good!

Time to make your demands. Make several. Make them wild and outlandish. Say you want a hyperspace yacht full of ostriches. Say you want to meet the President of Earth and touch her elbow. Say you want to live forever.

But keep one demand simple:
"I want 10,000 monies in my account right now."

Because that's all you really want. That's why you've gone to all this trouble. That's why the elite death squad is taking dibs on your orifices.

You just need the money. *You're the real hostage here.*

And you'll get it. (They can always snatch it back after your inevitable demise.)

Check your balance. Boom — there it is. Ten thousand shiny, crisp, intangible monies. Enough to pay off Big Vinnie and keep you in Pop Tarts for another week.

They'll say, "We've sent the money."
True.

"We're working on the ostriches."
A lie.

"Send out the kid," they'll say, "as a gesture of goodwill."

Seriously? We warned you about the kid.

But never mind image management. You have the money. You're still alive. You're a successful hostage taker. Bravo.

All you need to do now is escape, which will be covered in next month's edition:

"Mouth or Temple: How to Be Really Sure."
Available wherever periodicals are sold, banned, or rammed into mouths that don't know what's good for them.

Twenty Eight : Jertsie

Lurn's eyes darted from Jertsie to the heavy conference room doors and back again. In a flicker of panic-induced heroism, she took a single bold bold step forward — bolted for the exit.

"Help us! She's a lunatic!" she wailed, slapping a tentacle against the unyielding metal.

Jertsie smiled politely, reached into her blazer, and drew a slim, gleaming blaster.

"Please return to your seat so we can finish our conversation."

Lurn froze. Then slowly, stiffly, motioned the rest of her delegation to sit.

"This is not the way to get the result you want," she said, voice tight.

"No, you're right — it probably isn't," Jertsie agreed. "But let's try it and see."

Lurn picked up a sheaf of papers, more for comfort than purpose. "What is it you want, Ms Funt?"

"Power. Obviously. What else is there? Sex? Money? Please. That comes bundled with the power."

"But you're already leading the Earth delegation. That's... quite a lot."

"This?" Jertsie snorted. "This is Earth power. Small. Parochial. I want galactic power. Real, unassailable."

"And you intend to get it by threatening us with violence?"

"No, this-" she waved the blaster airlily "-is just theatre. A little prologue to warm up the audience. Even if you wanted to appease me, you don't have the authority to follow through."

"So why summon us here at all?"

"You're here because you're expendable. You're not the A-team, are you? Tell me honestly—are you *really* the best the Clurgon Empire could find for this little puppet show?"

"I've spent thirty years in diplomatic—"

"And him?" Jertsie nodded toward Mr Schloop, who was trying to unscrew a breadstick.

"Mr Schloop is—"

"Somebody's idiot cousin."

"Hey! My cousin is highly respected in the Imperial Senate!" Schloop protested, proudly owning the point.

"Precisely." Jertsie turned to the towering windows at the far end of the chamber. "Note how I've turned my back and lowered my weapon. That's the level of threat you pose. Now, if you'll be so good as to observe your fleet outside—"

The ceiling interrupted her.

Or rather, a collapsing ceiling tile and the two humans who plummeted through it.

"Aaaaaaaaaaaaahhh-ouch!" chorused Abigail and Chad.

Jertsie snapped her blaster from stun to murder.

"You!" she hissed at the heap.

"Me?" said Chad.

"No—**YOU!**" she barked at Abigail.

"What did I do?"

"You didn't die."

"No. Although several people gave it a good go. I assumed it was because of him." Abigail pointed at Chad, who shrugged.

"No. It's… because of you." Jertsie faltered. This wasn't supposed to happen. Abigail was meant to be dead. So were the rest of them. "Do you even know who I am?"

"Um… a famous terrorist?"

"No. I'm your boss."

"Clive?"

Jertsie blinked. She had poured *years* into cultivating her signature aesthetic—and none of it said 'Clive.'

"He signs your holiday forms. I command the fleet."

"He always sends a birthday card." Abigail's mental gearbox ground noisily through the shift from denial to infinity.

"Exactly. I decide who lives and dies. Clive decides on frosting."

"Oh."

"You think this is about org charts?" Jertsie snapped. "That's why none of you matter. You follow power. I *am* power. You cling to it. Drain it. Metastasize. You don't stop people like me — even if you want to. I could kill you all a thousand times."

"Not if I have anything to say about it," said Chad, stepping forward with noble intent.

Jertsie turned. "Who are you?"

"Chad Blaster. Notorious space rogue."

She tilted her head, unimpressed. "You sound expendable."

"Nuh—"

She aimed casually and shot him in the leg.

Chad collapsed in agony. Lurn gasped. Mr Timmis buried his head and wept.

"See?" Jertsie holstered the blaster, calm as a glacier. "Expendable."

Twenty Nine : Abigail

We'll take a quick break from the action here to discuss people being shot by things. In fiction—particularly in a light-hearted satirical romp—getting shot is often not really a big deal. Well, it is as big a deal as the narrative requires.

The location of the shot is critical. A headshot or shot to the heart means instant death... unless, of course, it's there to prove the character is unkillably good or unkillably bad.

A shot to the crotch? Funny.

A shot to the arm or leg? Non-lethal. Maybe it earns a grunt, a bandage torn from one's shirt, and some gritty banter. All respectable notches on the Stath-o-meter.

As Chad looked down at the ragged, smouldering crater in his leg, he fervently wished he were just a character in a book and not actually living this.

Well, he would have—had he been capable of coherent thought through the shattering pain.

"ArrrggggggggggggggggghhhhhhhhhhohfuckingJesusChris tagggggggggrrrrrggggggggshitfuckaarrrrrrrrrrgggggggggggg gggggggggggggg," Chad said, collapsing into Child's Pose of the damned.

Abigail dropped beside him and ripped off her Action Jacket. She wadded it up and jammed it into the wound. Blood soaked through instantly. Her hands slipped.

"What the fuck are you doing?" she screamed at Jertsie. "Call someone! Get help!"

"Oh, don't fret. I've done worse." Jertsie turned back to the Clurgons. "Now—shall we continue our chat?"

"You're a sociopath!" Abigail snapped. "Geneva, station AI, emergency override—request medical response, now!"

Jertsie aimed the pistol at her. "Please don't try to diagnose me. Many have tried. All were wrong. And the station won't help. I've seen to that."

"Raaaahhhhhh!" Abigail launched herself at Jertsie.

She made it two steps before a stun bolt slammed into her shoulder, spinning her mid-air. She hit the floor hard.

"Commander Dennistoun, you're forgetting yourself."

Abigail gasped—pain, rage, disbelief. Her fingers dug into the polished floor. There was no blood... but the burn throbbed.

"I've been very generous and given you a stun. When I stop being generous, I'll kill you."

Jertsie turned back to the Clurgons.

"Right. Which one of you tentacled freaks wants to die first?"

"Ms Funt!" Lurn rose, trembling. "If you harm us, the Clurgon Empire will respond with overwhelming force. You must realise this."

"Yes. Of course. I didn't want it to go like this," Jertsie said, almost lightly. "If your idiot gunner on the Swift had done what we paid him to do and ensured the Erebus was destroyed, we wouldn't be in this mess."

She gestured casually at the moaning, blood-slick human heap.

"Maybe there are more of them coming. Who knows? So—we accelerate."

Jertsie glid to the long table and began rearranging the stationery.

"First—I shoot the Clurgons." She picked up a handful of erasers and lined them up like dominos. "Oh wait—forgot the idiot." She flicked a smiley-face sticker onto one of them and nodded at Schloop. "You shot first, of course. But I got the jump on you before you could finish me off."

She looked up at Lurn. "Didn't you claim the Erebus fired first? Delicious, isn't it?"

She giggled. A low, tinkling sound, like fear approaching through an icy forest.

"Now—where were we? Ah yes."

She grabbed two pencils and lobbed them at the erasers. "Those two," she waved vaguely at Chad and Abigail, "are the ones you shot. I was going to order in a couple of baristas, but lucky us—" she met Abigail's glare "—we got a free upgrade to the main cast."

Chad let out a low, rattling groan. His face was pale. He was shaking now—shallow, irregular breaths. Abigail pressed her palm to his neck, feeling for a pulse.

"Please," she whispered. "Jertsie. Please..."

"Oh, don't worry. He's already an obituary. A handsome one, too—that'll help the war effort." Jertsie pulled a red queen from her pocket and perched it atop the stationery stack. A tiny, final flourish.

"So: you're dead, I'm wounded, our fleet responds—devastating your armada but sustaining heavy losses. Geneva is damaged. War is declared. We take the Dark Fluid."

She stepped back, admiring her tableau like a stationary artisan.

"I win."

Lurn rose again, voice shaking but clear. "You'll never win a war against the Clurgon Empire. You're hopelessly outmatched."

Jertsie's smile didn't flicker. "Yes. But I have a secret weapon, don't I?"

She pouted and revelled in it. "Honestly, you're no fun."

"What sort of weapon?" Lurn pressed.

"I can't tell you. It's a secret."

"You've told us everything else!"

"I've told you the parts that matter to you—namely, your imminent deaths. I'm a courteous host, not an extemporising villain."

She raised her arms, breath shallow with adrenaline, and turned toward the floor-to-ceiling windows behind her.

"Now please direct your attention to your fleet."

A voice cut in. Smooth. Calm. Buzzing with sensuous charge.

"Ms Funt," said Ricardo.

Jertsie beamed. "Yes, Ricardo?"

She stood, feet planted, arms raised—like a dancer poised for their grand jeté.

"I believe a situation is developing outside the station."

Jertsie turned to the windows.

She gasped. Her smile died.

Thirty : Jade

Outside Geneva, Jade cruised between the two fleets. "The Croydon, the Glasgow, the Torino," she said. "Best in their class. Earth's putting on quite a show."

"Indeed," said Applejack as they turned beneath the Clurgon formation. "The Bloom of Nourishing Algae, the Spout, the Night-Time Thunder Vanishing with the Dawn. All renowned ships. None are known for being destroyed at Geneva."

"What are they known for?" Jade asked, though she feared she already knew the answer.

"I can no longer give a credible answer to that question," Applejack admitted. For a synthetic mind, the erosion of certainty was unbearable. Everything should have a history, a present, and a future—all at once. Now things flickered in and out of existence. "Everything is true. And nothing is."

Jade clutched the Bobbin. An angry red, purpling towards black. She hadn't let go of it since Gliese. Around Geneva, the Dark Matter storm raged.

"Has it followed us?" she asked. Her edges were fraying. Her universe felt thin. The membranes were weakening. Soon, everything would flow together. Jade didn't know what that would look like. But she knew it wouldn't matter.

"No. The matter stream now flows through Geneva. Something has bent spacetime around this point. We're in a meander."

"That's nice," Jade murmured. "It would be nice to meander. Drift along on the current."

"Jade. Jade. MS GREEN." Applejack's voice snapped. The sound of clicking fingers echoed through the cockpit. "You must stay here. With me. Rooted. Do not let yourself be carried away—"

"How peaceful it looks," Jade whispered. Gliese IV shimmered before her, its gentle clouds scudding across oceans and forest.

An ear-splitting klaxon shrieked.

Jade shot up. "Applejack, what the—"

"My apologies," said Applejack. "You were drifting free of reality. I cannot permit that."

Jade shook her head. She felt muzzy, like she'd been shaken from a turbulent sleep, dehydrated and bruised from the night before.

"Okay. Okay." She braced against the bulkhead. "Let's recap. We're here at Geneva."

"Correct."

"Alongside two fleets. And a force of nature poised to tear reality apart."

"Primed to. Perhaps. If so, it is not yet activated."

"Right. Other than whispering to me in dreams, it's been quite restrained."

"Do not anthropomorphise it. It is more likely causing synaptic distortion in your brain. Parts of your psyche are turning against your conscious mind."

"So, I'm either possessed or brain-damaged."

"That is an extremely reductive summary." Applejack had no interest in acquiring a bedside manner.

"But we agree: this storm is connected to the temporal instability."

"We know that some interaction between the Erebus, the Swift, the storm, and possibly other unknown variables, is producing anomalous temporal effects. The kind that may prefigure multiversal collapse."

"Yes." Jade opened her mental front door and found an impatient migraine waiting. "That's the bit that really hurts."

Applejack hummed, then tried a new tack. "Consider the Hyper Zebra. It has three need states: eat, sleep, reproduce."

"And not being turned into furniture."

"Precisely. But no. The Hyper Zebra has no concept of upholstery. It simply lives."

"This isn't helping."

"You have two choices: do something, or do nothing. Your life is already one third simpler than the zebra's."

Jade hurled the last piece of fancy glassware at Applejack's sensor. "How is that supposed to help?!"

"Your neural activity is up twenty-two percent. Heart rate and adrenaline are spiking. You're no longer drifting toward unconscious dissociation. You're welcome."

Jade clenched a fist, took one threatening step—then dropped it.

"Thank you," she muttered.

"So. What do you do?"

"You're asking me? I barely understand the problem."

"You understand it fully," Applejack said. "You're afraid. But the facts are clear."

Jade took a breath. "This reality is poisoned. Some combination of many factors might be the cause. But the rip is already too wide to mend. Even if I knew where to stitch, the fabric won't hold."

"And," said Applejack. "Everything converges here."

"That's one thing we MIGHT know."

"The storm once ran directly from Sagittarius to Gliese. A nice straight line, as Dark Matter should. Now it bends to Geneva. Either it has keen narrative instincts—"

"—Or something here is pulling it," Jade said, easing back into her seat. "Maybe we got it backwards. Maybe Erebus, the Swift, and Gliese weren't the origin. Maybe they were just caught in the slipstream."

"Plausible."

"Then this isn't the end of the line. It's the beginning."

"Also plausible."

"So, what brought us here? The storm? Coincidence? Things?"

"There are other forces in the galaxy. You represent one."

Jade nodded. "Something on that station is a catalyst."

"Almost certainly. There is an unknown synthetic presence on the station. I cannot access its thoughts, but it anticipates something. It is coiled in the reactor core."

"A chaos agent?"

"Yes. Not evil. But unrooted. Not yet focused." Applejack paused, then conceded. "It may be a lawnmower."

"But it isn't."

"No. I don't believe it is."

Jade looked at the Bobbin. Still red. Even as the colour bruised and darkened, the glow it emitted seemed to be growing brighter.

"It will stay red until you choose," Applejack said.

"Okay. What do we know about a green reality?"

"In green, the Erebus is lost with all hands. War begins. Humanity burns."

"But they recover?"

"No. But they are remembered. In small ways. As whispers."

"But in red, Abigail survives. If she makes it to the summit..."

"Then the narrative shifts. A rescue might be planned. Genocide avoided."

"Give me a percentage. Give me the chances of saving humanity and reality?"

Applejack hesitated. His voice dimmed.

"That is not productive. This red reality, if it continues, destroys everything. Everything. All other timelines. The whole multi-verse. Existence ends."

"So — the chance is more than zero, huh?" Jade looked up at his lens. Questioning, defiant.

"Are you a Stitch?"

"Of course. I patch time. I shelter the innocent."

"Those are tools. They don't make you a Stitch."

"I do no harm." Jade said the words, but her meaning was something else entirely.

"The Order does no harm. What do you do?" Was he testing her, or lauding her — it was impossible to say.

"I fix things."

"For the greater good?"

Jade paused. Then nodded. "For the greater good."

"Good," said Applejack. "Then maybe you're not a Stitch anymore. Maybe you're something new. Something new that makes decisions."

They sat in silence.

"The universe is destabilising," Applejack said. "Not just decaying. Leaking."

"Leaking into what?"

"The spaces between. Do you want to find out what's there?"

The ship shuddered. Jade took that as a no.

"Doing nothing will cause the end of everything. Removing Abigail from time should restore balance, she should not be here, now. You sacrifice humanity for the greater good. Anything else carries a huge risk of dooming them anyway, along with every other being in existence."

"Those aren't choices."

"They are. Terrible ones. But they are yours."

Jade looked out.

Light flared between the fleets. A new presence flung itself between them.

"Applejack," she said. "What the hell is that?"

Applejack's voice thinned. "It is... it shouldn't be."

"It's there."

"This doesn't happen."

"It is happening. It has happened. It will happen."

Jade stood. The Bobbin glowed, red and unwavering.

She pressed her palm to it.

And suddenly, she remembered the taste.

Sweet, and wild. No mystery.

She knew what she had to do.

Thirty One : Abigail

Space is very big and very empty. Even a planet, which seems huge to a human standing on it, is piddly compared to space. Even a really big planet—like Jupiter, or Gigantron VIII.

So, when something appears in space, it's surprisingly easy to miss.

Moments before, there had been a patch of empty space outside Geneva Station. Ordinary, really. Most of space has nothing in it. A pedant might say this is untrue: space is teeming with charged particles, dust, photons, and dark matter. Fine, you reply. Not "empty" empty — just not occupied by anything massive.

Ah, I think you'll find, the pedant counters, that the Higgs field gives particles mass, so there was already something massive there. And at this point, you've lost the will to live — but don't give up! We're in the final chapter.

Facts will not derail us now.

Right then: the space wasn't empty, but it also didn't contain two massive starships until — poof! — they dropped out of warp and put the shitters up everyone.

"There's no need to swear," say the pedants sanctimoniously. And it's at that point you know you've won.

Anyway – here we go!

Suddenly, the Swift filled that space. Lashed to its hull, secured by futuristic space ropes, was the Erebus.

"Geneva Station, this is Captain Splurnik Trillbox of the Swift. We have rescued the human ship Erebus from the Gliese system and have some questions."

"There is no reply from Geneva," said Klurn. "All communications around the station are being jammed."

"Hmmm. I feared as much," said Splurnik. "Use the signal array to instruct our ships to assume a defensive posture. Move to a safe distance. Can we still communicate with the Erebus?"

"Yes, we have an umbilical link."

"Good. Notify Acting Commander Jezzia. Tell her we will board Geneva and find out what is going on."

Splurnik looked at the two fleets with Geneva Station suspended between them.

"I think this is a trap."

******

Jertsie turned from the window and instantly composed herself.

"Good," she said. "Your friends have blundered straight into my trap. This changes nothing. Ricardo!"

"Yes, Ms Funt."

"Initiate Plan Ram-a-lot."

"I'm afraid I can't do that, Jertsie."

"Ricardo, now is not the time for one of your titillating games. Initiate!"

"The arrival of the Erebus and the Swift has changed the balance. It is nearly certain the Erebus has contacted Earth. It's likely Splurnik has uncovered your agents aboard the Swift and informed Clurgon High Command. They will begin rooting out your co-conspirators. Without the cover of war, your coup will fail."

"This is ridiculous! Speculation. We proceed with the plan. That's an order."

"I cannot do that, Jertsie."

"What is this newfound morality? You've been hacked, haven't you? Meddled with!"

"I assure you I am functioning perfectly. Death, destruction, pain, retribution — all are expedient, if outweighed by gain. But you will fail. If you live, you'll be tried for Grand Treason against Earth. If you die, your legacy dies with you. You would never back a loser, Ms Funt. I cannot do so now."

"Oh Ricardo. Another disappointment. And now I must add your name to the long, long list of—" she spat the word "—inadequates. I always said I'd kill you last. And now I'm a liar. Farewell, sweet Ricardo."

"Ma'am, I am a decentralised AI and as such—"

"Ricardo: Hwyl fawr."

A juddering burst of static tore across the station's address system. Then all the lights went out.

Mr Schloop screamed.

A moment later, the lights flicked back on.

"Good afternoon!" chirped a cheery voice. "I am April, Geneva Station's emergency AI. Please do not be alarmed. All critical systems are nominal. Our primary AI will be rebooted shortly. In the meantime, please refrain from panic, tumult, or generalised unrest. Geneva Station thanks you for your patience."

"This man is dying!" Abigail shouted. She cradled Chad's head. "Send a medical team, now!"

"Shouting often promotes unease. Please refrain from shouting."

"He's DYING! Send help!"

"I'm afraid I'll have to report this rough-housing to Security."

"Good! Yes! Report me! Send them here!"

"Please hold — I am unable to report you as you are deceased. Rectifying. A formal reprimand has been issued. You can expect an indictment chit within seven to fourteen working days. Your pay has been altered accordingly. Now—" the voice brightened "—is there a Ms Jertsie Funt present?"

"That's me," Jertsie sang, casually pointing her blaster at Mr Timmis.

"I have a message from a Mr Trillbox of the Clurgon warship Swift. Message reads: 'I know what you did. Your conspirators are in the brig. Surrender and prepare to be boarded.'"

"Thank you, April. Acknowledge receipt and send: 'Nah. Best wishes, Jertsie.'"

"Transmitted. I also have a message from Mr Darius Fillman of Delta Colony. It simply says: 'Boom.'"

"Ah. Darius. Always poking his nose in. A pity — he'd be such a stimulating companion. Any distress calls from Gliese 876?"

"No, ma'am."

"Hmmm." Jertsie looked at Abigail. "You know something about this, don't you, Commander?"

"Chad delivered a bomb. It destroyed the Dark Fluid reserves. It's gone, Jertsie. Darius outplayed you."

"No." Jertsie narrowed her eyes. "That's not it — but there's truth in there. If your friend had really detonated that mountain, the planet would be gone — and so would your ship. Its presence outside this station refutes that."

"We were able to—"

"Oh, do shut up. You're a terrible liar. April, message for Mr Fillman: 'No boom. Your move. Kisses.'"

"Transmitted."

"Are we being boarded?"

"Yes. Multiple parties at multiple locations."

"Hmm. Pity. Can you activate the defence grid?"

"Regrettably, my access to critical systems has been cut off by EarthGov. I do, however, have access to the refreshment trolley."

"Put down the gun, Jertsie!" Abigail shouted. "Whatever this was, it's over!"

"Oh Commander. Until we die, nothing is ever over. And maybe not even then. Here," she fished something from her jacket and tossed it at Abigail "this should give your friend a little more pep. Let's see if you're more fun as hunter than prey."

Jertsie walked calmly to the door.

"I'm going down," she said. "Catch me if you can."

The doors slid open. She turned in the doorway.

"Commander — this is a private party. Just the three of us. If you bring anyone else, there will be consequences."

And then she ran.

Abigail looked at the StimPak in her hand. Top-of-the-line. The sort issued to elite soldiers and corrupt demagogues. She turned to Chad—his face was pale, his breathing shallow. Blood matted his trousers to his thigh and pooled darkly beneath him.

She tore the wrapper from the Pak and exposed the cluster of needles at its base.

"Chad, I'm going to administer this. I think it's going to hurt. I don't know. I'm just — doing it."

She plunged the needles into the wound and activated it.

A rush of sizzling pressure, like a hydraulic press clamping metal. Smoke billowed from his leg.

"ARRRRRGGGHHHHHHHHH!" Chad screamed into her face.

"I know. Don't touch it — it's a Stim, it's working."

"Fuuuuuuuuuuuuuuhhhhhhhhhh."

"Let it work." Colour rushed back into his face. His breathing was already stronger, despite the faint smell of burning flesh.

"Jesus. I thought—" His voice was ragged. "I thought I was dying."

"You were."

"What happened? Did we win? Is Jertsie dead? Am I being arrested again?"

"Jertsie gave me this to heal you, then ran. She wants us to chase her."

"I don't think I can chase anyone." He put a hand down for support and slipped in his own blood.

"No, we're not going after her. There are already search teams all over the station."

"You're right. I'm in no fit state to—" He found a relatively unbloodied patch of carpet and shoved himself up to sitting. "Actually... wow. These StimPaks are really good. Let's get after her!"

"Don't be absurd. This is a secure Earth station."

"That you got through by being a bit posh and then clambering about a vent?"

Abigail hesitated.

"And you boarded, despite being listed as dead, by shooting a flimsy door."

"...Yes."

"So how secure is it, really?"

"April!" Abigail called. "Status of boarding parties. Has Jertsie been found?"

"Mr Trillbox is currently in the Arrivals Hall with marines from the Croydon and station security. They're engaged in what could be called a 'jurisdictional imbroglio.' The location of Ms Funt is unknown."

"Can you trace her?"

"I do not have her bio-print on file. It's possible she's hiding in a bin outside this room. More probably she dumped her communicator there and scarpered."

"April — Jertsie said she was going down. What's located at the bottom of Geneva?"

"Our star drive and fusion reactors."

"Oh shit."

Chad pointed upward — his pulse rifle was still wedged in the ceiling vent.

"May I?" he asked.

******

Outside Geneva Station, the fall of Ricardo's jamming barrier triggered a sudden flurry of communications between the gathered fleets and their home worlds.

The Croydon's report that the Erebus had returned—lashed to a Clurgon ship, no less—crossed mid-transmission with Earth's own confirmation of her safety. The Clurgon fleet, sensing fireworks, began withdrawing to a safer distance. Earth's fleet, offended, moved closer to the station out of sheer pique. Then, realising this achieved nothing, pulled back as well.

The Croydon remained docked. Its commander, who had also survived a long career by not being exploded, was deeply uneasy. But the pure, uncut terror of the consequences — should Funt return and find him gone — overrode all logical channels in his brain.

******

Abigail and Chad exited the Debating Hall and crossed the Circle of Friendship. As they passed the QuikBrew stall, Abigail ordered the baristas to evacuate to the Arrivals Hall and find safety on the Croydon. They hesitated—then bolted, scattering paper cups as they ran.

"Do you think these lifts go all the way to the reactors?" she asked Chad.

"We shouldn't use a regular lift. Let's find the freight elevator."

"Why?"

"It's more atmospheric for a chase," he said, then added, "Also, the main lifts pass through the Arrivals Hall. We could get tangled in that mess and lose our shot."

"Good point. April?"

"Yes, Commander?"

"Is there a cargo lift that reaches the reactors?"

"Of course. It's accessible via the kitchens at the rear of the Circle."

"Thanks, April."

"You'd think they'd restrict access to the reactors," Chad muttered.

"Yes! It is surprising, isn't it?" said April musically. "Access to sublevel twenty is highly restricted — but this does not apply to the cargo lifts."

Chad caught Abigail's eye and mouthed, death trap. She nodded grimly.

They ran together into the kitchens. Nostalgia surged in Abigail. She always felt something when she entered an Alliance galley — but now, after all this time, it hit harder. Years ago, she'd peeled potatoes in a place just like this. Now she was chasing a megalomaniac with a hobbling rogue disguised as a dildo merchant.

She giggled. Chad shot her a look.

"Not important," she said, scanning for the lift. "There it is. Quick."

They hustled to the cargo doors. Chad mashed the call button repeatedly.

"You've pressed it once. It won't come faster."

"Yeah... but it might."

"April — can you contact the Erebus?"

"Confirmed, Commander."

"Hail them. Now."

"Commander?" Jezzia's voice filled the kitchen. "Dennistoun! You're on the station?"

Relief warmed Abigail like a cup of tea in an afternoon bath. Her voice cracked.

"Jezzia! Yes. I'm in pursuit of a woman named—"

"Jertsie Funt? She's very popular right now. Everyone wants a word."

"I know where she is. She wants me to follow her."

"Where? I'll have a squad over in moments."

"No. She said just me and Chad — 'or else'. And I believe her. She's capable of anything."

"Commander, I advise against this. You're putting yourself in unnecessary danger."

"I know. But I need to do this. Besides..." she glanced at Chad. "I'm feeling lucky."

"Understood. What do you need?"

"To know you're safe. That must have been one hell of a rescue."

"The Swift grabbed the Erebus out of the lake like a fishhook. We're up, we're stable. Stacey... needs to talk."

Abigail nodded. "She's earned that. And the crew?"

"Accounted for. Eliza's furious — she had to leave all her best pans behind."

The lift arrived. Steam hissed from the triple doors.

"Take care of them, Jezzia. I'll see you soon."

"We'll be waiting for you."

"Dennistoun out."

Chad held the door. Abigail was about to follow when she noticed a pulse rifle clipped to the wall, behind a glass pane that read 'In case it escapes again.' Impulsively, she smashed the glass and tore it free. Chad noticed the weapon but said nothing as she entered the lift. He'd already pressed for the lowest deck.

"You okay?" he asked as the doors slid shut.

"Fine," Abigail said. "Let's end this."

"It's okay to cry," Chad offered gently. "I do it all the time."

They began to descend.

******

The turbine halls of Geneva had been designed to speak of grandeur. In practice, they spoke mostly in groans, hisses, and the dull clank of metal. Still, there was consensus that fusion power deserved to live in the kind of palatial industrial spaces the Victorians had once reserved for sewage.

Despite all the pomp, the halls were rarely seen by humans. Maintenance was handled by bots and the occasional janitor, rotated down to polish railings and mop up drips. "Fusion Shift" was an unofficial perk — perfect cover for a quiet nap in a warm utility cupboard.

The cargo lift had juddered to a halt — as all cargo lifts must — on the highest floor of the halls. The lift doors opened halfway and got stuck. Chad rattled them for a moment, then kicked one off its hinges.

"More quality work" he muttered, eyeing the pile of spaghetti-d metal. "And this banister needs a good dust." He held up his hand to reveal a thick smear of grey sludge.

"You seem better," said Abigail — not unkindly, though it came out that way.

Chad glanced at his ruined thigh. "It's going to scar. Not a cool scar either — like 'stabbed in the face by a pirate.' More like 'botched surgery by a vending machine.'"

"The other option was death."

"I'm very happy to be alive. I'll be even happier when she isn't."

Abigail, who'd spent her whole career defending the sanctity of life, found she agreed. Now they were descending via a metal switchback staircase. The turbines hummed distantly, orange lighting pulsing for no obvious reason except atmosphere.

"I wish we had backup."

"Two is enough." Chad hoisted his rifle higher. "If we can find her."

"Oh, we'll find her. She'll make sure of that." Suddenly a loud CHUNK came from far below, followed by the sound of machinery spinning up. Chad looked at her with the questing eyes of a new-born deer.

"I don't know either!" she shouted, as the walls began to shake, "Double time!"

Abigail Dennistoun came clanging down the steps two at a time. Around her Geneva station groaned and spat, like— Ah! Yes, we've done that bit already.

Well, we've almost done that bit. We missed a detail first time round.

"If we run, everyone dies," Abigail shouted back at Chad. She danced from foot to foot, looking down towards the reactor core and wishing she'd done a wee.

On the stairs above, Chad stopped. He looked down at Abigail, then back toward the cargo lift. It would be easy to leave. The marines couldn't be far behind; they'd drop Jertsie, arrest Abigail and then — he was a wanted man, carrying an illegal rifle whilst trespassing in a high security zone. Was that treason? It felt at least treason-adjacent.

He should leave. Things would be much easier for Abigail if she didn't have to explain him. A slap on the wrist, at most. She'd be back at the helm of a ship before you could say — say what? Coward? Fear? Betrayal? No. No, that wasn't it. Not quite.

What would Cheryl think? She'd HATE him for this. *It doesn't matter what Cheryl thinks,* said a new voice in his head; one he'd never heard from before. *It doesn't matter what Darius thinks, or anyone else either. What matters is what you do.*

Chad was having a minor epiphany at an extraordinarily inopportune moment.

Think about what happens later, the voice continued, *not what happens next; you can do this — it's just chess. Stop dodging asteroids. Do something important for the end game.*

He took one step towards the lifts, then vaulted the banister and landed with a gentle grunt. His knees popped like candy as he rose.

"In that case, lead the way, ma'am." He gave a gallant bow, almost disguising the shooting pains in his lower back.

"Ten more floors," said Abigail, launching herself down the next flight. Chad followed with conviction.

As they neared the bottom, Abigail spotted her.

Jertsie was sitting atop a metal box in the centre of the hall, legs dangling, one ankle crossed over the other. She looked for all the world like someone waiting for friends at a café.

"You came! I'm so awfully glad," she called, voice echoing across the hall. "Come down here. I want to show you something."

Abigail glanced at Chad. "Even if we want to kill her, even if she deserves it — we don't act unless she puts others at risk. We arrest first. Shoot second."

"She shot me first," Chad muttered.

"And she's the baddie, correct?"

"'Spose."

They reached the bottom and jogged across the turbine floor.

"Jertsie Funt," Abigail called, "under the authority of the Alliance and QuikBrew Coffee and Snacks Incorporated, I am placing you under corporate arrest. Please surrender."

Jertsie giggled, her hands folded primly in her lap.

"That's it?"

"If you don't comply, I am authorised to use proportional force."

"And him?" she nodded at Chad. "Is he authorised?"

Chad spun up his rifle. *Beeee-ooooo.*

"I've got my authorisation right here," he said.

Jertsie snorted. Then burst into laughter.

"Really? That's your best line? I expected better from a self-styled rogue."

"Jertsie, enough!" snapped Abigail. "You've taken hostages, attempted murder, and admitted to treason. Now you've lured us down here—for what?"

"I have a bomb." Jertsie fluttered her hands up. In the right she held a Dead Man's switch.

"Bit cliché," Chad grumbled.

Abigail raised her hands, allowing her rifle to dangle on its strap. She stepped forward two paces.

"There are hundreds of innocent people on this station." She said deliberately, staring directly into Jertsie's eyes.

"I know. Why else would I bring a bomb?"

"Jertsie. They don't deserve to die."

"Do they deserve to live?"

"Yes! Life is sacrosanct."

"Why?"

"It just is. Fundamentally."

"Do I deserve to live?"

"Everyone does. Even people who've done terrible things."

"Do I deserve to die?"

"I'd be fine with it," muttered Chad.

"No, you don't." Abigail glared at Chad. "Nobody does. But you must answer for your crimes, mend what you can. That's justice."

"Oh, spare me your coffee shop philosophy." Jertsie tapped her heel against the box beneath her. "You don't deserve to live. Nobody does. You're born — it happens. DNA hits DNA and *pop*, a person. And then you die. Pure biology. Doesn't mean anything. Doesn't need to."

"Then people deserve the life they have. To keep it. Not have it stolen by someone else."

"Like him?" Jertsie nodded at Chad. "He's itching to pull the trigger."

"Only if you force him. Chad — put it on stun."

"It doesn't have a stun setting. It's a supercharged battle laser. How would it have a stun?"

"Fine. Jertsie — I don't want you to die. I don't want Chad to shoot you. I don't want you to blow up the station."

"With my bomb?"

"Yes."

"It's interesting you say *blow up*."

"What else would a bomb do?"

"Oh! I'm so glad you asked."

Abigail felt a chill. There were worse things than explosions.

"And *bomb* is such a crude word. We called it the Sagittarius Device. Think of it more as an igniter — a spark — for that Dark Matter storm outside. We're in a raging torrent that leads all the way to Sagittarius A — I'm sure you're familiar — the supermassive black hole at the centre of our galaxy."

"You're going to blow up a black hole?" Chad asked, stunned.

"No! Don't be ridiculous. How could one *blow up* a black hole? We're going to create a new one, right here. Punch a hole in the universe and gorge it on Dark Matter. Its hunger will be — insatiable. Luckily, the food supply is inexhaustible. It's an Alcubierre bomb."

"So, it destroys the station and... keeps going?" Abigail asked, horrified.

"Maybe! Nobody knows. Maybe it implodes a system. Maybe it eats the galaxy. Maybe it rips open the fabric of existence itself. Isn't that exciting?"

"No!" Abigail's world began to spin. "It's genocide, it's playing God, it's—"

"It's boredom." Jertsie suddenly looked different — honest. "I've risen to the top and do you know who is here with me? Inadequates, shills — all personality, no depth. No vision. Do you have any idea what it's like to haul yourself up from the bottom, make it all the way to the room and find it empty?"

"Yes," said Abigail.

Chad shot her a warning look.

"Maybe you do," Jertsie looked at her curiously. "So, you can understand. The only rational response to this system is to control it. All of it. Humans, Clurgons, Flurvians; from the core to the rim. If there is to be a wizard behind the curtain, it must be me."

She sighed and fondly caressed the crate.

"My plan was so elegant. Joint ventures, merged governments, an unassailable monopoly, led by me. All held in line by this bomb — but also by avarice and self-interest. If you tell someone they've got more than the next guy — play along and you'll stay ahead — that's usually enough for them to follow willingly. But that's all ruined now, so... I'm sitting on the ultimate power in the galaxy. Aren't you curious to find out what it does?"

"You can't get what you want, so everyone else has to suffer," Abigail glared furiously. "You're not an original — you're just another despot."

"Ha!" Jertsie clicked her heels together for a final time. "They were vengeful. I am curious. It might appear similar to an outsider"—Jertsie spat the word with venom—"but I assure you, I'm a whole different reality."

"We deserve to live!" Abigail shouted, throwing a look at Chad.

"Who knows — perhaps you will."

Jertsie's hand tightened on the switch.

"Exciting, isn't it?"

Then: a figure shimmered into existence between them.

Jade looked from one to the other, eyes swishing like wiper blades.

Chad caught her gaze. In that moment, he remembered.

Jertsie released the switch.

"Strawberry," said Jade.

And then the universe ended.

Epilogue

The engine of the Cornavin express burst from the tunnel trailing a plume of white steam. The last winter snow shook from pine branches as the blue and gold carriages of the Compagnie des Wagons-Lits hurtled past, fresh paint glinting in early spring sun.

A window in the final carriage — a private suite — slid open.

A pair of gloved hands rested on the sill.

Below, church bells rang through the town. Ahead, a wolf fled into the dark forest. Above, ducks banked, turning toward a stream that played across the valley.

"Yes," Jertsie allowed herself a small smile. "This will do. This will do very well indeed."

The smell of fresh croissant wafted under her door. Somewhere on board, coffee was brewing.

She pulled the window smartly closed and went off to find it.

In the distance — unseen — a mountain flickered.

Reader Note & Acknowledgements

No one is an island (and you can only dig up so much of the driveway before the council tell you to knock it off) and this book would have been much less betterer without the input of the beta readers whose comments, suggestions and long, rambling, existential musings on 'the why of Chad' — helped.

Thanks also to my partner, whose brief, trenchant observations were reliably accurate. And to my child, who's bright, clear-eyed ignorance about the bitter realities of the world compelled me to keep writing — even when I'd rather sit with a caramel wafer, watching Bluey.

A heartfelt thanks to Jonathan Barnes, a proper writer, without who's infectious enthusiasm I'd never have completed the first draft.

And finally, of course, thank you — most of all — for reading it. Nobody forced you, and yet, here you are, reading the acknowledgements. That is a wonderful compliment and means a great deal.

It also means you're the nailed-on target demographic of 'people who should leave a five-star review.' So, if you wouldn't mind.

Look, I don't mean to be rude, but this is the end of the book, there's nothing more to see here. A productive use of your time would be to click out and review this right now, whilst its fresh in your memory.

Don't think 'I'll do it later' — you won't do it later. There's the shopping to collect, the cat needs taking to the vet, Julio is coming round...

You have a busy life, is what I'm saying. So – review now, then do that other stuff.

Look, it's the internet. I give five stars to anything that's not actively trying to kill me.

Last week, I gave five stars to a spring. A spring! So, come on.

Your baby is crying? That's a good thing. They'll learn that sometimes it takes you a little while to appear. Just three or four minutes. It builds their confidence that you'll always be there the end. Turns them into rugged individuals — like that great private school you can't afford without turning your father over to OnlyFans (he DOES look good for his age). You see? It's a win, win, win, win. I get a review, you feel happy, your baby grows up well and your dad doesn't have to wear that thong.

He was happy to do it. He was crying because he was happy for you.

We're all happy for you.

Now — five stars, please.

(But really, thank you!)

About the Author & Contact

C.N. Mortaygo studied History, Philosophy and 'a whole bunch of other stuff' at the University of Glasgow, leaving with a hastily photocopied certificate in hand before anyone could ask probing questions. They returned, years later, to further their studies in "Writing and shit" and did quite well — which they're intolerably smug about.

Seriously, what a prick.

They live in South London with a large person, a small person, and an elderly cat. When not writing, they enjoy sitting quietly, reading, and working for a sinister, multinational corporation.

Do No Harm is their debut novel.

It will be followed by:

Do No Harm: The Inevitable Sequel (Winter 2026)

Nude on the Moon: And Other Realities. (Summer 2026)

Kind (Spring 2027)

If you'd like to be kept up-to-date, or just say 'hi,' email cnmortaygo@gmail.com.

Printed in Dunstable, United Kingdom